If You Say So

MEGAN REINKING

This book is a work of fiction. Names, characters, places, and incidents are either products of the author's imagination or are used fictitiously. Any resemblance to actual persons, living or dead, events, or locales is entirely coincidental.

Copyright © 2025 by Megan Reinking.

All rights reserved. No portion of this book may be reproduced or used in any manner without written permission of the copyright owner except for the use of quotations in a book review.

Editing by Jenn Lockwood

Proofreading by Sarah Ward

Cover Design by Lorissa Padilla

If You Say So is a contemporary romance that includes our main character, Sydney, and her grief journey while she navigates a relationship with her mother who has Alzheimer's. It also includes a parental abuse storyline involving an eighteen-year-old and his father. No violence is depicted on-page, but the direct aftermath is depicted and discussed briefly.

Please be mindful of these trigger warnings and of your mental health before reading if you think you may be sensitive to these topics.

For Laura A. and Laura J.
One of you I send 'remember when' texts to that go as far back as our high school days, and the other one I send memes to about parenting and being married to our husbands—who are basically a carbon copy of each other.
Thank you both for making it so easy to choose a name for Sydney's best friend.

ONE

Now

Week One of Renovation

I once read somewhere that lakes go through life stages, just as humans do. Over a much longer period of time, of course, but over the span of many years, a slow, gradual evolution takes place. The basins fill slowly with eroding material little by little until one day it's simply no longer a body of water, evolving from a large lake down to a pond, then maybe a creek, and down to nothing at all but land.

As I watch waves roll softly onto the sandy shore, this tidbit of information comes to mind, and an uneasiness settles in my stomach. Realistically, I know I'll be long gone by the time any drastic changes happen to a lake as large as Lake of the Woods, but the thought tugs on my heart all the same.

So many of my childhood memories happened here—admittedly ones I both yearn to remember and am desperate to avoid all at once. Regardless, I don't like the thought that so much of this lake will just be gone one day. Vanished as if it never existed.

A pelican flaps its wings, landing in the water next to the fish cleaning house, pulling my attention there. Inhaling a deep breath, I scan the length of the shore, taking in the beauty of Ruby Lodge's bay.

Several aluminum boats are tied to the large dock system that juts out into the water, and on the other side, there's another stretch of beach where a row of Adirondack chairs is nestled. The lake spans out for miles and miles without anything else in sight from this part of the island.

Lake of the Woods at its finest—a sprawling body of water that borders both Minnesota and Canada. With over fourteen thousand islands scattered across the vast lake, it's a scenic destination for many fishermen and folks looking to slow down their pace of life, both of which Ruby Lodge caters to. Many of the islands are small and uninhabitable with not much more than a slew of foliage sprouting from their bases. Others are dotted with cabins and resorts like the one Ruby Lodge is nestled on—Takini Island.

It's also home—along with the city of Baudette back on the mainland, where I grew up and my brother, Graham, and I went to school. We spent most of our weekends out here, helping my grandparents run the lodge. Eventually, our parents took over operations, often bringing us along to help, so to say this place is threaded into the very fabric of me is about as true a statement as I've ever made.

When I'm back here, the familiarity of it all drowns most of my senses. Every sound of a leaf crunching under a shoe or the soft chirp of a bird feeds my soul in a way that only the comfort of home can, not to mention the smell of campfire smoke and the faint call of a loon out in the distance. Or Graham's voice when he shouts a farewell to a fishing boat full of guests embarking on a morning fishing excursion.

A small, peaceful part of my soul thrives on being here.

But even with all its positive aspects, as I stand here with a tightness in my chest, I can't deny the negatives. Along with the ample number of happy memories, there are ones that fuel a steady grief that overshadows all of it. An ever-present subtle reminder of why I don't come back here often.

The slam of the door behind me brings me out of my nature-induced trance, and I give my head a timid quiver to clear my thoughts. Turning toward the lodge, I breathe in the fresh spring air, letting it ground me in its familiar way, and I do what I always do with this heaviness—push it down deep where it belongs.

Bounding up the steps with a renewed focus on the work at hand, I swing the front door open. As I walk across the worn entry rug, I can't help but think of the countless times I've crossed this very threshold. Passed through this same entrance on my way to find my parents going over paperwork in the office or to look for Graham in one of his famous hide-and-seek spots.

"Okay. I can do this," I tell myself under my breath in an upbeat tone, reminding myself that I'm fully capable of compartmentalizing my emotions. I've done it for years now.

"Hey, Syd?" My brother, Graham, looks up from behind the bar on the far wall of the dining area, shifting his gaze away from the coffee he's pouring just long enough to give me a side eye.

"Morning!" I smile at the sight of him as I cross the room to slide onto a barstool. One of the biggest positives of being here is seeing him in person, being able to talk to him without needing to use the phone.

"I mean this in the least offensive way possible...but what in the world are you wearing?" He smirks.

I glance down at the neon-yellow oversized hoodie that I've paired with forest-green leggings. Thick black wool socks peek out of camel-colored Wellie boots.

"What's wrong with what I'm wearing?" I ask innocently. I think I look cute today—bright and vibrant. While I may technically be here on business, since we're on a remote island in the middle of nowhere—where the general attire is 'mountain-man chic' at best—I made an executive decision and deemed casual wear to be appropriate.

"It's, uh...blinding," he mutters with a chuckle. Sometimes I forget that he's only one year older than me. He has an old soul and wisdom that often makes him seem much older to me than twenty-seven.

"It's called style." I flash him my best cheeky grin. "Fashion. You wouldn't understand."

With a miniscule shake of his head, he crosses to the other side of the bar where he places the cup in front of a guest reading the newspaper. Then he holds up a finger in my direction to signal he'll be right back before slipping through the swinging double doors into the kitchen. The old doors creak so much when they swing that I'm honestly surprised they haven't fallen right off the hinges.

I tap my fingers along the bar top while I wait, slipping my gaze over my shoulder and out the floor-to-ceiling windows that offer a view of the bay. The sun glistens across the top of the lake, a beam gleaming off the corner edge of the dock. The rustic beauty of this place is absolutely another positive of being here.

"Here you go," Graham says, placing a warmed cinnamon-raisin muffin in front of me. "Just a warning, you have about ten seconds before Shirley comes out to—"

He doesn't get a chance to finish his sentence as Shirley, our longtime family friend and head cook here at the lodge, comes barreling through the double doors, making a beeline when her eyes land on me.

"Sydney!" she squeals.

A grin stretches across my face as I jump off the stool mere seconds before she wraps me in a bear hug. I squeeze her back, savoring the embrace that brings me so much comfort.

"When did you get here?" She pulls back long enough to run her hands through my hair, then down my arms, inspecting every inch of me as if she hasn't seen me in ages—which would admittedly be true.

"Last night." My words come out slightly mumbled as her hands squish my cheeks, cradling my face. "Sam flew me in right before dusk. Graham said you had already turned in for the night, otherwise I would have come and said hi. How are you?"

"Oh, I'm just fine, dear." She gives a shake of her head and then releases my face, stepping back with determination. "What can I make you? How about an omelet?"

"Oh, I'm fine with a muffin, honestly," I object.

"Nonsense." She waves me off as she scurries behind the bar, rambling mostly to herself. "You used to love my ham-and-chive scramble, so that's exactly what I'll do. You have a very important job to do. I need to keep you well fed!"

She's halfway through the doors when she peeks her head back out. "Oh, I can't wait to see what plans you've come up with, Sydney. Such exciting times for Ruby Lodge."

With another squeal, she disappears into the kitchen before I can get a word in. Not that I tried too hard to stop her. I know her well enough to know that she's happiest when she's feeding the people she loves. Who am I to take that away from her?

"Speaking of plans," I say to Graham as I slide back onto the stool, "I'm having a meeting with Neal this afternoon to go over the tentative drawings I sent him. I'd like to start pulling permits so we can get the ball rolling on demo as soon as possible."

After months of poring over measurements and details, I'm anxious to finally get this project started. There's an unsettling urge inside of me to give Ruby Lodge some much-needed love and attention it deserves and so desperately needs. This means a lot to me. It's like this project is allowing me to return a favor in a way. To care for it, just like it has done for me so many times.

Sometimes it's hard to believe that, nearly a year ago, Ruby Lodge came so close to being shuttered for good. The list of repairs needed on the individual cabins was growing larger by the day while the amount of money coming in was rapidly dwindling. In a twist of fate, Graham and his fiancée, Blair, found an old trust that my grandparents had set up with more than enough money to do a full renovation, including adding on and expanding the property.

As one of the newest lead architects at a firm down in Minneapolis, that's where I come in—designing and overseeing this expansion project. One I'm honored to lead, even though it comes with a hefty dose of pressure and emotional uncertainty.

Was it necessary for me to stay on-site for the duration of this renovation? Not really. But being as I decided to be involved in every single aspect, including interior design, it only makes sense. Plus, I can work remotely from here, so despite my mixed feelings about it, I'm here to stay for the next three to four months.

"Is he flying or boating out?" Graham asks.

"He's coming by ferry boat, I believe."

"I'll be on the lookout to help tie up," he offers with a nod.

"Alright." I drum my fingers against the counter. "Catch me up on where we're at with the surrounding cabins. Have we secured the lots we need?"

"Well, we're looking good on the northern side of the property," he says. I gladly wrap my hands around a warm coffee mug as soon as he sets it in front of me.

"So far, Beckstrom and Halding have agreed to sell. Neither of them make it up here often anymore, so once the paperwork goes through, we're clear to start demolition in those areas."

"Excellent." The renovations I drew up are dependent on expanding into some neighboring properties, so hearing we bought those ones out is a relief and one less headache to worry about.

"The east side of the property, as you know, leads up to the community land," he points out.

Ah, yes. The portion of the island that belongs to all the Takini Island landowners. There isn't much more than a single wooden dock, a picnic table, and a barely standing pavilion set up on the property—and it's been that way for years—so I'm hoping we'll be able to cut into some of it. My plan for an expansive recreation area—complete with tennis courts, a beach volleyball space, and a large playground—depends on it.

"We need everyone's permission to acquire some of that community land," I explain, having already spoken with the city council to get details on that part. "They scheduled a town meeting to make an official ruling in two weeks. That was the earliest they could do."

"Oh, perfect." He nods. "Now, the west side of the island is another story. We've got two cabins that won't budge."

"Ugh, which ones?" My stomach drops, and my bottom lip juts out in a pout. Those properties are for my absolute favorite part of the renovation—ones I was banking on acquiring.

"The Gilbert place might sell if I can track him down, but it's a long shot. The cabin is boarded up, and it looks like he hasn't been back in a while. Nobody I've talked to has heard from him recently, so I'd probably count him out at this point."

I sigh, considering our options. That particular property is relatively small, so if we can't take ownership of it, there will only be a few minor tweaks to the overall plan. Nothing major, so no big deal, although it is unfortunate. The other property, on the other hand, is the one we definitely need.

"And the other one?" I take a quick bite of the muffin.

"You mean the one on top of the hill with the highest elevation, the amazing shoreline, and the best view on the whole island?" Graham gazes off, clearly envisioning it in his head, as I've also done myself plenty of times, before coming back to reality. "No luck. I tried yesterday, and he's already declined my offer."

"Oh no." I frown. "That one is crucial. Who owns it? Can we just offer him more money?"

"It's Cole Fredrickson's place now. He says he's too attached to sell."

My mouth goes dry, and a pang of almost tangible annoyance twists in my stomach.

TWO

Now

Cole Fredrickson.

The mention of his name alone makes my mouth turn up with disgust. I haven't heard his name spoken out loud in years. Not since shortly after he ran off and ditched town after…everything that happened. A deep, long-forgotten, unsettled feeling simmers in my gut. One that reminds me of yet another negative set of memories I've tried so hard to suppress.

Graham chuckles, shaking his head. "I figured you'd get a kick out of that one. You know, you never told me why you have beef with him—neither did he, for that matter. I never could figure it out."

I transform the frown into an inauthentic cheery smile, doing my best to look unfazed, although, truthfully, I feel anything but.

"I don't have beef with him," I flat out lie. "I don't feel any way about him."

"Is that right?" He gives me a pointed look, clearly not convinced.

"Absolutely. And we need that property for my vision. It's a must. There's no other way around it, Graham," I say emphatically. This whole renovation…it has to be perfect. It needs to be.

"Well, I don't know what to tell you. He already said no." He shrugs in a way that tells me he's already accepted this particular roadblock.

"Well, that's never stopped me before." I wave my hand, dismissing it as if it's nothing more than a minor hurdle. "In fact, I'll ask him to sell myself."

"Oh, you will, huh?" Amusement plays on his face as he runs a hand down the scruff of his beard. There's also a hint of complacency, knowing full well from experience that he can't stop me once I set my mind to something.

"Yeah, why not?" I brush my hands together to dispel any lingering muffin crumbs. "Is he staying there now, or did he leave?"

He shrugs. "As of yesterday, he was still here on the island, yes. But he's not exactly an open book. I have no idea how long he'll be here for."

"Good enough for me," I announce, hopping off the stool. "Tell Shirley I'll be right back."

"Syd." It's a half-ditch attempt to stop me, but I'm already halfway out of the room.

"I'm off to save the day! One cabin at a time!" I call back in a rush, pulling the front door shut behind me.

"I am a confident, persuasive, kick-butt-and-take-names kind of woman," I murmur enthusiastically under my breath as I make my way down the creaky wooden steps of the porch. Shielding my eyes from the glare of the sun that comes off the lake, I round the lodge to where the large shed is nestled against the woods.

"I am a persuasive, powerhouse negotiator." I'm not entirely sure if I'm saying these mantras to hype myself up or if it's to distract myself from the sudden nerves that are ruminating in my stomach, but either way, they seem to be a necessity, so I continue sputtering them off as determination sets in.

Seeing Cole was absolutely not anywhere on the list of things I expected to do today—or anytime in the near future, for that matter. If I'm honest, it's a reunion I'd rather not have.

Ever.

But alas, here we are. The fate of the new-and-improved Ruby Lodge is in my hands, so if I need to suffer through a few uncomfortable minutes, then I'll suck it up and take it on the chin as best I can.

The four-wheeler is parked right in front of the shed with the keys left in the ignition, so I hop on, ignoring the reminder in the back of my mind that I haven't operated one in years. How hard can it be?

"I am a capable, independent—ah!" The four-wheeler lurches forward as I ever so slightly give it some gas.

"Persistent…" Another lurch. "Graceful…" Lurch again. Luckily, it only takes two more small swerves before the four-wheeler steadies into a straight, smooth ride.

"That's better." I maneuver to the right of the main lodge and onto the gravel pathway that runs along the shoreline in front of a row of small log cabins, including the one I'm staying in, cabin number twelve.

Once past the cabins, I veer onto the trail that leads straight into the thick woods, following tree markings to get my bearings. I can't recall ever visiting this particular cabin, but I know the general area well enough to know what direction to head in. Besides, there aren't very many cabins on the island, so I should be able to find it by process of elimination if I need to.

The trail takes me on an incline as I narrowly swerve between thick, overgrown brush and towering trees. I pass Gilbert's cabin before spotting a wooden sign nailed to a tree that says *Fredrickson* on it.

Perfect.

That was easy enough.

Slowing to a stop at the clearing on top of the hill, I shift into park along the tree line. I breathe a deep sigh as I hop off onto the grass, mentally attempting to calm the uneasiness that's practically buzzing off me. As I make my way up the small hill toward the cabin, the lake catches my eye, and I can't help but admire the view from up here. It has the longest stretch of open shoreline of any property on Takini Island, with a gorgeous view of the lake from the hill the cabin rests on. It really is one of the best pieces of land.

Which is precisely why I'm determined to buy it.

I clamp down a sudden wave of nerves that threatens to overpower me and zero in on the clearly unkempt state of the cabin as I approach it. Overgrown bushes line the front porch, their branches encroaching haphazardly over the rickety stairs. Branchy vines twirl all the way up the wooden posts, and the porch is littered with sticks and debris. The roof looks like it's seen better days, and the windows have a thick layer of dirt covering them.

"Unbelievable," I mutter under my breath, swatting at the foliage as I carefully climb the stairs. For somebody who supposedly has a strong attachment to this place, he's certainly let the maintenance of it slip.

I rap on the solid oak door, shifting back and forth onto the balls of my feet while I wait patiently for any sign of life inside. A soft humming involuntarily comes from the back of my throat, an attempt to keep myself calm and centered.

A few heavy, muffled footsteps come from somewhere inside the cabin before the door swings open. What I see immediately steals the breath from my lungs.

Towering over me is an older, more manly version of the Cole Fredrickson I remember. A few slight creases frame his eyes and forehead, but to my annoyance, he's just as handsome as he was back when he was barely eighteen. He has a strong, tanned jawline and short ash-brown hair with eyes to match.

He has rugged good looks, made even more refined with age and an underlying graveness behind his eyes that seems to have not gone away. The kind of piercing depth to his stare that threatens both a good time and an emotional collapse all at once. A stare that I fell for once upon a time.

The apex of his jawline pulses with the deepening of his frown.

The feeling is mutual.

"Cole," I say cheerfully, albeit a bit sarcastically—if it's possible to be snarky while saying someone's name. I force a smile on my face, ignoring the way my throat suddenly feels thick.

Nope. No.

I've managed to make it this far without reflecting on what happened between us years ago. There's certainly no point in starting now.

Regaining my composure, I cross my arms in an attempt to display authority. Or maybe it's a subconscious way of protecting myself.

Could be both.

"Peterson." Somehow the way he smugly refers to me by my last name makes the kernel of irritation swirling in my stomach even more profound. Add that to the way he narrows his eyes in vague annoyance at my presence, and this exchange is officially the worst part of my day.

THREE
Cole

Now

"That didn't take long," I mutter under my breath, swallowing down a surge of irritation.

Sydney Peterson.

An entirely unwelcome blast from the past.

This right here... This is exactly why it's been so long since I've been back. I learned a long time ago that I can't go anywhere in Baudette—or on this island, for that matter—without running into people who remind me of a past I want no part in reminiscing over.

I huff, grabbing a baseball cap off the hook beside the doorframe. Sliding it on, I push right past her, not even bothering to pretend like I'm interested in hearing what she has to say.

"I'm here to convince you to sell," she announces matter-of-factly, pushing her frown into an over-the-top smile. Her tone is jovial and light, as if she's forgotten every last thing about our history together.

"I know," is all I say, barely offering a sideways glance while barreling down the steps of the porch. I've already been through this with Graham. If she thinks a mere conversation is all it'll take to get me to budge, she's sorely mistaken.

I slip on some work gloves that I left on the railing earlier, choosing to ignore her altogether. Then I start grabbing stray branches that lay erratically among the bushes. According to my conversation with Graham, several storms have passed through here since I've been back.

While tossing a few sticks into a pile, I try not to outwardly cringe at the disastrous state of everything. I was shocked at the amount of work needed when I arrived on the island yesterday afternoon. Of course I expected it to need some fixing up, as I haven't been up here to take care of it the way I should have been in quite some time, but seeing it in person like this causes a heavy layer of guilt to settle in my gut.

When my uncle first offered me the rights to his cabin, I vowed to myself that I would care for it the same way he did, out of respect for him and the solace he and this cabin once provided for me. It was the one place I could come to get away from all the heaviness going on back in the city. For a solitary reprieve with the only family member to ever mean a single thing to me.

"So should I do my song and dance now?" She cuts in with that same chipper tone, reminding me of her presence.

"Maybe list out all the reasons you should let it go? Put my negotiating skills to the test? I can be very persuasive...and stubborn," she admits after a pause.

I roll my lips in irritation, wondering if I'm going to be dealing with her chirping in my ear the whole time I'm here. I heave another sigh, contemplating what it'll take to get her to just leave.

"I already told Graham I'm not budging. Don't waste your breath," I say as politely as I can, but even I can hear the bite in my tone. I'm not trying to be a jerk, but I can't help that's how it came out. It seems to be an automatic response she brings out of me.

"Well, why not?" she asks, a little too sternly for my liking. Even without looking her way, I can feel her watching my every move as I rip at branches.

"Not interested," I say, keeping it short and sweet. I've never been known to be much of a talker in general, and I feel zero obligation to explain my reasonings—especially to her.

"But why?" she repeats. "Judging by what I see, clearly you're not here very often, unless you enjoy living in chaos and filth...maybe that's it. Wait, I thought you lived down in Longville?"

"I do," I grunt, crouching to reach between two bushes. I grab a handful of debris from under the porch before straightening, glancing up at her. "Keeping tabs on me?"

For the first time since she arrived, I pause and actually hold her stare, truly taking her in. She has the same almond shape to her eyes, button nose, and familiar oblong outline to her face that I remember studying once upon a time. The roots of her hair are the same shade of brunette I remember, but the rest of her longer hair has been dyed a dirty blonde.

It doesn't take much at first glance to see that she carries herself with the same sort of boldness she did then. A clear confidence in her stance alone. Although, underneath, I can detect the kind of weariness that comes with a few years of life experience under her belt. All of it covered in a ridiculously bright outfit that's vaguely reminiscent of the ones she used to wear.

"Absolutely not," she huffs in response, the faintest remnants of a blush swiping her cheeks. "Graham rambles sometimes. Trust me, you're the last person I've kept tabs on."

I force my stare away from her, wiping the sweat starting to form on my brow and feeling the same indifference toward her. I'd have to care what she thinks in order for her words to cut me. "What do you care if I sell, anyway?"

"I'm lead architect for the renovation," she announces proudly.

Graham never mentioned that Sydney was involved at all, though I had assumed she might be. But to be honest, if I had known she'd show up on my doorstep the day after I arrived, I would have reconsidered coming up here until after the renovation was complete.

"You don't need my land. You've got plenty of acreage down there," I point out, hoping I can get to the root issue and nip this whole thing in the bud so she can leave already.

She beams as if she's happy I made the point. She pans her open palms in front of her as if she's envisioning something magnificent in her mind. I raise my brows impatiently at her dramatics.

"This location, right here"—she points a finger to the ground as she beams—"is where the glamping tents will go. An extension of Ruby Lodge, if you will. This is the absolute perfect setting for an even more rustic getaway for those who want to enjoy the stunning view and be one with nature in the heart of Takini Island—while still enjoying the modern amenities that come along with glamping, of course."

My top lip curls in confusion at whatever she just described. I try to picture it in my head, but I draw a blank.

"I have no idea what you just said," I mutter, crossing to the other side of the stairs to grab the rake leaning against the porch railing. "But again, I'm not budging on this. You'll just have to rework your plans."

Her shoulders drop at the same time her face does, and she crosses her arms in a huff. "We'll have to see about that. I'm not convinced you even want to keep this cabin. You know how small this island is, right? I could come here every day and wear you down if I wanted to."

The threat makes my stomach swirl with irritation. I don't doubt her for a second.

"Are you done here? You got your answer. Go on back to wherever you came from." It comes out gruffly and with a bit more bite than I would normally speak to another human, but I'm finding it hard to feel bad about that at the moment.

"You don't have to be rude," she mutters after a moment of silence.

She stomps down the stairs in a huff. "Look, I know we've had our differences in the past—if that's what you want to call it—but we're both adults now. Don't you think we're perfectly capable of acting like it?"

I barely have a chance to open my mouth before she continues.

"You know, if anything, I'm the one who should be mad. In fact, I *am* mad."

She points her finger in my direction, a snarkiness to her tone. "You're the one who's being a jerk. With your attitude and your 'you can leave now.'" She says the last part in what I'm assuming is an imitation of me.

"But you don't see me pouting about it, do you?" she continues. "I'm perfectly happy to cast my dislike for you—and trust me, it's definitely there—aside for the greater good of this island."

I let her finish her soap box speech without interrupting, instead contemplating what I could say that she wouldn't use against me down the road.

Our gazes stay locked on each other like laser beams until, suddenly, her brows fly up, and a gasp escapes her mouth. "Oh, I know exactly why you're mad!"

She throws her arms up in disbelief. "I can't believe I didn't think of it sooner. You're mad about that stupid rumor, aren't you?"

All I can do is shake my head, my shoulders deflating with exhaustion at the mention of the rumor. I don't have nearly enough energy to rehash this right now.

"That has to be it...why else would you be all..." She waves her hand in front of my face, her eyes scrutinizing me. "Like this."

"I'd appreciate your finger being at least a foot away from my face, please," I bite out through partially clenched teeth.

To her credit, she snaps her finger back but keeps her gaze steady on me. She places her hands on her hips and clears her throat.

"Listen, I'm emotionally mature enough to apologize for my actions back then," she says.

"Oh, here we go." I pinch the bridge of my nose, squeezing my eyes shut.

"I did not think that me fabricating a teensy-weensy little lie would spread like it did. I truly didn't." She places a hand on her chest to show sincerity, but I'm not buying it.

"Sure, you did," I huff, moving around her, remembering the rippling fallout of her so-called 'teensy-weensy little lie.'

I grab the rake leaning against the railing, shake my head, and can't help grumbling to myself, "What kind of person tells the whole entire school that a student left due to a serious, unrelenting case of...what was it? Measles?"

"Chicken pox," she cuts in flatly, ignoring the fact that I wasn't speaking to her directly.

My head shakes at the sheer ridiculousness of it all, reminding me yet again of the root of my dislike for her.

"To be fair, I only told one person," she says. "And I had my reasons, obviously. It snowballed from there, and I just apologized for that."

She lifts a shoulder in a shrug, as if my forgiveness should be a no-brainer, but I pin her with a glare.

"Are you aware that an entire year after I left town, I ran into Mrs. Flitterman down in Longville? She had the nerve to ask how my skin transplant went," I say flatly.

She bites her bottom lip, pushing them together as if to prevent a laugh from escaping, further proving her insincerity.

"Mm-hmm," I continue. "Imagine my surprise when she filled me in on the complete gossip frenzy that was happening back home at my expense."

"So...I take it you're still mad?" She cringes.

"Yup," I quip. Now, I'm not childish enough to hold onto a grudge over something as juvenile as a rumor, especially one that happened several years ago when I had much bigger things going on at the time—like simply surviving.

However, her actions definitely wiped away any lingering trace of guilt I felt for the way things went down between us. That rumor followed me around for years. Anyone who stoops low enough to gossip like that isn't someone I'm interested in associating myself with.

End of story.

With a sigh, she shrugs her shoulders. "Alright. Well, I can see I'm not making any progress here today. Enjoy the rest of your time here, Cole. I'll be back. It's only a matter of time before you buckle under the pressure."

"Over my dead body," I mumble as she turns on her heels, offering a flippant wave. I watch out of the corner of my eye as she walks away, mumbling something to the effect of having that arranged. With a shake of my head, I try to clear the negative energy her little visit created.

I make it my mission to finish the work around here as fast as I can so I don't have to subject myself to too many of these encounters. I scoop up the large pile of branches and walk them over to the woods behind the cabin, not bothering to look back as I hear the ATV start up and drive away.

FOUR
Sydney
Then

Eight years earlier

The backpack hits the backseat of my Camry with a thud, teetering along the edge before dropping to the floor of the car as I fling the door shut.

"Are you sure you don't want a ride?" I shield my eyes from the sun as it flares just behind where Laura, my best friend, is standing on the sidewalk in front of school.

"No, I'm supposed to meet Ricky by the flagpole," she says. The mischief behind her wiggling brows isn't hard to miss, especially as she pops her gum with a crooked smile.

"Message received." I roll my eyes playfully, not bothering to hide my own grin. "See you tomorrow."

I sink into the driver's seat and watch through the windshield as she scurries off. When she disappears around the side of the high school building, my smile slowly fades, the same way my shoulders slump now that the distraction from the school day is over.

Sliding the gear into reverse, I take my time exiting the parking lot, not at all in a hurry to get home. The lot is mostly empty now that it's nearly an hour after the last dismissal bell rang. I had eagerly agreed to stay after school to help Laura put up posters for *Les Mis,* the end-of-the-year production she has a lead role in.

I linger at the stop sign, trying to come up with anything else that could delay me going home. Do I have any errands to run? Not really. Any friends' houses to stop by? Nope, they're all at after-school activities.

In years past, I've always been eager to head home after a long day at school. I couldn't wait to see my mom, who always had a tray of fresh cookies waiting, and debrief about my day. But this year, my senior year—the one that's supposed to be filled with excitement and anticipation—has been completely different. The vibes in our house, not to mention the overall tone of our family, has just been...off lately.

Resigned, I accept the fact that I've pushed it off as long as I can and take a right out of the lot.

I drive one mile under the speed limit on the country road as it curves, veering toward the main road that runs right through the heart of Baudette.

It's quiet and simple, my hometown. There's not much more than a hardware store, gas station, and a diner next to the marina where boats and a floatplane or two are typically tied up. There are rows of motels nestled along each side, where fishermen and weekenders come to stay before hitching a ride out to one of the islands.

I pass by each business before taking a left at the four-way stop just past the mechanic shop. After a mile on the winding road, I turn right and jostle with the car as it bobs over the uneven surface of our gravel driveway. Our farmhouse-style house, complete with a wraparound front porch, is nestled on the bank of the Rainy River, which is just barely visible from the driveway.

This sight used to fill me with peace and calm when coming home.

Lately, it's been filling me with dread.

Swinging the backpack over my shoulder, I reluctantly climb out of my seat just as dad's boots stomp down the wooden steps of the porch.

"Hey, Syd." It may be subtle, but I know him well enough to pick up on the exhaustion in his voice. It stands out to me because it's uncharacteristic of him. As much as he's been trying to keep his typical jovial way about him, a solemnity has been coming through lately despite his best efforts.

"Hey, Dad," I say as upbeat as I can, using quite a bit of force to make the words sound normal. If he can brush his emotions to the side, I can do the same.

"I'm heading out to the island to help Graham for a bit. He's been out there all day. I'll be back before nightfall," he says in a rush while trying to look reassuring. "Shelly stopped by to visit with Mom, so she's inside too."

I can see exactly what he's doing, playing it off as if Shelly is here for a normal, casual visit between two friends...but I see it for what it is.

After one of Mom's most alarming episodes to date last week, where she got 'lost' in the middle of the hardware store, and she worked herself up into a complete frenzy when she couldn't figure out where she was, he hasn't left her side since. That is, unless one of her friends conveniently happens to be stopping by for a visit for the same amount of time it takes him to run whatever errand he needs to get done.

Mom's memory has been slowly declining for a while now. What started a few years ago as forgetting minor details here and there has turned into more and more frequent lapses lately, leaving all of us confused and desperate as we search for answers.

Hence the uneasiness in the air and my reluctance to spend a lot of time here. It's uncomfortable and unsettling. You can't help but feel every tiny shift in a home when the heart of it has been faltering.

"Okay." I wave to Dad, who's already climbing into his truck. "See you later."

I take a steadying breath before heading inside, bracing myself for whatever state Mom might be in. It's been nothing short of jarring when she can't seem to remember things that a mother most definitely should.

I drop my stuff on the entryway bench and follow Shelly's soft voice into the kitchen, where she and Mom are baking cookies at the island.

"Hi, dear." Mom's eyes light up when she spots me, and I give her my best forced smile. It hurts just to look at her lately; not knowing what's going on inside her mind makes me feel sad and defeated.

"Hey, Mom. Hi, Shelly." I slide onto a barstool, reaching for a piece of cookie dough.

"How was Mrs. Jacobson's class today? Did she grade your term paper about the biology of the forest yet?" Mom asks calmly, and my stomach clenches.

"She did. I aced it," I say, even though that paper—and teacher, for that matter—was from my junior year. One whole year ago.

My gaze snags on Shelly's as she searches me, doubt of her own in her eyes. With a satisfied nod, Mom focuses on the ingredients in front of her, moving on, having no idea that her innocent question is wreaking havoc on me internally.

How does she not know what grade I'm in? How long will it be this time until she snaps back to now?

The amount of time it takes for her to shift out of her episodes seems to vary, with no rhyme or reason to them, which makes it all the more unsettling. I watch the two of them as they move around the kitchen, Shelly trying her best to act like things are normal. The uneasiness I feel practically burns a hole through my stomach until I physically can't take it anymore. A rising pressure in my chest adds to the mix and fuels me up and off of the stool.

"I'm going to get started on my homework." I manage a quick wave before retreating up the stairs, not bothering to wait for a reply from either of them.

These crushing emotions feel like they're eating me alive, eclipsed only by the worry I have for Mom, and I stomp up the stairs, hating every single thing about this situation all of us are in.

Closing my bedroom door, I soak in the quiet comfort of my room and remind myself that all I can do is focus on what I can control in my life. And that is finishing these last few months of school until I graduate—and then I can get some much-needed space from it all.

FIVE

Now

The morning sunlight sweeps across my cheek and over my eyes, bringing me out of my sleep. I groan as I stretch my body and point my feet, feeling them tug against the quilt that's still tucked tight around the bottom of the mattress.

Then I spread my limbs out like a starfish, breathing in the subtle smell of wood and pine. For a brief minute, I'm ten again, waking up on this same island with the sound of birds and sunlight bursting through the window, wide awake and anxious to jump out of bed and pull on my boots to see what kind of animals are also up for the day, scurrying to find breakfast of their own.

With a hint of a smile playing on my lips, I remind myself that I'm a twenty-six-year-old woman and not a child and push myself out of the bed. I grab a bright-green sweatshirt—in honor of Graham—out of my suitcase that's leaning against the loft railing, twist my shoulder-length hair up into a bun, and then trudge down the stairs to the small space that encompasses both the kitchen and the living room.

These individual cabins are small—something I debated making larger when I drew up the renovation plans. However, I ultimately decided to keep the bones of the cabins as they are. We intend to focus on new floors and cabinets, upgraded HVAC and plumbing, and a few other minor cosmetic upgrades on the interiors of each one. In my opinion, the cabins are small by genius design, forcing intimacy and a closeness between the guests—or at the very least, encouraging patrons to get outside the confines of the log walls and explore the island. Neither of which is a bad thing.

I think my grandparents, whose goal was to create a community here, would approve of that decision and of this renovation as a whole. I wouldn't be doing it if I had doubts.

I slip my toes into the slippers I left by the stairs and turn the Keurig machine on. I'm not much of a coffee drinker, not finding a need for the extra boost of energy most days, but I reach for a mug anyway. There's something special about breathing in the fresh morning breeze, feeling the wind on my face with a warm mug that keeps my hands snug despite the still-crisp air leftover from the cool temperature of the night. Needless to say, I find coffee to be a necessity when I'm here on the island.

After pouring a splash of creamer in, I bring the mug outside with me, the door creaking as it opens. I sit with bent knees on the swinging bench that hangs along the porch wall. The worn sage-green cushion feels stiff as a rock, but I swing the bench gently anyway, watching through the sparse line of trees as the waves softly lap onto shore. The lake stretches for miles on end, nothing but water in the distance, except the faint outline of Oak Island.

As much as I try to convince myself otherwise when I'm at my apartment in Minneapolis, I do admit that I miss the fresh air and solitude that comes with being up here. There's a specific peacefulness that I only get when I'm on this island. In the next breath, my eyes wander to the part of the horizon that, if I followed, would take me to the city where my mom currently is. The largest, most painful reason for my grief and general avoidance of this part of Minnesota. All at once, the peacefulness is gone, replaced by the ache that grips my chest.

With a sigh, I watch as a squirrel runs across the dirt path and climbs a tree, letting it distract me momentarily before heading back inside. I drop the mug in the sink, switch out my slippers for hiking boots, and head back out of the cabin in the direction of the main lodge.

I take my time, passing in front of the individual cabins, taking the dirt trail along the shoreline while I bury the persistent ache and focus on the tasks I need to complete today.

"It's going to be a great day," I mutter aloud to myself as I plaster on a smile, if nothing else to trick my brain into believing it.

When I get closer, the aroma of Shirley's bacon leads me directly into the lodge. As I bound up the steps, I spot Blair, Graham's fiancée, sitting at one of the tables on the patio.

"Sydney!" she exclaims, grinning as she meets me halfway for a hug.

"Ah, Blair. It's so good to see you." I squeeze her tightly. I may not make it home often to see her in person, but we've built a solid relationship in the time she's been with my brother. I'm lucky to not only call her my future sister but also my friend.

"I missed you yesterday," she says, pulling back. "It was my day to be at the law office in Baudette, and by the time I got back, you were already in your cabin for the night."

"Yeah, I crashed early. I forgot how much this fresh air takes it out of me." I laugh.

"Well, I'm glad you're here," she says sincerely.

"Me too. What are you working on?" I gesture to her computer and the pile of papers spread out next to it. "Legal stuff?"

"No, actually, I'm working on a little project I'm leading for the lodge." She smiles bashfully, excitement clearly brimming beneath it, but she's holding it back for some reason.

"What is it?" I inquire, wanting to know more.

"Graham and I are putting together a youth mental health wellness camp just for kids here on the island," she says softly, cautiously, as if she's not yet confident with saying it out loud.

"Really? That's an amazing idea, Blair," I gush.

She grins, the tightness of her features loosening. "Thanks. Yeah, I'm pretty excited about it."

"What do you have planned so far?" I inquire.

"We'll have daily activities like lakeside meditation, nature walks, journaling, speaking mantras out loud, making vision boards, stuff like that. Our overall goal is to put a focus on teaching them tools to foster their mental health." She beams, and I can tell how important this is to her.

"When do you start?"

"The first camp is this weekend, actually. It's fully booked! And don't worry, we'll keep everything out of the way of the renovations. You're starting on the east side of the property, right?"

"Oh, yes, I'm not worried." I wave a hand to dismiss her concern. "This is really awesome, Blair. It'll be a great addition to the Ruby Lodge experience."

"Thanks," she says just as my stomach loudly grumbles.

"Yikes. I guess I'm hungry." I cringe.

Blair laughs, waving me away. "Go on inside. Shirley made an amazing breakfast spread this morning for the group of guests that are staying here."

"Yum. Okay, I'll catch up with you later." I wave and smile, noting how seeing Blair has further fueled my good mood, as it always does.

In the dining room, I spot Graham behind the bar.

"Morning, Syd," he calls out as he pours coffee with one hand and clears plates off the counter with the other.

"Yes, it is," I say, nearly skipping to the barstool.

"Do you need fresh towels? Is the mattress okay in your cabin?" The crease between his brow deepens in the way it always does when he's overwhelmed with taking care of everyone around him.

"It's just fine. Stop worrying about me, please," I say, but he doesn't seem convinced. It's not until he catches sight of Blair through the window that he fully relaxes, a calmness overtaking him as he keeps his eyes on her.

I smile contentedly, sweeping my own gaze across the full room of guests until I catch sight of one particular brooding face in the back corner that immediately sours my mood.

"Ugh. What's he doing here?" I snap my head back to look at Graham.

"We're on an island, Syd," he says pointedly. "And we're the only place serving food. He's allowed to eat, isn't he?"

I push out my bottom lip as I contemplate how I can tweak the obvious answer to his rhetorical question out of spite.

"Of course he is," Graham replies for me.

"Well, I don't like it." I pout.

"You don't have to," he says with a smile before reaching for the rolled-up plans tucked under the counter. "I'll lay these out. You go make yourself a plate."

With a sigh, I twist my body in the direction of the buffet that's set up along the inner wall and follow my nose toward it. It only takes me a few steps to notice that Cole is now at the far end of the buffet, scooping scrambled eggs onto his plate.

Ugh. I did not prepare myself for an interaction with him so early in the day.

I falter, momentarily looking for the nearest escape, but ultimately, I resist the urge to turn around like I desperately want to. If I turn back now, everyone in here would see me avoiding him and therefore backing down...and I'm definitely not backing down.

With an internal grumble and a huff, I surge forward, determined to be the bigger person here.

"You're going the wrong way," I say, maybe a little too clipped, grabbing a plate from the left side of the table. His head doesn't move from where it's angled down at the food, leading me to believe he either already saw me here, or he's not surprised—or fazed—by my presence.

When he doesn't say anything back, I roll my eyes and shrug my shoulders. "Fine, have it your way."

I use the tongs to grab a muffin and then move on to the next dish.

"Hey, would you like to be included in our team meeting so you have a rough timeline on when we'd like you to fork over the keys to your place?" I say sweetly, our shoulders coming slowly together like a magnet as we both move in opposite directions down the buffet line.

At the very last second before our bodies would actually touch, I shift my body as he does the same, leaving us squared off next to the hash browns. His surly gaze peers down as he towers over me. The way he rolls his lips together makes it look as though he's trying to hold back his words, but he finally says a curt and simple, "No."

"That's too bad. You know, it's a shame you can't see that it's a great day to sell a cabin," I say. "The sun is shining. You could pack everything you own in that tiny little cabin and fly away in the sky before nightfall. I could even be talked into helping you pack."

He inhales, brows lifting as if he's contemplating my offer and about to concede...before his face falls right back to where it was. Cold and unemotional. "Nah, I'd rather not."

His teasing irks me, and I clamp my lips together to ward off saying the thoughts that come to mind out loud.

We square off for a few more silent seconds, each one tinged with growing animosity and disdain, until he dips his gaze, slowly raking his eyes over me, head to toe. To my utter annoyance, my body tingles under his intense scrutiny.

Traitor.

When his eyes reach mine, he holds them there for a mere second before turning nonchalantly to walk away. My nose scrunches together as I throw an imaginary dagger at the back of his head, then I spin on my heels and stalk back to the bar.

"Can you do me a favor and not kill him please?" Graham asks pointedly while leaning over the counter, clearly having watched our whole exchange. "I'm not well versed in the high school football handbook anymore, but I'm guessing it's frowned upon to let your little sister murder your former teammate."

"Hey, I'm not the one with the bad attitude." I shrug, sliding onto the stool, doing my best to mentally shake the frustration off.

"Whatever you say." He shakes his head with a smirk while he points to the plans laid out in front of me. "Alright, fill me in on your meeting with Neal yesterday."

I pop a bite of muffin in my mouth and nod. "It went well. He went ahead and put in a request for permits to start breaking ground on the east and north sides of the property, which should take a couple weeks, but in the meantime, his team will be out here on Monday to walk around and see what they can do before those permits go through. They'll prep the job site and solidify when they can start bringing equipment over via the barge. Stuff like that."

"And you're sure we can still keep operations running while this whole thing is happening?" He doesn't look convinced, despite our many conversations about it.

"Absolutely. At least for the first phase, when they'll be working on the addition in the back. Everything will be zoned off as we go, so the guests will have designated areas to stick to on the property—and it will get messy around here—but otherwise, the crew will do their best to stay out of your way."

"Okay."

"When we get to phase two, which is the main part of the lodge, then we'll need to close up for a while since we won't have a working kitchen, but that shouldn't take too long. Then once the lodge is fully functioning, we can open back up to guests! We'll just close each cabin down one by one as we work on them individually."

"Okay." He nods his head, his features relaxing, and I feel a surge of pride that he trusts me to lead this whole thing. I can't help but be overwhelmed with gratitude to even have this opportunity at all.

I take a bite of scrambled eggs and continue on, pointing out how the new state-of-the-art kitchen will be laid out and where the new library and workout room will go. All the while, as I talk, I have to put effort into ignoring the faintest sensation that a pair of eyes is burning into the back of my head.

SIX

Cole

Now

I stay firmly cemented to my chair in the corner of the dining room until I'm fairly certain Sydney won't be coming back. With one last cautious look around, I slide out of my chair to approach the bar.

"Thanks for breakfast, man." I throw more than enough cash on the bar top and lean on it, pushing my weight against my elbows.

"You bet. Hope you enjoyed it." Graham smiles wide before it fades into a straight line. "Hey, don't let Syd get you worked up, okay?"

A huff escapes my lips at the fact that he picked up on the animosity between us. At the same time, I can't help but wonder how much he knows about our history together. I'm positive he would have heard the rumor circulating about why

I left Baudette, as the whole town did, but I doubt he knows the plague-like-case-of-chicken-pox story started from his sister.

"She means well." He cringes. "Honestly, it's a bummer, but we completely understand that you don't want to sell. It's a lot to ask. I get it—no hard feelings whatsoever."

"I think she feels differently." I smirk. Not that I care what she thinks, necessarily, but I have a feeling she's going to continue making me aware of her thoughts whether I want to know them or not.

"She'll get over it. Hey, do you need any help around your property? I noticed a few shingles coming off the roof last time I was out there checking on things, but I haven't made it back in a while. I haven't seen your uncle in a while either, so just let me know if anything turns into more than a one-man job. I'm happy to help."

"Nah, I can handle it. Thanks, though. I always forget how much maintenance comes with having a place out here." I keep the conversation surface level, as I do with most conversations in my life, and shut down the opening to talk about my uncle.

"Mother Nature can definitely be unforgiving," he agrees.

"Hey, congrats on the renovation," I tell him. "This should draw some big crowds out here. Good for the economy."

"Thanks. Yeah, that's what we're hoping for, anyway—if we can survive the renovation process." He chuckles.

I smirk, silently agreeing with him with a nod of my head.

"How long are you in town for?" Graham asks.

"I'm not sure yet. My plan is to get the cabin and property cleaned up, and then I'll probably head out." I'm not sure where I'll be heading to next. I usually just see where I feel like going when it's time to move on. My job can be done from anywhere, so it's become a habit for me to wander around. I tend to swing in and out of Longville, where my house is, and then off to wherever the wind takes me.

Most often, I head over to Duluth to sit in a pub overlooking Lake Superior or over to The Boundary Waters with not much more than a canoe and a tent strapped to my back. Solitude and a few tools are all I need to get by in this life.

"Are you meeting up with any of the guys while you're here?" he asks. I assume he's referencing our football teammates from high school, most of whom I haven't seen in many years and haven't spoken to for even longer than that. Graham is really the only one I still talk to on a semi-regular basis, even though he was a grade older than me back then. Truthfully, if it wasn't for this island, I probably wouldn't keep in touch with anyone from that time in my life.

"Maybe." I shrug, pushing off the counter. "I'll let you know if I do, though. See ya later."

"Have a good one." We nod at each other before I head back outside to where I parked my uncle's old ATV.

I can't help it when my eyes flick around the entire area surrounding the lodge. It's subtle, and not at all something I do on purpose, but I scan the property for any signs of a feisty woman who might follow me home—or maybe even sabotage my trek. I wouldn't put anything past her, truthfully.

Once satisfied that she's nowhere in sight, I rev it up and head onto the trail. As I ride past the row of cabins and into the dense woods, I let my mind zone out. Taking in the true beauty of this island is something I don't often appreciate as much as I should. But every time I'm back here, I'm reminded why my uncle chose this serene island for his home in the first place.

Eventually, I reach the property and bring the ATV to a stop next to the barely standing shed that's tucked back by the line of trees. I climb off and head toward the cabin.

My cabin.

It's been years now since Uncle Paul signed the papers over to me, but I have yet to see this place as anything more than his. In my mind, it will always belong to him. My attachment to it is largely out of respect for him and the sanctuary this place has provided me.

I push the door open with a loud creak, kicking my boots off on the faded rug. Instantly, I'm enveloped by an aroma that conjures up a hefty dose of nostalgia. The cabin air smells like earthy wood with a subtle hint of cinnamon and worn rubber from the rain boots that still sit in the front closet. There's a dampness to it—likely due to moisture in the walls somewhere—but it adds to the overall somber vibe of the place.

All of it evokes a comforting sentiment that's hard to accurately put into words. This place was a reprieve for me—a safe haven—back when I was just a pawn under my father's thumb without autonomy of my own life.

A coil of heavy anger runs up my spine at the thought of my father, the same way it always does when he crosses my mind. The fact that I let him affect me after all these years of no contact only deepens the anger, twisting painfully like a knife. I sit with it for a breath, allowing myself to feel it, and then I bury it.

This cabin was built as a one-story open floor plan way before that particular layout was trendy. To the left of the front door, there's a small couch and a worn La-Z-Boy chair surrounding a TV that hasn't worked in years. Beyond that, tucked in the back corner, is a queen-sized bed with a single nightstand on one side. A small bathroom is nestled against the back wall that runs into a few kitchen cabinets, a rusty old stove, and a fridge that doesn't have a single thing in it. The whole cabin is dimly lit with just two small oil lamps for lighting.

There's not much to it—definitely worthy of being torn down—but that doesn't make me any more inclined to let go of it.

As I sit on the edge of the bed to adjust my socks, I wonder where in the world Uncle Paul is at this very moment. It's something I wonder almost daily ever since the last time I saw him—over five years ago.

It's never been hard to pinpoint where I get my wandering tendencies from. That man has never stayed in one spot for more than two days for as long as I've been alive. For a while there, he would come to Baudette to check in every so often when he came to spend a day or two here, but ever since he signed the cabin over to me, it's as if he released himself from needing to come back. I haven't seen or heard from him since.

With a grunt, I shove off the mattress, running through my mental checklist and pondering what chore to get started on first for the day. I shove my feet back into my boots and head outside. At the bottom of the porch stairs, I grab a rake that I left propped up against the side of the cabin and head down to the beach to finish the cleanup I started there yesterday.

SEVEN

Then

"Ugh, shoot." I curse under my breath as the stack of papers from my English folder scatters to the ground, with a few stray pieces floating to land all the way on the other side of the hallway. Footsteps fade away as all the other students rush to their classrooms, leaving me alone as I struggle to get my act together.

Just as I bend to reach for one of the papers, my heavy biology book slips out of my arms and slams to the floor with a loud thud.

Come on.

My head feels frazzled and foggy as I frantically grab at papers. Since when have I become such a walking disaster?

When everything started happening with Mom, I made a point to not let what was happening at home affect my school-work so I can still graduate on time...but I don't think I'm doing a very good job at that anymore. The last several days have been harder to get a grasp on.

"Need help?" a soft, deep voice says out of nowhere behind me, causing me to jump. I twist my neck enough to look up and see a guy who looks vaguely familiar.

Graham's football teammate?

Wait...that's right. And the mayor's son.

This school is small enough to be aware of pretty much everyone, at least on the surface, but he and I definitely don't run in the same circle. I can't recall a single other fact about him.

My gaze snags on a subtle seriousness behind his stare as he holds mine. A quiet, mysterious vibe to the nonchalant way he stands there, completely unbothered by being late for his own class.

He bends to pick up one of my papers, and I realize I haven't answered him yet.

"Uh, thanks," I say, regaining my composure. "Cole, right?"

I take a few steps to grab the farthest stray paper, and then we rise to stand at the same time. He stretches a hand out to give me the stack of papers, but keeps my biology book under the crook of his arm.

"Yup." The corner of his mouth tilts up in the slightest of ways, but he doesn't ask me anything in return. He simply stares at me with an intensity that somehow leaves me almost lightheaded.

"Sydney Peterson," I offer, never shy about meeting new people, no matter what emotional state I'm in. He nods in a way that tells me he might have already known that bit of information.

"Going this way?" he asks, pointing down the now empty hall.

"Yeah," I say, falling into step next to him. "I'm late for biology. I can't seem to get my crap together today."

"Happens to the best of us." He dips his head, a crooked smile breaking through his hard exterior. A hint of warmth soothes my stomach at the way something visibly eases inside of him. I get the feeling perhaps his smiles are hard-earned.

"Where are you off to?" I try not to make my perusal of him obvious as I note the lack of his own books in his hands.

"Study hall," he answers simply. Nothing more.

Alright, then. He's definitely a guy of few words.

"My class is right up here. You don't have to walk me if you don't want to." I point to my book he's still carrying.

He simply shrugs, again completely unbothered. "I don't mind."

Something about his quiet confidence draws me in as I study him as nonchalantly as I can, wondering what his story is. The rest of the walk is silent, nothing but the sound of our footsteps echoing in the air. I slow to a stop as we reach my classroom.

"Well, thank you," I say, holding a hand out for my textbook.

"No problem." He places it in my hand and holds my eyes for a beat longer than normal before dipping his head. As if stuck in a trance, I watch him walk back in the direction we came from before I slip inside the classroom.

"Dang it, Jimmy!" Laura shouts, clutching at her chest as if she's just seen a ghost.

A laugh escapes me as I shove him back into the line of trees he just jumped out of, breathing through the sudden spike in my own heart rate.

He howls a cheer with a fist pump in the air, clearly proud of his clever antics to scare us.

"That was unnecessary." I fix a glare on him as he falls into step beside us.

"Sorry, I couldn't help it." He shrugs menacingly. "You guys are late. I got bored."

"We're not late. The sun just went down," Laura points out.

It's a well-known fact for the entirety of our senior class that sunset is the unofficial start time for the standing Friday night field party at Rayna Phillips's family farm.

"I've been here for thirty minutes already," he complains.

"Hanging out in the woods, huh? Looking for a repeat make-out sesh with a certain brunette, I presume?" I wag my brows. "Eager much?"

"Hey, I'm not above desperation." He smirks.

Stray sticks crunch under my feet as we follow the sound of voices. Just past the edge of the treeline, a clearing opens up to where a large campfire is already roaring to life. Groups of people are standing around the fire while a line of pickup trucks are backed up around the outskirts of it, tailgates down with coolers resting on top.

It's a typical Friday evening setting for us in Baudette—one I've been looking forward to all week. The persistent heaviness that's been weighing me down in an overwhelming way has me picking up the pace, making a beeline straight for Jimmy's truck.

"Beer?" I hop onto the tailgate, fishing a cold can out of the cooler. I hand it to Laura before cracking one open myself.

"I'd love one, thank you," Jimmy mimics, retrieving one for himself.

I flash him a wide-mouthed smile, trying to reach the part of me that is able to joke and be playful, but it's too far out of reach. I take a long chug, focusing on how the ice-cold liquid travels down my throat, hoping it'll drown out the heaviness in my chest. With a deep exhale, I pause to let the first numbing tingles from the alcohol start to rush through me. I relish it—the way it softens the edges of the sharpness I'm feeling inside.

"Are you good?" Laura asks softly, hopping onto the tailgate next to me.

"Yeah," I lie. We've hashed out every possible scenario about my mom together over the past couple days, and I've opened up about my fears with her, but the last thing I feel like doing tonight is talking.

Tonight, I want to forget the fact that, when I go home, my own mother might not be lucid enough to remember me.

Dramatic, I know. But her episodes seem to be getting worse and more frequent. To be honest, I don't think I'm doing a good job of handling it.

I don't know how I'm supposed to.

"Let me know if you want to bail, go somewhere quiet," she offers with an elbow nudge.

"I'm okay, really," I say with as big of a smile as I can muster before taking another swig.

"Did you hear that Theo was running his mouth today?" Jimmy asks us, coming closer to the truck. Laura and I both shake our heads. "Apparently he's looking for a rematch with Dylan tonight."

"One fist fight isn't enough for those idiots?" I grumble, recalling the pathetic brawl they took part in last week that looked more like an ego-stroking display than anything else.

"Apparently not."

"Oh, there's Ricky," Laura exclaims, a grin taking over her face as she spots him across the fire. She glances at me to gauge my reaction, her way of asking permission, which I appreciate.

"Yeah, yeah, see you later." I push her off the truck bed, and she blows us a kiss while rushing away.

"Pathetic sap," Jimmy mutters in his teasing tone, although he and I both know he eats up every little bit of our romantic drama as much as we do.

"Says Mr. Desperate," I tease, elbowing him.

He rolls his eyes dramatically but doesn't respond. Instead, we fall into a quiet silence as we watch the crowd grow larger.

I consider opening up and telling him about our concerns for my mom, which I haven't done yet. I even open my mouth a couple times to do so, but I just can't find the steam to push it out. Again, no part of me feels like acknowledging it right now.

The blaze-orange glow from the now roaring fire becomes more vibrant as the sky completely darkens, offering a black backdrop that surrounds us.

"Well, you're a ball of fun tonight, but I think I'm going to mingle." Jimmy crushes his can and grabs a fresh one before walking backward, pointing a finger at me.

"I'll be right back," he promises.

I wave him off just as I did Laura and zone out, my eyes fixed on the smoke coming from the top of the fire.

Without anyone left to distract me, my mind hyperfocuses on Mom and how in the world I might be able to get time to speed up so I can leave for college already. A part of me feels like I need to get some space in order to be able to process this all in the right way.

"You again," comes a deep, steady voice on my right. A quick tilt of my head, and I find Cole leaning against the side of the truck. Without a word, I watch him for a second, taking in his solid stature and the bulky red sweatshirt he's wearing, even though it's been an unseasonably warm spring.

"Two times in one week," I chide. "Are you following me?"

A hint of a smile cracks his serious face, and the sight of it brings the same out of me.

"That's a weird way to say, 'Thank you, Cole, for your help,' but I'll take it," he says softly.

The subtle gleam in his eye holds my attention, and the intensity of it sends a trill down my spine. Add in the numbing effect of the alcohol, and the sensation feels good. Or maybe it's the fact that I'm feeling something other than apprehension that feels good.

Either way, I welcome it.

"Aren't you supposed to be over there?" I tip my head over to the other side of the fire where some of his teammates are tossing the football. Others have their arms slung around doting cheerleaders, happily staking their claim for the night.

Something tells me Cole doesn't quite fit in with that crowd.

"Nah." He shrugs.

"Most guys on the team follow each other around, proudly touting their letterman jackets as their way of announcing their inclusion in the 'cool kids' club," I mutter, perhaps letting my bad mood shine through. "Yet, here you are, lurking in the dark—sans jacket too."

Another hint of a smirk. "Football isn't my life like it is a lot of theirs."

"You just enjoy playing the game?"

"It's just something to do." He shrugs.

I take another swig, intrigued by his answer. He hasn't given me much to go on, so I find myself wanting to know every little detail about him. What makes him tick? What does he do for fun that isn't just something to occupy his time?

"You're one to talk. Why are you over here all by yourself?" he asks, flicking his eyes up to meet mine. Again, I feel a flush from it unlike anything I've ever felt before by simply making eye contact with someone.

It's my turn to shrug. "Don't feel like socializing tonight."

He nods. Something in his expression tells me he empathizes with that, which intrigues me even more.

"Anyway, I gotta run. See ya around," he says, holding my gaze for just long enough to steal the breath from my lungs before disappearing into the night.

I can't help but keep my eyes on where he stood, intrigued by the mystery of him. Wondering why I feel this yearning to peel back his layers one by one. Wondering why I would even try with everything else I have going on in my life at the moment.

After a deep sigh, I take another sip, turning my attention back to the crackling fire.

EIGHT
Cole

Then

"Hey, Fredrickson."

The strap of my backpack slips off my shoulder as I twist to look behind me. Standing on the corner of the sidewalk I just stepped off is Sydney, wearing a bright-yellow hoodie and a black headband that's nestled between her wavy locks.

Behind her, students are swarming out of the school in a rush to get to their after-school destinations. But she simply stands there, clearly not in a hurry to get anywhere fast.

My heart ticks a few beats faster at the sight of her. She's a stranger, really, but I've been around her enough now to know this interaction with her will likely be the only bright spot left in my day.

"Now who's following who?" I ask, the corner of my mouth tipping up. I slide my hands into my pockets and shift my weight onto the balls of my feet as I wait to see what she'll say.

The juxtaposition of her sunshiney outward demeanor and the sullen pain I can see underneath was something I picked up on right away and has kept me curious enough to wonder what her life is like.

Her playful grin is visible even as she dips her head toward the ground. There's something about her... An aura. An energy. Even as she stays firmly in one spot, it's as if she's got some sort of vivacity that bubbles from the inside out. A zest for life that I'm self-aware enough to know I've never had and probably never will.

"I saw you walking." She shrugs. "Figured I'd say hi."

I stare at her for a long pause, trying to figure her out, before offering her a simple, "Well, hi."

Her smile falters slightly as the silence stretches between us. She flicks her gaze back down as she kicks at the dirt, a hesitation in her stance. When she looks back up, there's a subtle question in her stare, as if she's searching—or waiting—for something. But I'm at a loss for what that could be.

"You want to walk with me?" I offer, feeling stupid as soon as the words leave my mouth. Of course she doesn't.

"Okay," she says almost immediately. A flash of something close to relief passes on her face. It's a familiar enough look I know all too well.

A distraction, then.

That's what she needs.

"Where are you heading?" she asks, a bit of a zip back in her step as she falls into place next to me. "Do you walk to school every day?"

"Not every day," I answer, continuing down the road. I surprise myself when I feel the urge to keep talking instead of giving the bare minimum I usually do in conversations. "Only on days like today when I have the afternoon shift at the bait shop. It only makes sense with the shop being so close to school. I'll walk back to get my car at school when I'm done."

"The bait shop, huh?" she inquires.

"Yup." It's hard to hide the disdain in my voice as I grumble, "It's a dream. Nothing quite like wrangling minnows and smelling like nightcrawlers when I leave."

She snorts. "Do you like to fish?"

I shrug. "About as much as any other guy around here, I guess."

"That doesn't sound convincing. What do you do for fun, then?"

"What is this? Twenty questions?" I huff a quiet laugh, but it's not lost on me that not even a tiny bit of me minds her interest. In fact, I might even be enjoying it.

I'm used to being on my own, as I've always been somewhat of a loner. I'm self-aware enough to know I keep it that way mostly out of self-preservation. The last thing I want to do is let anyone get close enough to unravel the truth about my home life.

She only smiles expectantly, waiting for me to answer.

I roll my lips together, casting my gaze downward as I share something I hardly ever admit aloud to anyone else, but for some reason, it feels okay to do with her now.

"I like to make stuff. Out of wood. Woodworking." I stumble on the words, not liking being vulnerable enough to talk about myself.

"Oh, that's cool! What's the last thing you made?"

I swallow, kicking at a rock, watching it ricochet off the curb.

"Um, I finished a chess board yesterday."

"That's impressive." She smiles, shifting her backpack on her shoulder. "I love chess."

"What about you? Do you have a job?" I ask as we follow the curve of the road that heads straight for town.

"I help out at Ruby Lodge any chance I can. That's my family's fishing resort out on Takini Island." She offers the explanation, even though she didn't need to. Even if my uncle didn't have his own cabin on the same island, I would still know where Ruby Lodge is. You'd have to live under a rock in this small town to not know where every single business, resort, or restaurant within fifty miles is. Besides, I remember when Graham had to skip practice a few times last year to run out there and help with an emergency or two.

"I answer the phones, book reservations, or help in the kitchen. Basically, pitch in wherever I'm needed," she explains.

"Sounds like a better gig than the bait shop," I comment.

I catch her smile out of the corner of my eye as I run my fingers through my hair out of habit.

"What happened there?" I follow her pointed finger to my wrist, where a black-and-purple bruise wraps around it. I immediately tuck my hand back into my pocket, feeling caught off guard.

"Oh, uh...I ran into the corner of my desk in my room," I lie.

"Ouch." She cringes. I don't expand on it, and thankfully she doesn't press with any further questions.

Once again, we fall into a comfortable silence. She sure likes to talk, which I don't seem to mind as much as I do with other people, but I'm also finding the quiet feels good with her too.

I wait patiently for her to bring up my dad, as everyone always eventually does, and I've already got a backlist of several different ways I can redirect the conversation away from that particular topic. Talking about my family isn't something I do. Period. Maybe if my mom hadn't run off when I was a kid and my dad wasn't such an asshole, I would think differently.

But here we are.

I'm pleasantly surprised to reach the sidewalk in front of the bait shop with no mention of them. I turn to face her, feeling unsure of what I'm supposed to do now. Obviously, I can't offer to walk her back to school, but it doesn't feel right to just leave her. Do I really just go inside while she walks back alone? That doesn't sit right with me.

"Well, thanks for letting me tag along," she says cheerfully.

"I feel bad that you have to walk all the way back now," I say, forcing my thoughts out in the open.

"Nah." She waves her hand in dismissal. "I don't mind. It's a nice day."

She starts backing away but keeps her gaze on me. A comforting warmth spreads in my chest as I hold her stare. The possibility of a genuine friendship—maybe even something more—blooms faintly in my chest.

I clear my throat, a silent warning to myself to not hope for too much. My life has always gone a certain way, and this will be no different. I can almost bet on it.

"Well, see ya around." I tip the corner of my mouth up in a small smile before heading inside the bait shop.

NINE
Sydney
Now

Week Two of Renovation

"So, the new exterior wall will come out to about here." I step back, my foot sinking into the dirt, and make a marker with my arms, not necessarily to ask Neal for confirmation, but more so to acknowledge the plan out loud. To make sure we're all on the same page moving forward.

"Yup." Neal nods as he, Graham, and I examine the space directly behind the lodge, visually placing the changes to be made. He points to the back wall. "Graham and Blair's apartment expansion will take up that whole side of the building directly behind the dining room and kitchen. And a proper office and upgraded library will be in the middle section. Then the utility room, laundry, and exercise room are carved out for the far side."

"Sounds great," Graham says enthusiastically. I can practically see the wheels turning in his head. I can envision it too. How this place will look with the updates. How it'll be able to serve so many more guests in so many different ways. I just know my grandparents would have been thrilled with this—and that makes it all worth it.

"Once we get demolition of the neighboring cabins out of the way, we'll start in the back of the lodge here and work our way forward so you can keep operations running until we reach the front half of the building," Neal says.

"Perfect," Graham says. "And Syd and I went over the schedule of blocking off reservations for each of the cabins in staggering weeks. Just let me know if the timeline looks different for that so I can adjust as needed."

I nod, agreeing with Graham as Neal turns his attention to me.

"What's the latest on the glamping tent area? When can we get up there?"

I actively choose to remain professional, so I keep the irritation in my mind instead of outwardly rolling my eyes. "It's not looking good, actually. We might not be able to acquire that land...but I'm not giving up yet, so just hold tight on that portion."

"Okay." He points to the woods behind us. "We always have this area back here if we need to revert to plan B and do it on a smaller scale."

A squeeze of panic grips my throat at the thought. It wouldn't be good enough that way. It wouldn't be perfect.

"Yup," I agree with him as the three of us start walking back around to the front. My boots slip through a muddy spot before I have the chance to skirt around it, but it doesn't bother me in the slightest. Getting a little muddy is par for the course out here.

"So, your next job will be to clear everything out of that shed," Neal tells Graham, pointing to the structure as we pass. "We'll have to move the whole thing back a bit to fit the expansion."

"Roger that." Graham salutes.

"I've got a barge coming out tomorrow morning with an excavator, a Bobcat, and a team of guys who are going to start clearing anything we're allowed to before the permits come back, which should be any day now. Once we get those, we'll hit the ground running," Neal explains.

"Sounds like a plan. Thanks for your help executing this, Neal," I say with a smile as we reach the steps of the front porch. Shielding the sun with my hand does little to combat the glare as it beams off the lake, but I do my best to keep it out of my eyes.

"You bet," he says with a smile. "I'll run in to grab my things. Sam should be flying in to pick me up any minute here."

"I'm actually hitching a ride with you into town," I tell him. "So, I'll see you on the dock."

With a wave, Neal heads inside the lodge.

"What are you doing in town?" Graham asks as soon as Neal is out of earshot. A wave of guilt and heartache hits me like a brick wall at his question. I know what he's hoping to hear, and I hate that I have to burst his bubble like this again—just like I do every time he asks.

"I'm meeting Laura and Jimmy at The Saloon for happy hour. I haven't seen them in ages, so we're making a point to catch up since I'm here," I say with a tentative smile.

"So, you're not seeing Mom, then?" To his credit, he tries to hide his disappointment, but I feel the weight of it regardless of the neutral expression on his face.

"No," I say softly, looking down.

He nods, pushing his lips together. We do this often enough over the phone that I know he won't push me on it, but man does it hurt to feel his disappointment in person.

"I have to go change before Sam arrives," I say gently, pointing in the direction of my cabin.

"Alright. I'll keep an eye out for him." He heads toward the stairs while I turn on my heel, making a beeline down the trail to my cabin.

I'm able to do a quick outfit change and clean up my makeup in record time. I even have time to spritz some perfume on my wrist, even though I know the mosquitos will swarm me later because of it.

My phone buzzes with a text message just as I'm heading out the door.

Graham: *Sam's here.*

I rush to the docks where Sam and Graham are holding the floatplane in place.

"Sorry. Coming!" I yell as I jog, ignoring the small voice from my childhood in the back of my mind that reminds me not to run on a dock.

"Your chariot awaits." Sam smiles, offering his hand to usher me into the open door on the side of the plane. I give Graham a quick kiss on the cheek and take Sam's hand to climb inside.

"Hey, Neal." I settle next to him, sinking into a cloth-covered seat, pulling the seat belt tightly across me. Sam says farewell to Graham and follows me inside, closing the plane door behind him.

I watch with fascination as he starts pressing buttons and pushing levers to bring the plane to life, and a small swarm of butterflies flutters inside my stomach. No matter how many times I've flown in a floatplane—and that would be too many times to count—it just never gets old.

We slowly bob across the water as Sam takes the plane out of the bay. Then another exhilarating rush runs through me as he accelerates, lifting us off the water and up into the sky.

I peer out the window to watch Ruby Lodge as it gets smaller by the second. I never waste a chance to admire it like this from up here. There's something special about getting an aerial view of a place that holds so many of your memories. In the same breath, it can also be a devastating reminder of the present day that looks nothing like the past you once knew.

Neal and I chat mindlessly for the twenty-minute flight, and before I know it, my stomach flips again as we land and approach the marina in Baudette.

"We're good to go," Sam announces from the front as he climbs out of his seat to open the door for us. He exits first, offering a greeting to the dock boys who are holding the plane steady, and then he offers a hand to help me climb out.

"Thanks for letting me hop in, Sam. I really appreciate it," I tell him.

"Anytime. We need to leave by 5:30 to be able to get back before dark, though, so just text me when you're ready."

"Okay!" I wave and call out a quick goodbye to Neal before rushing off the dock toward town.

As I head up the inclined sidewalk toward the main road, the familiar weight of both nostalgia and grief settles over me. The city of Baudette holds the most painful memories for me, much more than Takini Island does. Even now, I can't walk this sidewalk without the stark awareness of my mom—and dad—being only a few short blocks away. It's a complex and strange feeling to be so close to something and yet still feel so mind-numbingly far away at the same time. The reality of the thought alone creates a heavy knot in my stomach as I swallow, trying to push past it.

A quick right takes me to The Saloon, a bar that opened five years ago. I've never actually been there, but Jimmy recommended it. I take in a calming breath, channeling my focus on the excitement of seeing my friends, and head inside.

"Syd!" Laura's voice immediately calls out from the back corner, and I find where she and Jimmy are sitting on barstools.

"Eek!" I shriek, doing a little happy dance as I run into her open arms for a much-needed, long-awaited hug.

"Ah, I missed you," I say into her hair before pulling Jimmy into a tight embrace as well.

"Well, look what the wind blew in," Jimmy marvels. "Miss hot-shot architect. It's about time you came home to say hi."

A twinge of guilt twists in my gut. Admittedly, avoiding home has had an effect on all of my relationships, not just the one with my mom.

"I know, I know." I cringe. "I'm sorry."

I slide onto the stool next to Laura and ask, "When did you get in?"

"Only about twenty minutes ago. It took me an hour this time to drive from International Falls—not bad!"

"This is the first time she's been back in a while too," Jimmy complains, hooking his thumb at Laura.

"Hey, I come home at least once a month, so don't start." She points a finger in his face, and I laugh, realizing how much I've missed them.

"Yeah, yeah. Do you want a drink?" he asks, waving the bartender down for me.

"Just a soda water and lemonade please." I smile at the bartender, knowing I recognize him from some small part of my past here but not enough to officially acknowledge or make small talk with him.

I can feel my two friends' stares on me, as my non-alcoholic beverage choice is a far cry from what I would have ordered back in the day, but I don't feel the need to explain.

It's not that I don't drink at all, but I'm self-aware enough to know that I've used alcohol as too much of a crutch in the past. I've leaned a little too heavy on it at times. I feel enough on edge just by being here that I don't feel like adding it to the mix. Besides, I don't need it to have fun.

I twist in my seat, facing both of them, and grin.

"So, what's new? Tell me everything," I say to neither of them in particular.

"Laura was just telling me she got promoted to regional manager at the paper mill," Jimmy offers.

"Laura! That's amazing! Congratulations!" I grip her shoulder and squeeze. "And how's the wedding planning going? Last time we spoke, you mentioned Ricky was absolutely no help at all."

"He still isn't." She huffs, but I revel in the enamored glint to her eyes that I always swear I can see whenever we talk about him over the phone.

"Either way, it's going to be great. I can't wait," I tell her honestly while taking a sip of my drink.

"What about you, Jimmy?" I turn my attention to him. "Is the gas station business everything you hoped it would be?"

Staying in Baudette after graduation to join his family's legacy in the service station industry was always the expected route for him—at least that was his plan and dream for his life for as long as I can remember.

"Everything and more." He says it sarcastically, but the look on his face tells me he's truly happy, and that's all I need to know.

When I take my next sip, my eyes wander around the bar, and I catch sight of none other than Cole walking our way, appearing just as he has every time I've seen him since I've been back—grumpy and irritated. It's ironic that seeing him seems to make me feel the exact same way.

"Ugh," I grumble to myself.

"What's with the face?" Laura asks, turning her head in the direction of my displeasure.

Cole looks over, and our gazes connect, two matching scowls that zone in on each other. There used to be a time when the sight of him was intriguing and electrifying. Now all I feel is aggravation and disgust.

"Cole," I say curtly in greeting as he slows to a stop in front of me.

"Peterson," he replies, nearly under his breath.

"Did you come to concede on the sale?" I ask as chipper as I can muster. "We could have done that on the island, you know. No need to follow me into town."

He huffs, shifting his weight on two feet while arching a brow. "Believe it or not, my every move does not, in fact, revolve around you or your renovation plans. Shocking, I know."

I roll my eyes so hard it physically hurts, and Laura chokes on her laugh, hiding it in Jimmy's shoulder, who I believe is also grinning.

Just as I'm about to turn in my seat to brush him off, recognition flashes across Laura's face as she examines Cole.

"Wait a minute," she says, tapping a finger against her lip, visibly struggling to place him. I mentally sigh, knowing exactly where this is heading.

Cole deepens his scowl as he pushes his lips together and offers her a simple word, "Measles."

My mouth goes dry as Laura snaps her fingers. "Yes! That's it!"

He ever so slightly lifts his brow at me as if to prove some point—which is noted.

"Chicken pox," I correct in a defiant whisper. Laura whips her eyes to me in the next second when the rest of the realization of who he is sinks in.

Cole keeps his piercing stare on me as I try to come up with words in my defense, but unfortunately, nothing comes to my mind. My brain goes all fuzzy, and I can't think straight when he's staring at me like that.

"Alright, then." He dips his head, acknowledging the three of us before continuing past. We all watch the back of his head in silence until he disappears inside the bathroom.

"Cole, right?" Jimmy asks me in a hushed voice, as if he might be able to overhear us through the wall. "The former mayor's son?"

"Yup," is all I can say.

"Dang, he aged well," he breathes. I want absolutely nothing to do with talking about how handsome he is, which, admittedly, he is...but it does nothing to overshadow the truth of his character. I clear my throat and change the topic.

"Alright, tell me about the latest honeymoon plans, Laura."

Her eyes light up as she delves into their top three destination picks and their pros and cons list for each one.

As the next hour passes by, I try to soak in the rare time with my old friends as much as I can. However, I end up focusing an annoying amount of effort on batting away the hyperawareness I have of the man who's sitting across the bar.

TEN
Cole

Now

The scrape of my chisel as it runs against the wood is the only sound that hangs in the air. The only one that rivals the wind rustling through the woods behind the cabin. Two sounds—along with the soft pat of wood shavings as they fall to the ground—that I would happily live with for the rest of my life in place of any other.

I exhale with the next push, releasing some lingering tension from yesterday, as I work on turning this slab of wood into a birdhouse for a client. The last-minute order came through yesterday morning, and I decided to go ahead and complete it here in between cabin repairs instead of waiting until I get back home.

Working with my hands like this always gives me an escape, and I can feel the tension melting away with each stroke. Being in Baudette yesterday was too much. It's one thing to be on

Takini Island, but I tend to avoid the city altogether when I'm here. If there was a closer city with a hardware store, I would have gladly avoided the chance to immerse myself back in that environment at all.

Even though my father moved away several years ago, Baudette is riddled with ghosts of him and our tumultuous, mostly hidden, father-son relationship. I've moved on about as much as a person can from a childhood like that, but it doesn't mean I enjoy being surrounded by the memories. I'm all for avoiding it if I can.

Running into Sydney obviously didn't help my mood either. Talk about adding insult to injury. Although, I have to admit, her friend recognizing me as the guy from the rumor—effectively pointing out the reasoning for my irritation—was pretty satisfying.

Pushing any thoughts of her out of my mind, I set the chisel down to inspect my work in progress. It's a standard birdhouse with an A-frame roof and a single hole positioned above the perch. A faux chimney stack sits atop the roof with a hook on top.

With a satisfied nod, I set the birdhouse on my workbench with the goal of sanding and staining it later this afternoon. I need to get moving on repairing the cabin, otherwise I'll never get out of here.

Dusting any leftover slivers of wood off my jeans, I head to the shed that looks like the whole thing could blow over with one strong breath.

The door actually does fall off its hinges when I pull it open, and I curse under my breath as I let it fall onto the grass.

"For Pete's sake," I grumble, shifting through the random, unorganized contents inside. A cracked shovel leans against the wall, and a disassembled rake is scattered between discarded buckets. Debris and foliage dust every single available surface inside.

Once again, I'm fully aware that I have no one to blame but myself for this mess. This is exactly what I get for not putting more energy into maintaining this place.

Making a mental note to add fixing this shed to my to-do list, I grab the small step stool ladder buried way in the back and get to work on the roof.

Then

I slam my bedroom door shut and slump my weight against the frame. My back slides down to the floor as my chest heaves with staggered, painful breaths. My bicep aches from my father's harsh grip, and my cheek still stings from that last blow of his fist. I squeeze my eyes shut, every inch of my body feeling too exhausted to move.

His truck revs to life outside my window, no doubt disappearing to blow off steam like he does every time we get into an altercation like this—that part, at least, is predictable.

What's not predictable is what I do to trigger him in the first place. That's something I've been trying to figure out my entire life. His behavior has become more and more volatile lately, and while I used to be able to at least sense when he was in a mood, I can't seem to anticipate it as well anymore.

An overwhelming heaviness squeezes my entire chest as I hang my head, not feeling mentally strong enough to keep the whirlwind of conflicting emotions at bay.

Shame.

Anger.

Defeat.

Hurt.

All of it washes over me in waves. Anger screams the loudest in my head—I absolutely hate that he has this effect on me. That I don't stand up for myself. That he left me yet again with my soul just as bruised as my skin.

As a kid, I felt hurt and confused more than anything when he would lay his hands on me. I couldn't understand why someone who I knew was supposed to love us could hurt my mom and me the way he did. That was way back before Mom left, on days when I had to watch him put on an act in public and then squeeze her arm with a little too much force inside the confines of our home. A little shove here and there that he reasoned his way out of at first before the aggression toward her slowly escalated—and eventually expanded to include me.

At this point, a few months out from graduation, it's hard to feel anything but infuriated. I'm furious that he can hide it so well in front of the entire town who was dumb enough to elect him mayor. Angry that none of them have a clue what he's like behind closed doors. I'm also livid that he ran Mom off years ago, forcing her to leave town with not much more than a train ticket and an addiction problem.

Most of all, though, I'm angry at myself for not being man enough to stop any of it.

With a grunt, I push myself off the floor, swiping my palm against a rogue tear I hadn't noticed fell down my face. When I pull my hand back, it comes away covered in blood from a cut on my cheek that he must have made with the wedding ring he still wears for show.

I stumble across the room, press a Kleenex to my cheek, and pull open the drawer of my nightstand. There sits the one glimmer of hope I've been clinging to all week.

A letter from my uncle Paul.

The only person in the world who knows the truth about the man he calls his brother. He's been off roaming the country for some time now, but he sends me a letter from time to time to check in and keep me updated on where he is. I cling to them like a buoy in stormy waters. This one in particular came a few days ago with the postage stamped from Albuquerque.

Hey there, slugger. Greetings from New Mexico! I hope you're doing okay. Just think, you're almost done with school. A high school graduate, can you believe it? I'm so proud of you. I can't wait until I can take you on adventures with me. Show you the world and get you out from under your dad's thumb. Soon enough. You won't believe the beauty I've found in so many different places. You're going to love it, I promise. I'll write again soon.

Hang in there.

Paul

I fold the letter, letting his words comfort me the way they do every time I get a message from him.

A few more months.

Then I'm free.

Free to leave this town and go meet up with him—wherever he'll be at that point. It doesn't matter where. All that matters is that I get out of here.

A few more months... I can handle that.

ELEVEN
Sydney
Now

I wasn't prepared for the way the sweet sight out the lodge window would draw me in, keeping me locked on Blair and the small swarm of children that are spread out on the beach. Today is day one of her first three-day youth mental health wellness camp, and I'd say so far it looks like it's going well.

Eight kids are settled, with their legs crisscrossed, on individual beach towels for this morning's beachside grounding meditation. With their eyes closed and palms up on their knees, not only is it adorable, but they make it look so relaxing I'm half tempted to join them.

"This is great, isn't it?" My dad appears at my side with a wistful look about him.

"Which part?" I ask, a perma-smile glued on my face.

"All of it," he breathes, his own smile growing. "What you're doing with this renovation. You being here. Young life out here at the lodge. It's a beautiful thing."

I nod into my coffee as I take a sip, not quite able to let the compliment sink in all the way, but appreciating his words, nonetheless.

"I mean it," he insists. "Your grandparents would be so proud. They would have loved to see this."

"That's why I'm doing it," I say softly, meeting his eyes. A moment of tender understanding and respect for our shared history passes between us.

"Are you ready, Dad?" Graham calls from behind us, emerging from the kitchen.

"Yup. He's giving me a boat ride back to the mainland," he explains to me as we head toward the front door.

"That was a quick trip," I comment.

"Yeah, I only needed to drop off a few things for Graham. It's time to get back to your mother." The way he says that last word makes my heart feel like it's ripping in two. Nothing gives me this fresh of a reminder of my grief more than when I see my dad, especially here.

"It's good to have you here, Syd." He slides an arm over my shoulder. It's comforting and genuine, but I hear the words he's holding back clear as day.

When are you going to come see your mother?

He doesn't have to say it out loud for it to have an effect on me. Guilt crushes my chest.

Why can't I do this?

My throat feels tight, and I bite my lip to distract myself from the emotions that threaten to overcome me as we walk onto the dock.

"It's good to be here, Dad," I whisper. The words only feel half true, but I say them anyway.

"Well, I'll be back out soon," he says as he climbs in one of the fishing boats still tied to the dock.

"I'll be here for a while," I remind him. Behind me, Graham gives Blair a quick kiss on the cheek before jogging to the boat. He grips my shoulder in passing as he unties the ropes and climbs in.

I wave as they take the boat out of the bay, a part of me screaming to jump in and go with. To just rip the Band-Aid off and go. But this stubborn grief keeps my feet firmly rooted in place, and I watch as the boat gets smaller until it completely disappears into the horizon.

As nice as it is to see my dad, I can never shake the nagging thought of knowing I'm disappointing him by not going to see Mom. It happens every single time.

I let my eyes drift closed, soaking in the minuscule amount of comfort the gentle wind in my hair and the warm sun on my face gives me. Blowing out a sigh, I turn and head off the dock where Blair crosses the sand to meet me at the end of it.

"Morning," she says with a warm smile.

"Hey. Looks like the kids are having fun," I say as upbeat as I can. The kids are each now set up in Adirondack chairs with blankets covering their laps and journals in hand.

A serene, thoughtful look comes over Blair's face as she watches them. "Yeah, I think they are."

I need to head back to my cabin to put the final touches on the interior design board for the cabins, but this mix of emotions swirling inside me has me reluctant to move.

"Hey, are you okay?" Blair furrows her brow.

I force a smile, but I'm not sure how genuine it comes across. "Yeah. I'm just tired, I think."

She nods sympathetically and then starts heading back toward her campers.

"Hey, Blair," I blurt out before she gets too far. It's like a panic response I hardly consider before it comes out.

"Yeah?" She twists back.

Emotion surges inside me, the words all at once demanding to be let out.

"How does he do it?" I manage to squeak out, tears pricking at my eyes.

"Who? Do what?" She closes the space between us again, worry etched on her face.

"Graham," I whisper, swallowing hard. "How can he see her like that?"

Instantly, her face softens, and sympathy creases her features. I hate getting attention like this with every fiber of my being, but at the same time, a small part of me feels relief at being vulnerable out loud with someone I know I can trust.

She reaches forward, gripping my hand gently, and gives me a reassuring smile.

"It's not easy for him," she says with a squeeze. "It never has been. But I think, for him, he does it because a part of him feels like it's his duty. As a son, as a man. Graham is also a caregiver at heart, so it's become sort of a natural thing to do. Plus, I think it helps when he brings her photos and memories—he feels like he's caring for her somehow."

"Yeah," I choke out, looking away as I blink back tears. It's not lost on me that I feel the same way about this renovation—this is me caring for it somehow. For the memories and for an important part of my past. I just don't know why I can't seem to do the same for her.

"It's okay that it's hard for you," she says softly. "It's okay to do what you need to do to take care of yourself. There isn't a rule book for these kinds of situations."

Her validation cracks me open a little bit more, and I feel a lone tear run down the side of my cheek despite my best efforts to hold it back. I swipe it away immediately and purse my lips together, giving my head a slight shake.

This is exactly what I was worried about when I decided to come back here. There are too many unresolved emotions here that are lurking and ready to pounce on me. How in the world am I going to do this every day? I'm already exhausted.

"Maybe one day you'll be ready," she offers gently, running her hand down my arm.

I sniffle and heave a deep breath, nodding.

"Maybe I need to borrow one of those journals you've got," I joke, wiping the remaining tears from my face.

"Do you want one?" Her eyes perk up, clearly eager to help. "I have extra."

"No." I shake my head. "I was just kidding. Thank you, though. I'll be alright."

"Well, if you change your mind, let me know."

"I will. Anyway, I'll let you get back to it. We can chat more later."

She immediately wraps me in a hug I didn't ask for, but I feel grateful for it all the same. I grip her tightly for a squeeze and then pull back, ready to shift my focus back to work.

With one last smile, I leave her on the beach and head toward the trail that leads to the cabins on the west side of the property. As I pass by the lodge, my arms wrapped around myself, my gaze flashes up to where I could have sworn a flannel-clad figure just moved away from the window.

TWELVE

Then

Early-onset Alzheimer's.

The words out of the doctor's mouth this afternoon have been at the forefront of my mind for several excruciating hours now. While I'm definitely inebriated enough to make the edges of my world blurry, I'm apparently not drunk enough to block the words out like I hoped it would.

We knew this diagnosis was likely, but nothing could prepare me for the blow it would bring to actually hear the words out loud. It was a gut punch straight to my core that felt both heavy enough to cement me to the floor but also left me with an indescribable urge to run. It didn't matter where to; I just needed to get away from it all as fast as possible.

Which I did as soon as we got out to the parking lot and Mom urged me to go. She's always known that I need space to process big news in my own way. The fact that she acknowledged it and selflessly supported me in this way, especially in a moment like this, somehow made the grief—and guilt—even worse.

I came straight out to Rayna's field, an entire hour earlier than anyone else, which explains why I'm currently a few too many beers deep, sitting on the trunk of my car, watching people just now starting to arrive.

As the cars drive across the field one by one, I mindlessly repeat the diagnosis in my head and zero in on the way the buzz of the alcohol is almost comforting—how it takes away some of the sharpness of the sting.

An entire hour passes, and eventually, the fire is roaring to life and rambunctious voices fill the air. All the while, I've barely moved a muscle. Firmly planted in place, I've been watching it all happen through a hazy blur.

"All by yourself again, I see."

I recognize the voice immediately without needing to turn my head, and the quiet intensity in it seems to have the same effect as the alcohol. Another wave of warmth courses through me as I turn my head to watch Cole slowly inching his way toward my car.

His hands are tucked into the pockets of his jeans, and he has the hood of his sweatshirt pulled over his head. It takes me a few seconds to find his gaze now that the sky is pitch black around him and my vision is this unclear.

"Yeah, my friends ditched me," I say against the mouth of the can before taking another sip.

Truthfully, I'm happy Laura and Jimmy both have dates tonight. I want them to enjoy their evenings without worrying about me, which is exactly why I didn't tell either of them about Mom's official diagnosis yet. I can already picture their looks of pity clear as day. There'll be plenty of time for that later.

"Where'd you come from?" I ask, feeling proud of myself for not slurring my words—at least I hope I didn't.

"Bait shop."

I rest my drink on my thigh and give him the smallest hint of a smirk.

"For what it's worth, you don't smell like worms...at least not from here."

For a split second, the way he presses his lips together to stifle a full-blown smile sends something brand new down my core. Something other than heartbreak and grief. Something I think I want more of.

"Are you going to hover over there all night, or do you want to sit with me?" I tap the metal trunk beside me in invitation.

He rolls his lips. "I'm still trying to figure out if you want me to. To be honest, you're giving off a pretty intense 'don't mess with me' vibe."

I huff.

"It's been a day. Come on," I say simply, smiling to myself as he stalks closer, enjoying the dip of my car when he climbs on.

He shifts, and the solid warmth of his body as it settles next to mine gives me something tangible to focus on—a beacon in the midst of this storm I'm in.

"You want to talk about it?" he asks quietly.

As I inhale, I consider how that makes me feel, what it would feel like to open up to him. Aside from a few rumors and chatter around town, nobody knows my mom's official diagnosis yet. I give that all of an entire day to last. A diagnosis like this is big news that's sure to spread like wildfire once it's out. I already dread the looks of pity and stares we'll inevitably get at every corner, and if I could somehow keep anyone else from finding out, I would.

But at the same time—as inexplicable as it sounds—in this moment, it feels okay to exist in a world where Cole knows. I clear my throat, mustering enough courage.

"You know the phrase 'fight, flight, or freeze'?" I ask quietly, staring over at the flames of the fire.

"Yeah." I can see the dip of his hoodie-clad head in my peripheral vision.

I sigh. "I'm pretty sure I'm a flight kind of person."

He waits quietly, doing nothing but pushing his hands into the front pocket of his sweatshirt.

"My mom was diagnosed with Alzheimer's today." Saying the words out loud feels like a sharp knife in my side, and I struggle to inhale a steady breath.

"I'm sorry," he says so quietly I'm not even positive he said it out loud.

When tears start to prickle at my eyes, I clear my throat, immediately gaining composure.

No.

I don't want to go down this road right now. I can't.

"I don't want to talk about it." I shake my head. "Quick, distract me."

"Go on a date with me," he blurts out.

"What?' I snap my head to him, wondering if I heard him correctly or if the alcohol has officially become a terrible idea.

The outline of his face is a tad fuzzy as my head swims, but I pick up on something behind his stare that keeps my eyes glued to his. A vulnerability that I latch onto with all my might. It's a shared moment between us that ignites a flurry of new emotions somewhere deep inside of me.

A bearing of souls. An understanding. A validation of sorts that I'm instantly consumed by.

"Go on a date with me," he repeats, firmly this time.

"Okay," I whisper immediately, as if the words are pulled impulsively from somewhere deep inside.

He stares, his brows creasing together, a question on his face. There's a slight hesitation before he drops his gaze to my lips and inches slowly closer.

Air gets stuck in my throat and my heart beats rapidly. I respond by boldly closing the rest of the gap between us, pressing my mouth gently to his.

All at once, I'm completely consumed. It's not entirely clear to me whether these butterflies are real or if my brain is tricking me into latching onto—and fueling—anything that might cause a distraction right now. Either way, I can't seem to get enough.

I twist my torso, slipping my hand inside his hoodie, cradling the base of his neck. He runs a warm palm up my outer thigh, settling at the very top of it.

The kiss is overwhelming in the simplest of ways. It's gentle. It's pure. And it's life-giving to me in this moment.

When he gently pulls away, I flutter my eyelids open and bite my lip as I process this newfound feeling. The corner of his lip curves up into a slow smile, and I mimic it with one of my own.

Words don't come to mind—for either of us, it seems—as he presses the side of his body against mine. A silent show of support.

We quietly watch the fire as I sip my drink. Eventually, the world starts to spin a little too fast and a little too out of control.

"I need to go," I announce, hopefully in a casual way, but in this state, I'm not entirely sure.

My foot snags on the bumper of my car as I attempt to climb off, and suddenly Cole is directly in front of me, holding me steady.

"Whoa, easy there," he says.

"I'm okay," I mumble, struggling to find my footing as the world spins around me.

"How much did you have to drink?" he asks, keeping his grip strong. He asks the question so quietly that I'm going to assume he's asking himself and not actually me.

I can't seem to form words anymore, so I stay quiet, allowing myself to slump against him as he wraps his arm around my waist to hold me up.

"Come on, let's get you home."

The sound of tires rolling against gravel faintly registers in my dream state. Then the brush of a cool wind against my cheek causes my eyelids to flutter open, waking me from a deep sleep.

It takes a few more seconds to push through the brain fog to become aware of where I actually am. The soft cushion of the front porch swing shifts as I sit upright, a wool blanket falling off my shoulders. My head throbs with a pounding headache, and my stomach feels uneasy.

With a groan, I close my eyes again as vague memories from last night shuffle through my head. The doctor's office. The field party. The beers. The way the world was going blurry at the edges.

The interaction with Cole, though—and the kiss—is clear as day, and butterflies swarm my stomach at the memory of it. From the kiss on, the night gets fuzzier, but I vaguely remember bits and pieces of Cole driving me home in my car and tucking me in on the porch swing.

Ugh. How embarrassing.

"Did you sleep there?" Graham asks from the driveway, slamming his truck door shut.

"I guess so," I croak, my throat feeling scratchy.

"You're looking like a ray of sunshine this morning." His voice is teasing in a gentle way.

I rub my eyes with my knuckle. "Look who's talking. You're just getting home."

"I slept at the lodge with Mom and Dad last night, actually."

"Oh." A twinge of guilt hits me. I should have been there with them.

He gestures for me to move my legs out of the way before lowering next to me onto the swing. Then he slowly rocks us with his foot.

"Oh, don't swing, please," I whisper, bringing a hand to my head. I can feel his eyes on me as I blink through the blur, barely noting an eagle that flies over the river behind the house.

"How are you feeling about everything?" he asks gently.

"Obviously not great," I admit.

To his credit, he doesn't try to invalidate or rationalize my feelings. He only nods, running his hand through his hair as his own shoulders slump.

I shift my feet to the side so I can lay my head on his shoulder, taking comfort in knowing at least there's one other person in this world who knows what this feels like. Who knows how much losing Mom hurts.

As we swing in silence, I contemplate how our lives are about to change. The doctor said every patient progresses with the disease at their own pace, and there's no true timeline. It could be slow and steady over the course of years, or it could happen rapidly. The unknown of it all is one of the hardest parts. How am I supposed to prepare for something if I don't know exactly when and how it will happen?

"You know I'm here if you want to talk about anything," Graham says quietly.

"I know." I offer a sad smile.

"We'll get through it together." He nudges me with his elbow in a supportive-big-brother kind of way that I appreciate. A crushing heaviness threatens to blanket me, and for a few moments, I like the way it feels when I let it.

When a text message notification dings from somewhere under the pillow, I slide a hand underneath to find my phone.

Laura: Meet for coffee?

Sydney: Sure, give me twenty.

The uneasiness deepens, knowing that I plan to tell Laura about the diagnosis. I guess this morning will mark the beginning of everything changing—more accurately, the outside world changing the way it treats us.

Our world changed yesterday.

"I'm going to get cleaned up," I tell Graham as I climb off the swing. "We'll chat later?"

"You bet."

I hold his stare, a moment passing between us that doesn't involve words but says enough about the support we're willing to provide for each other.

Then I head inside to change.

THIRTEEN
Cole

Now

"Oh, great. Must be my lucky day." Sydney's voice drips with sarcasm from somewhere on the dock behind me.

I mentally sigh at her attitude, keeping my focus on the outline of the trees on this side of the island. She steps onto the ferry and immediately crosses the boat to the open space that's clear on the other side of the platform—the one farthest away from me, of course.

"Hey, man." Graham follows behind Sydney, choosing to sink into the seat next to me instead of following behind her.

"Morning." I slide over to give him room as the ferry crew unties us from the dock, and the captain takes us out of Ruby Lodge's bay.

"Where are you heading?" he asks with a smile, making two of us who are ignoring the pointed glare coming this way from across the boat.

"I need to pick up some planks of wood at the hardware store," I tell him. "I'm working on rebuilding the shed on my property—it needs to be a little more solid."

"Yeah, that thing has seen better days." Graham chuckles.

"How about you?" I ask.

He points to Sydney. "We're heading over to City Hall. We need to submit the proposal to buy out a portion of the community land and make sure the town hall meeting is still on as planned for the approval of it. Apparently, that needs to be done in person."

"Sounds like things are moving along nicely," I say.

"They are. The crew got all the equipment brought over, and they're starting to level the ground in the back today. It's fun to see. It brings a sense of excitement to the lodge. Honestly, I owe it all to that one." He points across the ferry. "I wouldn't be doing any of this if she wasn't the one at the helm of it all."

When I glance in Sydney's direction, our eyes meet for half a second before she whips her head the other way.

For some reason, it almost makes me want to smile. The animosity she has toward me is obvious to anyone with a set of eyes, but if I were completely honest with myself...my own is starting to soften.

When I saw her talking with Blair on the beach yesterday, I was caught off guard by the way my body completely froze at seeing the look on her face.

It was a look of vulnerability laced with heartbreak. A look I would never judge someone for. In fact, it was one we bonded over once.

It gripped me and brought me right back to when we were two kids just trying to get through hard situations. I take responsibility for my own actions back then, and if she needed to badmouth me in order to get through…then, honestly, who am I to judge?

If she wants to hate me, I can live with that. But I'm not sure I have it in me to fight with her anymore.

"Hey, I have a favor to ask," Graham says, pulling my attention back to him.

"Yeah? What's that?"

"I'd love to commission a wood statue for the lodge. Would you be interested in making something like that for me?"

"Absolutely," I say almost immediately. It would mean staying longer on Takini Island, of course, but I can do this for him before I leave. "What are you thinking?"

"I was thinking a bear statue. A big one. To put right in front of the lodge so people can see it from the lake."

"I like it. That sounds good. We can discuss the details later on if you want."

The ferry slows its speed, and I look up, surprised to see we've already made it to Baudette.

"Great. Thanks, man. Catch ya later," Graham says with a dip of his head, and I wave, following the handful of people stepping onto the dock. Sydney scurries past me from behind and makes speedwalking look like an angry activity while she catches up to Graham.

I slip my hands into my pockets and slowly walk up the sidewalk, not at all in a hurry as the cloud from being physically in this city starts to slowly loom over me.

With my truck back home in Longville, I plan to walk the few blocks to the hardware store. Typically, when I travel to the island, I charter a plane to take me directly there—that way I can manage to forgo going into the city altogether.

With each step across the concrete, I take in my surroundings, noticing that, although much has stayed the same, there are some small but notable differences since I last walked these streets.

There's a mini wine bar I've never seen before that was put in next to the gas station, and across the street from that is the new law office that I'm assuming belongs to Blair.

Not enough changes to have me seeing the town differently as a whole, but maybe enough to have hope that perhaps someday I could—for the few times a year I'm here, anyway.

Finally, I reach the hardware store and head inside to grab a flat cart to wheel over to the lumber aisle. I pick out the slabs I need for the shed and am placing them gently on the cart when I notice a vaguely familiar face looking at me like a deer in the headlights.

"Cole!" Mrs. Hines exclaims, acting like I'm a long-lost relative and not a student from her second-grade class she hasn't seen in many years.

"Good afternoon, Mrs. Hines." I dip my head, feeling wary under her attention. Nobody ever gets this excited to see me, but I suppose when you're a teacher in a small town, it's not hard to remember every single one of your students. Still, I'm not used to the level of delight on her face.

"Oh, I'm glad you're here. Would you be a dear and help me reach that wood on the top shelf? I need two of those planks to fix my chicken coop."

"Sure thing." I reach up and slide the boards down. She looks up at me with doe eyes, watching my every move with appreciation.

"Is this all you need? I can take them up front for you," I offer, placing them on top of my cart.

"Oh, that would be great." She happily falls into place beside me while she rambles off a whole lot of gossip and life updates from my old classmates, all of which I silently pretend to be interested in. I don't mind doing favors to be nice, but that doesn't mean I'm always comfortable partaking in conversations.

When we reach the registers, I help her get her boards scanned and paid for. She waits patiently by the door while I pay for my own. Apparently, I'm also helping her get them loaded up. I schedule a time for them to deliver my wood to the island via the barge and turn to Mrs. Hines.

"Do you have a truck or another vehicle to bring these home in?" I ask as I wheel her boards outside.

"Sure do. Right over here." She points proudly to a rundown green pickup truck. I follow behind her and get the wood loaded up.

"Thank you for your help. It was so good to see you, Cole," she gushes before climbing into her truck.

With how talkative she seems to be, I get the sense that she says the same thing several times a day to whoever she comes face to face with. But for some reason, I think she might actually mean it.

"Maybe I'll see you around!" She waves as she reverses. I doubt that will be true, but I offer a smile and a wave anyway. Then I make my way back to the ferry.

FOURTEEN
Sydney
Now

Week Three of Renovation

I narrowly divert my step to avoid crushing a package as I pull the door of cabin twelve shut behind me. In the middle of the rug is something rectangular wrapped in honeycomb packing paper with a red-and-black checkered ribbon tied delicately around it.

Picking it up with one hand, I check my watch on the other. My daily progress meeting with Neal is in a few minutes, but I do have a little time to spare.

Sinking onto the edge of the porch swing, I pull at the ribbon to open it. Inside the package is a floral ballpoint pen and a leatherbound book of some sort.

I fan the pages with my thumb to discover that it's a journal. Tucked between the cover and the first page is a note written on a lavender notecard.

Syd,

Just in case this might help.

Blair

I smile, noting that this is absolutely something Blair would do. I'm not sure I know how to use a journal, or if it would be of any benefit to me, but in some small way, it feels comforting knowing I have one now.

I set it inside on the kitchen table where it's safe and scurry off to meet with Neal, making a mental note to thank Blair when I see her later today.

A short while later, after the meeting with Neal, I find myself sipping coffee at the lodge window with a scowl on my face.

I should not be scowling.

I know this.

What's unfolding in front of me is enough to make any logical woman swoon and go weak at the knees. There's a man out on the beach—one who would be considered devastatingly handsome by any standards—knelt down, surrounded by a swarm of children. He's teaching them how to safely start a campfire in the fire pit, and it's admittedly the most adorable thing I've seen in a while.

Except, that man's name is Cole Fredrickson. And I know more about the truth of his character than I'd like to. I know that underneath that rugged exterior is not someone who's approachable and adorable with kids, as he's clearly trying to fool people into thinking he is. Nope, I know firsthand how dismissive he's capable of being. Careless and cold. Feigning sympathy to lure you in and then—bam—throwing you out like trash in the wind.

"Cute, huh?" Shirley says, breaking me out of my glowering.

"That's one word for it," I grumble. Without so much as a sideways glance, I can feel her studying me. I'm not sure what Graham has told her, if anything, about the tension between Cole and me, but I know that she's always been a quiet observer around here. I'm guessing she knows more about what goes on around this island than people give her credit for.

"I knew his uncle, you know," she says quietly, folding her arms around herself.

"Oh yeah?" I feign disinterest, but the truth is, I am actually a little curious about his uncle. Other than a casual mention of him years ago, Cole never said too much about him.

She slowly nods her head as we watch Blair return from the woods with an armful of sticks, handing them off to Cole.

"We were friends in high school." Shirley says it with a hint of subdued nostalgia in her tone. There's also a twinge of somberness to it. Like she knows something I don't.

Cole bops one of the kids playfully on the nose, and I swear I can't hold back the way my lip turns up in disgust. Shirley sighs, her gaze burning into me. She places a hand on my arm as she turns.

"Go easy on him," she whispers before walking away.

I barely have time to register her words or why she would be saying them to me before Graham emerges from behind the bar.

"You ready?" he asks me.

"Yup." I push my hands into my pockets, mentally making a note to process Shirley's words later.

I grab my crossbody purse from the back of a chair, slip it on, then follow him out of the lodge.

"We'll be back in a few hours," I hear Graham say to Blair, to whom I offer a smile, having already thanked her for the journal earlier today.

As for Cole, I manage to walk right past him without so much as a fleeting glance his way.

One hour later and I'm fighting to keep my eyelids open with my head slumped against Graham's shoulder. I'm not sure if it's the sound of Terry, the head counsel's, voice or if this is the comfiest folding chair I've ever sat in, but either way, I'm drowning here.

It's a good thing this town hall meeting should be short and sweet—at least our portion of it, anyway. All we need is for Terry to read the proposal out loud, take a show of hands for a vote, and we should be on our way.

It's been years since I've been to one of these town hall meetings, but it's comforting to find that they haven't changed much.

Our case should be up any minute now. We've already discussed the new lowered speed limit through town that will go into effect next week, and we voted on the flavor-of-the-month ice cream for Mrs. Bishop's ice cream shop.

"The next order of business is the ruling for a potential buyout of a small portion of the community land on Takini Island to Ruby Lodge," Terry says. I perk up in my seat, tapping my manila folder with spreadsheets and statistics to present if needed.

"Per the proposal, Ruby Lodge would like to acquire three acres of the community land to install a recreation area for the lodge." He pauses, pushing his bifocals up on his nose with a finger. "Island residents must be present to vote—and it needs to be unanimous. All those in favor, say aye."

"Aye!" I say with a grin, shoving a hand into the air. Graham and three other residents who are scattered about the room also offer ayes of their own. I offer a smile to as many of them as I can as a show of thanks.

"Wonderful. I'm not anticipating any opposition, but out of technicality, all those who oppose the purchasing of the land, say aye."

I smile, feeling giddy at being able to wrap up and move forward with this part of the renovation, and tuck the folder back under my chair.

"Aye," a grumpy voice comes out of nowhere on my left. My head snaps that direction as shock runs through me.

"What?" I sneer just above a whisper.

"You've got to be kidding me," Graham grumbles in my ear. "Gilbert."

"No," I breathe, catching sight of Mr. Gilbert, the owner of the boarded-up cabin on Takini—the one who hasn't been heard from or seen in the better part of a year.

"Mr. Gilbert?" Terry places an inquisitive hand on his hip. "How long have you been back in town?"

"Since I got wind of this meeting," he murmurs, both indignation and boredom in his tone.

"Alright. Do tell us...why are you opposing this motion?" Terry asks.

"It's community land. Rightfully part of my land. It's been exactly the way it is for decades. There's no need to change it now."

"That's your reasoning?" Graham cuts in, his voice rising.

"Why should the community have to suffer just because you want to run some hoity-toity resort?" he barks back.

"When's the last time you used that part of the island?" I ask, cutting into him with my glare. "Haven't really been around much, have you? Your place is boarded up, for Pete's sake."

His face grows red.

"Yeah, well, look who's talking," he spits. "Everyone knows you're hardly ever here. Not even to see your mo—"

"Hey, that's not fair," Graham says in a rush of anger as he rises to his feet. My cheeks burn with anger of my own, and a lump forms in my throat as another person calls out from the very back of the room.

"Pipe down, Gilbert." The sharp voice cuts through the room like a knife. I swing my head in its direction, but I already know who it belongs to.

Cole sits in the very last chair in the far corner of the room, a menacing glare fixed directly on Mr. Gilbert.

What's he doing here? Did he boat or fly over?

"Alright, alright." Terry lifts his hands to gain control of the room. Voices are hushed, and Graham reluctantly sinks back down into his chair.

"Everyone calm down," Terry says pointedly before fixing his gaze on Mr. Gilbert. "While you're legally entitled to a vote, do you really think I haven't noticed that you've been behind on property taxes for the last two years?"

"I—" Mr. Gilbert barely gets a word out as he fumbles for an answer.

"Do you have a legitimate reason for that?"

Again, he stutters.

"Uh-huh." Terry dismisses him with a wave of his hand, and hope dares to bloom in my chest. "Well, for that reason, I'm counting your vote as invalid."

Mr. Gilbert's huff is audible, along with his grumbling, but I bite the corner of my lip to hide a satisfied smile. Then Terry points to the back of the room.

"Mr. Fredrickson, you did not offer your vote on the matter. As you are the rightful owner of a cabin on Takini, you do have a say in this. How are you voting—for or against the sale of the land?"

Just like that, the hope vanishes.

No.

He's going to ruin this just to spite me, isn't he?

I keep my stare fixed on the floor in front of me as I hold my breath, waiting for it all to crash down again. After a few very long seconds of silence, Cole finally offers a small but firm, "Let them have it."

Relief rushes through me, followed by a wave of confusion as to why he would go along with this. I've heard nothing but negativity from him about the renovation efforts since I arrived.

I rotate my head ever so slightly to the side, and when his gaze connects with mine, I clamp my mouth shut, whipping my head forward, not quite sure what to do or say. This whole situation is catching me off guard here.

"Excellent," Terry says, pounding his gavel with a loud thud. "Consider the proposal passed."

He moves on to the next order of business, but I haven't a clue what it is about. I spend the rest of the meeting ruminating on what I should say to Cole on our way out. How I can thank him without tripping on the foreign words as they come out of my mouth.

But when the meeting ends and we finally get up to leave, he's already gone.

FIFTEEN
Sydney
Then

My tiptoes push against the wood floor of the porch, softly moving the swing back and forth. I bite my lip to taper a wave of adrenaline running through me while I wait as patiently as I can.

The text from Cole yesterday—and this looming date—has proven to be the only source of distraction from my grief, despite how hard Laura and Jimmy have done their best to cheer me up. There's only so much talking it out and ice cream dates I can do. I just want more of the way I feel when I'm with Cole.

I flip through my messages, wanting to look at it again for the hundredth time today, and find the one from this morning.

> **Cole:** I'll pick you up at seven. Wear comfortable shoes.

I have no clue what we'll be doing, but I'm hoping I made a decent choice when I opted for a sundress and tennis shoes. There are only so many things to do in Baudette, and every single one of them that I can think of can be done in a pair of tennis shoes.

I set the phone on the cushion and drum my fingernails against the wooden bench, clearing my throat simply for something to do. I follow the path of the river as it winds behind our house, seeing only a glimpse of it, but I'm able to watch a large log as it gets swept along in the current.

My parents' voices carry from inside the house, low hums of back and forth chatter. They're undoubtedly doing the same thing they've been doing for the last several days now...taking advantage of what's left of Mom's lucid moments to go over any possible life or medical-decision scenarios they can think of. They've also been throwing in many discussions about the future of the house, the lodge, and of course, Graham and me.

Conversations I've been a part of as little as possible, if I'm honest.

I push thoughts of my mom's diagnosis out of my head, holding my emotions at bay while I wait for the sound of tires to eventually come down the driveway with bated breath, anxious to soak in the reprieve I know that sound will be.

I had no way of knowing at the time that moment would never come. At first, an entire hour passes without a word or car in sight—and then it becomes two. All the while, I barely move a muscle, stewing in a rapidly increasing haze of anger and shame.

Could he still be coming? Where in the world could he be? Maybe he got tied up with something. Is it really that hard to send a quick message explaining what could have possibly happened?

A part of me refuses to accept that I really just got stood up, especially from Cole, someone I thought I could trust. Maybe I've read him wrong this whole time. In a split second of panic, an awareness hits me that this is the absolute last thing I need right now. I'm fully aware that this anger is probably not healthy to be adding to my mix of emotions. I feel unstable enough as it is.

Another hour passes without a word, and the sky is now completely dark. As the grasshoppers chirp their nightly song, I finally work up the courage to send a simple text.

Sydney: Thanks for the date…

As much as I'm tempted to lay into him and grill him with a ton of questions, I decide against it. Honestly, what's the point? I closed myself off to him the moment I realized he wasn't coming.

I kick off my tennies and curl my legs up onto the swing. Laura and Jimmy are off doing their own things tonight, and Graham is out on the island. The last thing I want to do is go back inside and get sucked into the emotional vortex of being around my parents, who are working through grief of their own. So, I stay on the swing and rock mindlessly back and forth.

Feeling utterly alone.

"Are you alright?" Laura asks for the tenth time in as many days, pressing her shoulder into the locker next to mine.

No, I'm not.

"Fine," I tell her, attempting to once again ignore the ever-present heartache that feels like it's been crushing me a little more every day. She knows me well enough to know that, underneath my outwardly positive attitude, I'm barely staying afloat. Things at home have been unbearably heavy, and I'm not sure how much more I can take.

"Yeah, well, that half-ass response might work on someone else but not on your best friend," she says pointedly. "How about some ice cream after school? It's definitely been a double-scoop kind of week, don't you think?"

"Sure, I guess." I shrug, attempting a sorry excuse for a smile. A double scoop of rocky road actually does sound somewhat appealing, even if I had the same thing last week.

"Don't shoot the messenger, but I have some intel," Jimmy announces hesitantly, appearing on the other side of my locker. There's a slight cringe to his face, which tells me he's probably about to bring up the other factor causing my terrible mood this week.

"Is it something that's going to help or hurt our mood?" Laura asks, nudging her head in my direction as if I can't see her clear as day.

"Honestly? Probably hurt?" he says slowly, pushing his lips together. "It's about him."

My eyes dart directly to his.

"Cole?"

He nods, assessing me slowly. I didn't think it was possible, but my chest feels even heavier at the mention of his name.

"Tell me," I demand at the same time Laura speaks his name as a warning.

"I think he's gone," he says in a hushed whisper.

"Gone? Like, left town gone?" I ask, even though I already know the answer to my own question. Word on the street, from what I've heard, is that nobody has seen or heard from him in the last week. He definitely hasn't been showing up to school—not that I've been looking or anything.

"I guess," Jimmy cringes sympathetically. "The rumor going around the gym locker room is that he has a girl down in Bemidji that he would go visit on the weekends. They think he left to go see her."

"Great," I mutter, slamming my locker door shut. Of course he was seeing someone else. All of that enticing mystery surrounding him was bound to have at least a few secrets.

"I'm sorry." Laura puts a soothing hand on my upper back.

"It's fine." I shake my head then plaster on a fake smile that I know she can see all the way through. Shifting my biology textbook in my arms, we head down the hallway.

As we walk, I take notice of the many posters adorning the hall that boast of the various senior year activities and end-of-the-year celebrations coming up. As much as I'm really trying to push through and enjoy what's left of my time here, despite everything going on, I'm not sure that is within reach anymore.

I know he's just a boy, and I have a mantra that I try to live by—to not give someone else the power to ruin my day—but...something was different about Cole. Whatever connection we had reached a part of me I didn't know was there. It touched on an emotional chord that was as soothing as it was igniting. It was intoxicating for the brief time I felt it, and I had hoped that meant it could be something remarkable.

The heaviness lingers as we walk to class, and I find myself once again feeling overwhelmingly ready to leave this place. To leave it all behind.

Just a few more weeks. That's all I need to get through...and then I can finally give in to this primal urge I've been trying to ignore that's been telling me to run.

SIXTEEN
Cole

Now

With a grunt, I twist the heavy end table I just completed into place next to the couch. I stand back to admire my work, and a sense of contentment settles over me. One of my favorite parts of what I do is seeing it all come together at the end. The final product after all the meticulous, often tedious, work to get there. From traipsing into the woods behind the cabin yesterday in search of a wide enough tree to cut down, to using the chainsaw to cut it into pieces, all the way to sanding, drilling, and applying a natural finish. It gives me a sense of accomplishment I never seem to find anywhere else.

The only problem with this end table is that it looks wildly out of place next to the other furniture in here. Everything else is old and tattered, worn at the edges, except for the kitchen island that's been given new life after I sanded and resealed it yesterday.

I didn't necessarily plan to make furniture for the cabin while I'm here, but working helps to quiet my brain, and I found myself needing to do something extra with my hands this week now that most of the exterior work is done. Besides, I've been surprised at how good it feels to be fixing up this place. It might be helping to assuage my guilt for abandoning it for so long.

Just a few more pieces of furniture in here, and finishing the bear piece for Graham, and then I should be ready to head back to Longville. With a sigh, I take a look around to pinpoint which piece to make next.

The faint rumble of an ATV comes from somewhere outside. It's quiet enough to tell me it's still a ways away but increasing enough that it's definitely heading this direction. My chest tightens, having mixed emotions about how I feel about interacting with Sydney today.

Do I know for a fact that it's her coming up the path to my cabin?

No.

But I would sure bet money on it. She's the only person to ever show up on this doorstep—at least since I've owned it—aside from Graham when he comes to check on things, which obviously doesn't happen if I'm here. Besides, after the town hall meeting yesterday, I've been anticipating a run-in with her.

I'll admit, I've been watching her lately. Not in a creepy way. More of a 'we're staying on the same island and there's only so many people to look at' kind of way. I'm drawn to her more than I am to anyone else.

In doing so, I've gotten glimpses of the way she carries herself. A hint of the person I briefly knew for a moment in time. She's a spitfire. A bubbly, talkative force that draws people to her. But even with all that positivity, she has an emotional depth that she thinks she's hiding from others.

I can see it clear as day.

It's easier for me to connect with people when I can see the vulnerability underneath the mask they wear. The way a person exists when they think no one's watching.

The ATV shuts off, and through the thick log walls of the cabin, I hear boots as they clank on the steps. A soft mumbling voice recites something along the lines of being a mature adult, one who is fully capable of a civil conversation.

With a subdued smirk, I pull the door open before she has a chance to knock.

"Oh. Hi," Sydney says in surprise, clearly caught off guard.

"Peterson," I say in greeting, dipping my head.

After a quick timid smile, she stands in place, fiddling with her fingers, looking down at the ground as if she's not sure what she even came for.

What *did* she come here for?

"What's up?" I ask, leaning against the doorframe.

She clears her throat then steels herself, standing taller. "I came to say thank you."

The look of pain on her face almost has me smiling.

"I can see that was very hard for you to say. Thank you for what?" I know darn well what she means, but I want to hear her say it. Just because I don't have animosity toward her doesn't mean I wouldn't enjoy watching her trip over her words, just for a minute or two—for the sake of the rumor she started.

She rolls her lips then swallows hard, as if the words are getting stuck in her throat. "For your support yesterday. It, uh...it means a lot to us."

The effort she's making is written all over her face, and for a moment, I can see the crack in her armor. The slight thawing of her iciness toward me.

"Do you want to come in?" I ask, extending an olive branch of my own.

A flash of surprise dances across her face, and she clamps her mouth shut. Our gazes meet, and we hold them there for a brief moment of honesty.

A moment of truce.

"Sure," she whispers, a slight nod of her head.

I push the door open with my foot before retreating back toward the kitchen.

"Nice place," she remarks from behind me. I can't tell if it's genuine or the more likely option—sarcasm. I wait for her to inevitably comment on the actual dump that it is and for her to try yet again to get me to sell.

"My uncle didn't exactly leave me much." I pull a jug of homemade apple cider I picked up in town out of the fridge, placing it on the island.

She nods, running her fingertips along the back of the couch, perusing every little detail in here. I can't decide how I feel about her roaming around, studying everything.

"Cider?" I ask.

She strolls past the bed in the corner, toward the fireplace, and tilts her head toward me to answer, "Sure."

I hand her a mason jar when she makes it to the kitchen, and she places a hip against the island across from me.

The air in here feels...tense. As if she's sucking up all the oxygen somehow and leaving little left for me. I study her as she takes a sip, noting her hair pulled up in a high pony and a red Ruby Lodge sweatshirt that accentuates a slight tint of red on her cheeks from the ATV ride up here.

Then I wait for her to say something. Anything.

"So," she finally says. "Judging by your vote yesterday at City Hall, does this mean you're on board now with the reno?"

"I never said I wasn't," I point out.

"Enough that you're willing to sell?" A gleam in her eye sparks as she smirks at me.

There it is.

"Nope," I reply immediately, watching the disappointment fall across her face.

"Why'd you do it, then?" she asks as she takes a sip.

"It was fair. Nobody uses that community land," I say with a shrug. What I don't say out loud is the real reason behind my outburst at Gilbert—that I got defensive. High school may have been eight years ago, and our interactions then were admittedly fairly minimal, but that doesn't mean they didn't make an impact on me.

I remember every single second of our time together, especially sitting on the back of her car that night by the fire as she opened up to me about her family. When I heard Gilbert bring up her mom in that way, I snapped.

She eyes me, as if acknowledging there's something I'm not saying, and I hold her stare. For a brief moment, we're not two jaded adults with complicated pasts. I'm seventeen again. Face to face with someone who feels...comfortable. Who feels easy. As if the energy that was once between us might still be there.

She breaks our connection first, her eyes dipping down. I keep mine trained on her, waiting cautiously to see how the rest of this visit will play out. What she'll say next. She sets the glass down and runs her fingers along the island. I can't help but watch her fingertips as she grazes them against something I just put so much effort into fixing up. It makes me feel a certain way...though I'm not sure what.

"This is nice," she comments, tapping on the island.

"Just finished restoring it."

Her brows furrow as she looks deep in thought. Then her gaze trails to the end table—the only other piece that looks updated—and her eyes widen.

"Wait...did you make that?" She points to the table.

I watch her for a second then simply nod.

"Huh." She hums, a hint of a smile appearing on her face. "I remember..."

She trails off, stopping herself from finishing the sentence. I watch as she crosses the room and runs her fingers along the table, inspecting my work.

Something very similar to pride flashes behind her eyes, and I'm caught off guard when it sends a twinge of warmth to my chest.

She clears her throat, and I wait quietly, content to simply watch her every move.

"Anyway, I'm leaving tomorrow." She reaches for her boots to slip them back on. "Heading back to Minneapolis to check on my apartment and a few things at the office."

"Okay," I say with a nod as she pulls open the door.

"Don't worry, I'll be back, though—I know you're going to miss me." She flashes a wide smile, her tone laced with a teasing glint.

"Terribly," I mumble.

She hovers by the door for a few seconds, and I hold my breath, waiting to see if she'll offer anything else. A slight twinge of disappointment hits me when she opens the door.

"See ya," she calls out before pulling it shut behind her.

In a slight daze, I'm left staring at the spot she just stood in for long after the ATV noise disappears.

SEVENTEEN
Sydney
Now

After signing off on an email to an associate, I tilt my laptop shut and lean back for an early morning break.

The window in my apartment kitchen nook offers a sweeping view of the Stone Arch Bridge with the sprawling Mississippi River flowing steadily underneath it, capturing my attention as it always does when I attempt to work from this spot.

The Minneapolis skyline stands tall just beyond it, and I know without a doubt that I could sit here forever and never get tired of it, especially when I can watch everyone walking the trail on the sidewalk next to my building. I love imagining a life story for each of them, trying to guess what the rest of their day will look like.

Being this close to the energy of a big city served as a fresh start for me when I came down here for college. The only memories it holds are positive ones for me—memories of a life far away from the heartbreak that home held. A place that aided in my tendency to deflect and avoid my piercing emotions.

Before jumping back into my emails to check on the delivery status of the furniture I ordered for Ruby Lodge's dining room, I head to the kitchen to get rid of my empty tea cup.

As much as I've enjoyed watching the Ruby Lodge renovation begin to come to life—and seeing Graham and Blair on a daily basis—it feels really good to be back home in my own space.

With a smile, I look around the room, taking it all in. It's not hard to note the vast difference compared to the environment at Ruby Lodge. Stark-white paint covers every square inch of wall space, offering a modern blank canvas as a background. Of course, I wouldn't feel at home here without adding my signature pops of color.

There are several cascading plants hanging in almost every corner of this main living space. A mauve-and-cream vase adorns the middle of the kitchen island with a beautiful faux bouquet of flowers whose colors pop against the white cabinets.

Off to the right, my beloved thrifted sage-green couch frames the outline of the living room, with mustard-yellow accent pillows neatly settled on each side. A bundle of colorful tissue paper flowers adorn the wall—I made those myself—hanging above a muted orange-gingham bookshelf.

Bright and vibrant. Exactly how I like to keep my space.

An email pings from my laptop, and I head back to the table to check it. There, I find an email from my boss, inquiring about an update on a development project I'm slated to start working on after Ruby Lodge is complete.

While I type a reply email, a call from Graham comes in.

"Hey, Graham," I say with a smile, realizing how much I've missed him in the span of only a day.

"Syd." There's enough of a panic in the way he says my name to instantly wipe the smile off my face.

Mom.

"What is it? What happened?" Fear grips my chest in a fierce chokehold. If something happened to her and I've wasted all this time not being there, I'll never, ever forgive myself.

"Neal's team was digging near the back of the lodge this morning, and a pipe burst," he explains in a huff.

Both overwhelming relief and an entirely different kind of panic wash over me.

"How bad?" I demand.

"The entire main lodge is flooded."

"Oh no," I groan, pinching the bridge of my nose. "Are you serious?"

"Well, seeing as I'm currently standing in two inches of water, I'd say I'm pretty serious."

I close my laptop with a thud and shove it into my carrying case as fast as I can.

"I'll be there as soon as I can."

In my rushed haze, I almost forget to thank Sam as I jump out of the floatplane.

"Thank you," I call into the wind, securing my backpack onto my shoulders while breaking into a run off the dock. The panic in my chest hasn't let up since Graham called to tell me the news this morning. I rushed to gather my things and got here as fast as I possibly could.

When I hastily rip open the door of the lodge and step inside, my boot immediately slushes through at least an inch of standing water.

My stomach drops with a heavy thud that threatens to bowl me right over, and as much as I try to keep it at bay, emotion starts to prick at the corners of my eyes.

Not like this... It's not supposed to happen like this.

"Hey," Graham's voice cuts me out of my spiraling thoughts as he comes out of the dining hall, carrying a bucket. "Here, give me your backpack. I'll set it on the bench outside. Everyone is in the kitchen where the water is the worst."

My mouth falls open to reply, but no words come through the fog in my brain. How can he be so calm about this?

He uses his free hand to slide my backpack off my back for me, and then he exits through the door behind me. I numbly follow voices toward the kitchen, stunned at the mess that surrounds me.

The water deepens with each step I take as I go behind the bar and through the swinging doors. The kitchen doors are propped open, and Shirley, Blair, and Neal are forming an assembly line, passing buckets between themselves. I barely register Cole in the very back, helping to scoop water.

"Hey," Blair says when she spots me. She sounds as exhausted as she looks.

"This is..." My voice trails off.

"A disaster," she finishes for me when I can't.

"Sorry to throw a wrench in your plans, Sydney," Neal says, regret obvious on his face.

I shake my head, offering a wave of my hand that I hope makes it clear I don't blame him. Accidents happen, especially in construction zones.

My breathing quickens into deep erratic pants as my eyes fall to the floor. The wooden planks my grandfather once laid by hand are barely visible, submerged under water. The floor that my family—the people who mean the most to me—has walked on tirelessly and countless times over many years...now completely ruined. Not salvageable to be repurposed like I had originally planned.

A sharper grip of panic seizes me as my mind replays the memories built between these walls. The love that was woven into the very fabric of my family's name. All of it tarnished.

"Hey." Graham's warm hand on my shoulder gives me something else to focus on, and I swing my panicked gaze to him.

"It's okay," he whispers, his brows furrowing as he takes my current panicked state in.

"But..." Once again, my words trail off as I struggle to work through this visceral reaction.

He places a hand on my back. "Look, I know it's not ideal, but...we're re-doing all of this anyway, right? Renovating it?"

"Yeah," I say weakly. "But not like this."

I planned to have time to say goodbye to each area before it was torn down. I wanted to salvage original pieces and mementos to help gradually smooth the process of change and repurpose what we can. Rebuild and restore the lodge. Not have a big part of it taken so abruptly like this. I didn't even have time to take some pictures.

I wasn't ready.

Blinking back tears, I try to rein in my emotions while I run my fingers through my hair. I'm overwhelmed, and my mind is racing a million miles a minute as I span the kitchen once more. My eyes lock on Cole in the back. His hands are moving the bucket to scoop water, but his dark eyes are pinned on me, studying me with concern in his brows.

"How about we take a break and figure out a plan now that Syd's here?" Graham suggests.

"Good idea," Blair replies.

The water sloshes as we all move out of the kitchen. Graham puts an arm around my shoulder, providing a steady frame for me to slump against as he leads me out.

When we get out to the porch, we circle around a table. The fresh air helps to quell some of the overwhelming emotion I have, leaving a lingering heaviness as I try to switch my brain to crisis-management mode.

"Alright, give it to us straight, Neal," Graham says.

Neal heaves a heavy sigh. "Well, we'll get the water remediated, but there'll likely be water damage to the floors. I wish I could say there's a quick fix to make the space operational, but truthfully, there's no point in putting resources into fixing it up until we're ready for the official renovations we had planned. That won't be for another couple weeks."

"So, the main lodge is officially out of commission," Graham says.

"I hate to say it." Neal cringes. "But yes, it's not operational, unfortunately."

"Okay." Graham nods, his brain clearly doing a better job of processing this than mine is. "That means the kitchen is down. And the cabins are full of guests we need to feed."

"Thankfully, my latest group of campers left two days ago, so we don't have any children on-site," Blair points out. "But we had a big group of people come in for a fishing retreat yesterday. What do we do with them?"

"My guys have double-checked—all cabins are still fully operational," Neal confirms.

"But how do we feed them without a kitchen?" Blair asks.

"Can Shirley prepare food from a different location? What about my cabin? Could we set up a makeshift kitchen?" I ask. My brain finally seems to be working.

"Too small." Shirley cringes.

"Any chance Gilbert would let us use his place?" I already know the answer, but I throw it out there anyway.

That earns me several chuckles.

"Not a chance," Graham murmurs.

"Use mine," Cole offers from where he's standing off to the side against the railing.

Silence falls as we all turn toward him.

"Say that again?" Graham asks as if he didn't hear him correctly.

"I'm serious. It's not much, but it's bigger than these cabins. And it's got a fully functioning kitchen. It's all yours if you want it."

"That might actually work... We could shuttle guests back and forth from here with the ATV? Have them eat in shifts?" Graham asks no one in particular. "Are you sure, Cole?"

"Absolutely." Not a hint of doubt or regret is found in his tone, and I study him, too emotionally spent to hold any animosity toward him at this moment. All I can do is appreciate his selflessness.

"We'll probably need Shirley to stay onsite, then, if that's okay? She can set up a home base there so her schedule is disrupted as little as possible." Graham looks at Cole, who nods his approval.

"Okay, this could work," Blair chimes in. "Maybe Graham and I can take Shirley's cabin, then, since we can't stay in the apartment anymore?"

"Of course," Shirley agrees.

"But wait, where will Cole stay?" Graham asks the question that popped into my head a few moments ago but haven't spoken aloud.

A sudden mix of anticipation and dread fills my stomach all at once when several heads slowly turn toward me.

EIGHTEEN

Sydney
Now

"I'm not going to feel guilty about giving you a cot and not the bed," I say into the silence, knowing full well he's wide awake, just like I am. The cabin lights are off with only a faint glimmer of light coming from the small lamp on my nightstand.

"Didn't ask you to," he mutters calmly from down below. I pull the comforter all the way up to my chin, appreciating the fact that at least I don't need to see him from all the way up here in the loft.

Do I love that I'll be sharing a small space with Cole, of all people, for the foreseeable future? Absolutely not. Will it be uncomfortable to have him stay here? Probably, yes.

But...he's done a lot to help us out lately. I suppose it's the least I can do. Luckily, I've had a lot of practice with compartmentalizing my emotions.

I close my eyes, willing sleep to come. With all the work we got done today, one would think sleep would come easily, but as I lie here, hyperaware of his presence, tired is the absolute last thing I feel.

In the span of a few short hours, we used every last minute of daylight to get as much done as we possibly could. Shirley is officially moved into Cole's cabin and has a fully functioning kitchen all ready to use in the morning. We set up picnic tables on his grass for the guests to eat their meals on, and Blair and I even created a sign pointing where to go if any non-guests stop by looking for food. We put it right next to the *Excuse our mess* sign that's been hanging by the lodge entrance. Arrows now line the path to Cole's cabin, and the ATV will be making continuous runs back and forth.

It's not ideal, but I suppose that's life when trying to operate through a renovation. We're doing the best we can.

The cot squeaks from down below, groaning under his weight as Cole shifts.

My mouth parts to ask if he needs anything, but I promptly clamp it shut, fighting a war in my head. I was raised to be a good hostess—it's in my blood. But this isn't just anyone sleeping on my cabin floor.

It's *him.*

I roll my lips, trying to make sense of his presence and how I feel about it, while he clears his throat. I hold my breath, waiting to see if he'll speak, but there's nothing but the faint whistle from the fan whirling overhead. I force my eyes closed once again.

"Thanks for letting me stay here." His quiet voice has my eyes flying open.

I bite back a comment pointing out it wasn't exactly my choice. I take the high road instead and offer a simple, "It's no problem."

"I would head down to Longville to get out of your hair, but I need to finish your brother's statue first," he explains.

"Is that the lump of wood I saw down by your beach?" I suppose some conversation wouldn't be the end of the world.

"That would be the one."

"What will it be? Graham didn't mention anything about a statue."

"A bear."

"He loves bears." I smile to myself, remembering the time we went camping as kids and came within forty feet of a brown bear. The look on Graham's face was one of pure joy, while Mom's, of course, was the polar opposite.

A knife twists in my heart, and I squeeze my eyes shut, breathing through the sudden spark of grief for the way things used to be. For the innocence of my childhood that's long gone.

I'm reminded, yet again, that I can't escape thoughts of my mom like I can when I'm home in Minneapolis. She's everywhere here, at every corner.

Pushing the memory far in the back of my mind, I roll onto my side as silence falls between us again. This time, exhaustion feels heavy, and I reach over to turn off the lamp.

My legs slowly creep out of the comforter one by one as I roll onto my side, ever so carefully attempting to get up without waking Cole. I roll the rest of myself out of the bed as quietly as I can. Once fully upright, I tip-toe my way to the small powder room at the edge of the loft wall. The absolute last thing I want to do is allow Cole to catch sight of me with bedhead and a sleep-creased face, so I need to figure out where he is in order to avoid him.

Peering over the edge of the railing, I crane my neck to make as small a part of me visible as possible.

Down below, I find Cole fast asleep on the cot. He's sprawled on his back, his head turned into the crook of an arm that's bent behind his head. A white T-shirt stretches against his tanned skin, and a blanket lies haphazardly across his waist. He's entirely too big for the cot that it's almost laughable.

I almost feel bad.

He stretches, and I duck out of view, crawling the rest of the way to the powder room. Once my hair is brushed, my teeth are clean, and I'm dressed in leggings with an oversized button-down, I make my way down the stairs.

As I reach the bottom step, I find Cole awake at the kitchen sink, scratching at the base of his neck. Instantly, the room feels entirely too small, as if any move I make will be in the direct line of his own path.

I clear my throat, announcing my presence, as if there's any way he didn't just hear me come down the creaky steps.

"Morning," he says without so much as a head turn my way.

Alright, then. Instead of mumbling my thoughts to myself out loud, like I normally do in the morning, I keep them in my mind as I convince myself that we can co-exist in this small space. Easy peasy.

"Morning," I say back, not bothering to snark down my tone as I typically would with him. There's enough on my plate right now. I don't need to be worrying about stoking the animosity flames toward my new roommate.

Approaching his side, we both reach for the hanging coffee mugs under the cabinet at the same exact time.

"Oh, shoot," I say at the same time he mumbles, "Sorry."

We both snap our hands back as a half-laugh escapes my mouth. He gestures for me to go first, so I take a mug and get the individual Keurig machine going, feeling unusually frazzled.

"Sleep okay?" I ask him, folding my arms around myself as I lean a hip against the counter.

"Yup," is all he says, but I don't miss the bags under his eyes.

We trade places, almost tripping over each other as we do, and I move toward the fridge so he can make his own cup of coffee.

I pull some cream out of the fridge and scoop some sugar into my cup.

Then I take a sip, savoring the warm drink as I watch him move around my kitchen.

"I'll leave those out for you," I tell him, gesturing to the counter. "You look like a sugar-and-cream kind of guy."

He huffs, a whisper of a smile tugging on his lips. I swallow, not liking how the sight of it seems to have a certain calming effect on my nervous system—the same exact way it did back then.

We finish our coffee around the same time, mostly in silence, before he moves to fold up the cot.

"I'm going to go see if anyone needs a ride to my place on my way up there," he says, sliding his wallet and phone into his jeans.

I nod and gather my own things to go check in with Neal.

"I guess I'll, uh...see you later then," I say as he opens the door.

He twists his head back to look at me and gives me a dip of his head before walking out the door. I groan when he leaves, allowing myself a moment to lament on how weird this is going to be. Then I head out to see Neal.

NINETEEN
Cole
Now

Taking a step back, I slide the safety goggles off my head and shield my eyes from the sun to inspect my progress. I used the chainsaw to form a general outline for the statue, priming it for tomorrow when I can go in with the carving bar to begin carving the bear's features.

I give a satisfied shrug. Not too bad for a day's work.

Loading up the supplies I brought with me down to the lake, I head up the hill toward the now empty picnic tables that are set up in front of my cabin. Working this far away from the shed isn't exactly ideal, but I wanted to be out of everyone's way, so I did what I could to make it work. I suppose there are worse places to carve than steps away from a lake.

"Hey, Cole. Thanks again for letting me barge in here," Shirley calls, coming out of the cabin as I walk past.

"Not a problem. Everything work out okay today?" I slow to a stop to chat while she leans against the post.

"Yeah," she says with an exhausted nod. "We managed. Everyone was fed, anyway. I don't think anyone minded the extra-scenic transportation coming up here for their meals either."

"Good to hear."

"You've got a special place out here." She looks past me with a look of endearment on her face. I wait, wondering if she might shoot her shot in convincing me to sell too.

"I think so," I agree.

"Your uncle thought so too," she says softly.

I lift my gaze to meet hers. "You knew him?"

"Once upon a time." She huffs, looking down at her hands clasped together.

"Still keep in touch?" I hold my breath, not sure if I want to hear that he's been keeping in touch with anyone else but me.

"No, not for many years now."

I nod as a wave of sadness hits me. Man, do I miss him.

"Anyway, I'll let you get back to it," she says before reaching behind her to grab something off the chair. "I saved you some dinner. Pot roast and veggies. Make sure you eat it while it's still warm."

My chest warms at the fact that she thought of me. It's yet another thing I'm not used to.

"Thank you. I appreciate it," I say sincerely, grabbing the to-go container.

"My pleasure," she says warmly. "Do you need a ride back down?"

"I've got my ATV. Thanks again. I'll see you tomorrow." With a dip of my head, I head to the newly built shed, where I place my tools, then hop on the vehicle to head back to Sydney's cabin.

As I drive down, balancing the plate of food on my lap with one hand, I attempt to calm the mixed feelings I have about staying in such a small space with her—someone who clearly hasn't been very fond of me.

I park behind cabin twelve and round my way to the front porch, dinner in hand. As I reach for the knob, I hesitate. Am I supposed to knock? I'm thinking I probably should. Although, I wouldn't put it past her to leave me out here out of spite.

I settle for knocking, waiting a few seconds before pushing the door open. I find Sydney at the small, round kitchen table, an array of puzzle pieces laid out in front of her. Her elbow is propped up on the table, her chin in the palm of her hand as she peers up at me. I look for any sign of animosity that I might need to brace myself for, but there isn't a trace on her face.

"Hey," I say quietly, shutting the door behind me.

"Hi," she says just as softly, focusing back down.

I take two steps to reach the table and slide into the chair across from her, needing somewhere to sit to take my boots off. I slide my plate of food onto the table and pull my boots off slowly and cautiously. I'm well-aware this is her space, and I'm just encroaching on it. The atmosphere in this tiny place feels apprehensive...that if I make one wrong step, our fragile truce might be shattered.

"Did you already eat?" I ask her.

"I did. The pot roast was really good. You'll love it," she says simply.

As she puts a puzzle piece into place, I notice a stack of paintings leaning against the back wall by the utility closet.

"Are those from the lodge?" I point to them, taking a risk on starting a conversation as I peel the tin foil cover off my food.

She twists her head, following the direction of my finger, and nods.

"Yeah. I took everything off the walls today. Kept a few things for myself." Her mouth twists up in a nostalgic smile while a layer of something close to pain lingers behind it.

While I certainly don't have any right to know the ins and outs of her family relationships, it's obvious how much this place means to her. How important it is to be doing this renovation the right way.

"Did Neal get everything under control?" I ask, taking a bite of the warm food.

"Yup. They were able to fix the pipe and finished grading the rest of the soil. The plan is to start framing the addition within the next day or so. Graham and I got everything out of the lodge and kept anything that didn't have water damage."

"Did you find a new place for your camping tents?"

"Glamping tents," she corrects.

"That's what I said."

I don't miss the slightest of eye rolls. "I have a backup location. That'll be the very last part of the reno, though, so I'm still hoping I might be able to get you to change your mind."

I roll my lips before meeting her eyes, saying as honestly as I can, "I can't do that."

She holds my stare, and her face softens. For the first time, she doesn't push or try another tactic to get her way. It's a moment of quiet acceptance. Of honesty. It's one that I appreciate.

When she breaks the stare, my own gaze falls down to the puzzle. It's still mostly in pieces, but the box tells me it's a scenic picture of a loon floating on a lake among lily pads. A quintessential rustic lake scene.

"Can I?" I ask, looking for her approval before I pick up a piece that might fit on the outer corner she just started.

"Be my guest." She smirks as I rotate the piece, pressing it firmly into place.

I lean back, satisfied.

"Once again, you don't strike me as the puzzle-doing kind of guy," she remarks.

"And what kind of guy do I strike you as?"

Her eyes flick back up to mine, and she seems to consider her answer, while her attention makes my body flush.

"I still haven't figured you out," she mutters, looking away.

Well, that makes two of us.

As I eat my dinner, we alternate taking turns placing pieces on the puzzle, and the energy inside this small cabin slowly shifts from apprehensive to what I can only describe as a certain sense of calm. It's become quiet and light—soothing in a way.

I soak it in, enjoying the way my brain feels like it can finally slow down, until my eyes start to feel heavy.

"I'm beat," I say, cutting into the silence. "Mind if I turn in?" I motion to the cot that's folded up along the wall.

She shakes her head. "Go ahead. I'm going to stay here for a bit longer if that's alright with you? I'll turn the lights off when I'm done."

I hold her gaze for a moment longer than I probably should, not able to help myself from being glued to it momentarily, before saying, "Of course."

I cross the room to grab a pair of sweatpants out of my backpack and then hit the bathroom. I change—pulling my button-up off, leaving just the undershirt—brush my teeth, and head back to roll the cot to the middle of the living space.

A slight groan escapes my lips as I settle onto my back with my feet hanging off the end of the cot. As I shift, I'm starkly aware of her presence a few short feet away from me, finding it hard to focus on anything else.

My eyes drift closed, and I fall asleep to the soft noise the puzzle piece makes when she snaps a new one into place.

TWENTY
Sydney
Now

Week Six of Renovation

"It's looking great, Neal." I duck under a wooden beam and lift the hard hat off my head once I clear the main construction zone.

"It's coming along," he agrees. "We've got a ways to go, but you've got to start somewhere, right?"

"That's right." I grin back at him.

"Oh, I noted the slight change with the beam in the north bathroom on the plan, per your request, so we're good to go there," he says. "And I've got a team over at the community land this morning, prepping to get started there this week."

"Perfect. Let me know before you dig anything over there, though, okay? I want to make sure everything's mapped out where it needs to be."

"You got it." He nods.

"Great. I'll be back this afternoon to check in. Thanks, Neal." I hand him my hard hat and wave before rounding the side of the lodge. Instead of heading straight back to my cabin, I head for the beach. I'd like to try something before moving on with the rest of my day.

Thankfully, the beach is pretty much empty, as most guests are either out fishing or are up getting food with Shirley. The noise from Neal's crew working in the back is fairly loud but nothing I can't tune out.

I choose an Adirondack chair that faces the lake and settle into it, pulling my knees up to my chest. After a moment of quietly watching the way the lake laps onto shore, letting it calm me, I pull Blair's journal out of my bag.

I run my hand over the leather binding, feeling an uncomfortable apprehension settle over me. The lake is rolling, a bird is chirping somewhere in the woods, and aside from the faint roar of Neal's machines behind me, it's quiet. So, in theory, this should be an ideal place to get in tune with my emotions.

But as I focus on my mom and the overwhelming feeling of grief that inevitably comes along with it, I find my emotions to be anything but clear and concise enough to write down.

I try anyway and open to the first blank page, hovering my pen above it. I reach up to grip my favorite snowflake necklace between my fingers, and I realize I'm not quite sure how to use this journal. Am I supposed to write down my reasons for not wanting to go visit the nursing home? Or do I delve deep into the truth of my emotions surrounding Mom's illness and attempt to unravel them enough to make sense? Both topics leave a heavy pit in my stomach and an ache in my chest enough to block the urge to do so.

Instead, I jot down three words that encompass my thoughts toward both facing my emotions and going to see my mom.

I'm too scared.

I stare at the words for a while, sitting with them, wondering if I'll ever be able to push through, until soft boot steps break me out of my thoughts.

"Hey," Cole says, approaching slowly from the direction of the cabin. In his hands are two to-go coffee cups.

"Morning," is all I say as he gets closer, closing the journal.

He slides into the chair next to me and offers me one of the cups.

"An official peace offering." His mouth turns up in a genuine half-smile.

"Thank you." I can't help but appreciate the gesture and the way my own mouth slightly turns up. It's weird to me that I truly don't mind his presence. In fact, I might even be happy to see him, which is nothing short of confusing to me since there's still a solid source of anger I feel toward him.

"I need this after you kept me up all night with your obnoxious snoring," I chide, hiding my smirk behind the cup as I take a sip.

"I don't snore," he replies with a straight face.

"Oh, yes you do." The urge to laugh threatens to burst out of me, but like I've found myself doing often lately, I hold it back. A few walls may have been broken down between us, but there's still one firmly stuck in place for me.

This tug-of-war between my thoughts has been constant ever since he moved into my cabin. I find myself wanting to give in to the easy way it feels between us, for the sake of what could be a genuine friendship, but my brain won't let me get past the elephant in the room. The one I've let fester in the back of my mind for so many years.

Being around him the past few days, living in the same space as him…it feels natural…but I can't move forward with a friendship while not knowing the truth.

I may not be brave enough to go see my mom, but I think I can find enough strength to address this today.

"Listen," I start slowly, "I'm more than willing to accept this peace offering and call a truce on this whole thing between us…who knows, maybe we could even be friends."

He ever so slightly smiles at that.

"But…" I look down at the sand in front of me. "If I'm honest, I'm having a hard time moving past the root of my anger toward you."

His brows etch together as he studies me. I clear my throat and muster more courage.

"My hurt," I clarify. "If I ask you something, can you do me a favor and tell me the truth?"

He nods, nothing but authenticity and promise in his eyes. "Sure."

My voice drops to barely a whisper. "Why did you leave? Back then. Why did you disappear without talking to me?"

His gaze softens, and he swallows as he leans back in the chair.

My heart races uncontrollably. I bite my lip, immediately wondering if I made a mistake, if I really do want to know.

Unable to look at him, I draw my gaze back out to the lake while he shifts in his seat next to me.

"My, uh..." The hesitation is clear in his voice as he leans forward, running a hand along his jaw. "My father liked to paint this picture that there was a solid father-son unit between us. It was the two of us against the world, helping each other get by, despite the abandonment of my mother. That's what he told the town, anyway."

My breath gets stuck in my throat as I wait with bated breath for him to continue, confused at where he's going with this.

"When in reality, he drove my mother away with his fist. Eventually, he ended up doing the same with me."

My stomach drops as I snap my gaze to his. I'm not sure what I was expecting, but it was definitely not this.

"He was nothing more than a weak man who resorted to physical violence within our home."

I seem to have no control over my hand as I reach out to lay it on his forearm. Or the way my thumb brushes against his skin.

"Cole..." My voice trails off as he heaves a deep inhale.

"I hadn't told him about my plan to leave Baudette as soon as I graduated to meet up with my uncle Paul. My father had a strained relationship with his brother, mostly because my uncle Paul was the only other person who knew the truth about his character. He was the only one to ever intervene and protect me as much as he could. Even when he was out of town, he always checked in on me."

Tears rim my eyes as I recall bruises on his skin that I thought nothing of at the time. The truth of what they were horrifies me as emotion catches in my throat.

"Anyway, my father found a letter from my uncle that mentioned me going to live with him after graduation, and it set him off. I'd never seen him that mad."

He runs another hand over his face as he swallows, pausing as if the memory is too hard to relive.

"It was the final straw for me, Sydney. I no longer cared about waiting until after graduation. I took my duffel bag—and broken jaw—and fled."

A tear runs down my face as I search for the right words to say. Nothing comes to mind as he tilts his head over to me, his gaze darkening with concern as he notes my tears.

"I am sorry for not explaining it to you at the time. I should have," he says sincerely.

I shake my head and manage to force a few words out in a whisper, "No. I...you didn't owe me anything."

He sighs, settling back in his chair as if a weight has been lifted. A resigned calmness takes over him, but my mind is left reeling. How could I have thought the worst of him with no proof? Guilt settles in my stomach as I recall the rumor

I flippantly started and watched spread like wildfire with no attempt to stop it.

"So, there was no girlfriend down in Bemidji." It's more of a realization than a question.

"What?" He acts like it's an absurd thing to say, then he shakes his head. "Of course not."

"Hmm." I let the truth settle as I watch a pelican fly in to land in the bay.

"I've never told anyone that before," he mutters, and I can hear the authenticity in his voice. I rake my gaze over him as my mind continues to process this newfound information. I'm heartbroken for what he had to go through. And for how long he's had to live with the weight of it.

It's then that I realize my hand is still resting on his forearm. With a subtle squeeze, I remove it and pull my knees closer to my chest. I wrap my arms around them, resting my chin on my knees.

We sit like that for what feels like an entire hour, just the two of us, watching the waves roll in. One of us, I'd guess, feeling the relief of sharing the weight of a years-old burden...while the other lets it atone for the past.

TWENTY-ONE
Cole
Now

"She never misses, does she?" Blair raves across the picnic table, looking adoringly at the blackened ribeye strips on her plate. Beside her, Graham shakes his head, his mouth too full to do anything other than grunt his agreement.

I pick at my own empty plate, having ravished my meal already. Blair is not wrong. I've never had food as good as the kind Shirley makes. I don't know what she puts in it, but whatever it is, it has some kind of magic. A home-cooked meal has always been a rarity for me, so I have to admit I'm soaking this up while I can.

"Neal finished framing the walls today for your new apartment," Sydney tells them from where she sits on the other side of Graham. "You'll have to go check it out in the morning."

Blair gasps. "Ooh, that's so exciting."

Graham slides his arm all the way around Blair's shoulder, letting his hand hang in front of her as he buries his face in her hair.

"I can't wait," he whispers, words clearly meant just for her. I look down at my plate, feeling like I'm intruding on an intimate moment between them.

"Hopefully the rest of the lodge reno will go fast," he says to me as he straightens. "Sorry again for displacing you, Cole."

"It hasn't been so bad." I shrug. Sydney looks up from her own plate, meeting my eyes for a split second before looking away.

It really hasn't been terrible staying with Sydney. There's an easiness between us now that is reminiscent of the way it used to be, especially after opening up to her yesterday about my past with my dad, which I was surprised to find ended up being a sort of cathartic release for me.

I didn't realize how much I was needing to speak that part of me out loud, how much it needed to be released from the deep cavern I've kept it in until now.

I also didn't realize how much my hasty exit back then would have affected Sydney—and how much it still affected her opinion of me now. Of course she crossed my mind once my life settled down and the wounds healed, but at that point I got wind of the rumor and was too annoyed to do anything but write her off for good. I truly didn't think much of it until she showed up on my cabin doorstep.

But I'm man enough to pinpoint my faults, and leaving Sydney hanging is definitely a relevant one. I don't like that I unknowingly hurt her like that. Not one bit.

"Are you ready?" Blair asks Graham while climbing out of the picnic table. "It looks like there's a line forming for rides back down to the cabins."

"Yup." Graham wipes his hands in a napkin and rises.

"See you both later," he says to Sydney and me.

"See ya," we say at the same time.

When it's just the two of us left, Sydney slides her plate over until she's directly across from me.

"Hi," she says quietly, as if being alone requires an entirely new greeting. It brings a crooked smile to my lips.

"Hi," I say in return, setting my fork down. I'm done eating, but I might as well stay until she's done to offer her a ride back.

"How's the bear statue coming?" she asks.

"I'm almost done. I just need to put some oils on it over the next day or so."

"Really?" Her brows fly up and pure excitement flashes across her face. "Is it here? Can I see it?"

Her reaction catches me off guard. "You want to see the bear?"

"Of course," she says with a look as if it should be obvious that she does.

It's not obvious to me.

"Uh, sure."

"Let's go, then." She grabs her plate and climbs over the bench seat. I do the same, following her to the garbage bin. All the while, I convince myself that she probably wants to see the bear to make sure it's perfect enough for the lodge. That's the most likely reason.

I lead the way down to the beach, feeling weirdly unsettled. There isn't usually anyone that I share my projects with, especially at the unfinished stage. I'm not exactly sure how to feel, but it feels an awful lot like I'm putting a piece of myself on display. I don't know why, but showing it to her when it's not yet complete feels vulnerable in a way I didn't expect.

Midway down the hill, I turn to face her. "Okay, no peeking."

I move behind her to cover her eyes with my hands. I'm aware that I probably shouldn't, but I can't help zeroing in on the way her skin feels under mine. Soft and warm. Grazing it feels forbidden in a way, knowing what her feelings of me have been until recently.

Clearing my throat, I lead her the rest of the way down to shore, making sure there aren't any stray branches she could trip over on the way.

"Are your eyes closed?" I ask.

"Your hands are glued to my eyeballs, so I would say yes," she mutters.

Lining her up with the statue, I release my hands and step aside.

"Okay. Open," I tell her, sliding my hands into my pockets as a way of bracing myself.

Her eyes fly open instantly, and all of a sudden, I'm grateful for this clear view of her face. Watching her reaction—the way she lights up—sends a flush of something down my spine. Her jaw drops open, and a wide smile spreads as a giggle comes out of her.

"Cole," she says in a half-laugh, half-whisper, "this is incredible."

I swallow down a grin of my own as another wave of warmth rises in my chest. She steps closer to the statue and runs her hand along the surface, covering every detail line and curve of the bear.

"I mean it." She looks over at me earnestly. "I absolutely love it."

Seeing the look of admiration on her face does something to me—more than just physically. It creates a sense of pride for my work that I don't normally feel. I feel content with the work I do, sure, but I've never been one to fully take in the glowing reviews I receive. For whatever reason, I don't let the praise settle deep enough to believe them.

I choose to ignore the lingering question in the back of my mind of whether this feeling is from having anyone admire my work...or if it's because that person is her.

"Thanks," I say, shifting my weight.

"I mean, your end table is nice, but this..." She smirks. "This is next level."

I huff a soft laugh, not knowing any other way to take the compliment.

"How did you do this?" She runs her hand along the outstretched arm.

"Do you want a step-by-step tutorial?" I smirk, watching her every move as she circles the bear again.

"Maybe," she says cheekily.

"Well…" I run my hand along my jaw. "First I gather my tools—"

"I'm just kidding. I won't make you explain it all." She beams as she walks toward me.

"Something tells me if I did, you'd go out and carve a whole animal just to prove it's better than mine," I mumble.

"You're probably not wrong." She shrugs pointedly, standing next to me as we watch the sun start to set behind the bear.

"It's starting to get dark," I point out.

"Let's go," she says, walking off the beach.

I follow her back up to find Shirley is already inside the cabin for the night, and there are no guests left outside. Sydney beats me to the ATV and climbs on the back while I slide between her and the handles.

It might just be my imagination, but I swear she slides ever so slightly forward, closing the distance between us until her legs are flush with the back of mine. Any other time I've given her a ride, she's kept her distance, so I immediately pick up on this subtle movement.

I start the machine up and take us back to cabin twelve. On the way, I realize I might just be starting to grow fond of staying down here by the lodge. Cabin twelve feels a lot less lonely than my own cabin does.

Once inside, I slide my boots off while eyeing the puzzle she's clearly made headway on. The loon's entire body is finished, with just the frame and outer pieces left to be filled in. I happen to spot a piece that might fit, and before going to pull out the cot, I quietly slide it into place.

The faint sound of angry mumbling brings me partially awake, but it's the slam of the front door that causes me to bolt upright.

"What the—" I grumble.

A surprised shriek bursts out of Sydney as she falls against the now closed door.

"Oh, I'm so sorry." She clutches a hand on her chest to catch her breath. "I figured you'd be awake and gone by the time I came back."

"That was quite the wake-up call," I mumble, stretching my neck side to side and twisting my back to loosen my stiff muscles from sleeping on the cot.

"My bad." She cringes, placing what looks to be a journal of some sort on the table.

"What were you mumbling about?" I ask, rising to put the cot away for the day.

"The wrong flooring was delivered." She sighs. "Five pallet racks of the wrong floor color are currently sitting next to the lodge."

"And you can't just use it?"

"No," she says pointedly. "It's three shades too dark and would throw off the whole aesthetic of the lodge. It has to be perfect...and this is not it."

I nod, staying quiet to let her vent.

"It's too late to replace—it would take too long to deliver from Minneapolis—so now I need to run into town and pick out something from the hardware store that's in stock and can be loaded on the ferry by Monday."

She slumps in the chair, sighing again. Then she flicks her eyes to me. "What are you up to today? Want to come with me?"

"To Baudette?" My brows furrow, clearly still not fully awake.

"Yeah." She shrugs. "It might be nice to have some company. Besides, you might actually be of some help. You're good with wood and all that stuff."

"I'll take that as a compliment." I have to put another coat of finisher on the bear, but I can do that this afternoon. And truthfully, I don't hate the idea of spending more time with her.

"Sure, I'll come with."

"Alright, hurry up. The ferry will be here soon."

"Have you always been this bossy?" I huff.

"Yup," she says but with a smile this time.

I get myself put together for the day and make us two to-go coffee cups while she works on her laptop. Then I meet her at the door, offering her one of the cups.

The sound of a nail gun driving nails into wood and the faint sound of a Bobcat behind the lodge becomes more prominent as we get closer to the docks. Neal's men are stationed in and around the lodge, not hard to miss with their neon-yellow safety vests and hard hats.

"It's looking really good," I say to Sydney, pointing to the lodge.

"Besides the floor," she says flatly. "It's not perfect."

As we load onto the ferry, I wonder how much pressure she feels to get this right, how much of the weight of this reno she's putting on herself.

I climb in and settle into the spot next to her. As we pull out of the bay we fall quiet, listening to the hum of the motor and the howl of the wind that brushes against our faces.

The boat ride is uneventful, aside from pointing out some random birds flying low above us. As we reach the marina, I notice the slow sweeping breaths she keeps taking. I recognize it because it's usually the same thing I do when I'm bracing myself to head into town.

"After you." I let her climb onto the dock before following after her.

There's a strange sort of nostalgic feeling when we make our way onto the sidewalk. That feeling you sometimes get when you feel like you've been in that exact situation before. Not too long ago, she was walking by my side along this same sidewalk to the bait shop. I remember it as if it was yesterday.

As we get closer to the hardware store, I pick up on the way Sydney keeps flicking her eyes to the road that travels east out of town—toward the nursing home.

"Is that where your mom is?" I ask, then immediately regret blurting it out. "I'm sorry. We don't have to talk about—"

"No, it's okay." She gives me a soft smile before looking down at the ground. "Yes, she's there. I, uh...haven't been there in a couple years."

Her words might be innocent to most, but I see them for what they are. An opening. A confession of sorts in this volley of truths we seem to be baring. Perhaps it's her turn to share a piece of her story I wasn't a part of.

"I came back often after I left for college—a lot, actually. Every single weekend, I'd come home. But eventually, once she couldn't remember who I was anymore, it just...got too hard," she admits.

"I can see how that would be really hard," I mumble quietly.

She doesn't expand and I don't push. We walk the rest of the way without talking, knowing that words aren't always necessary. Sometimes silence is the better option when the world can be so loud as it is.

"Let's find you the perfect floor, huh?" I hold the door to the hardware store open and follow her inside.

TWENTY-TWO
Sydney
Then

"You'll want this pair of rubber sandals for the dorm showers. Promise me you won't set foot in those things unless you have some sort of sandals on, okay?" Mom places them inside the duffel bag that's next to her on the edge of my bed.

"Okay." I offer her a smile, but I know it doesn't come close to reaching my eyes. Tears prickle at my eyes like they do so easily these days with the heavy mix of emotions I feel sitting right at the surface. I'm desperately aching for the moment I'm able to flee the pressure and grief of the reality here and find some space to breathe at college. I need to get away before it crushes me whole.

At the same time, I'm also hyperfocused on the fact that I should be soaking up every lucid moment I can with

Mom—while I still can. What kind of daughter does this make me if my strongest urge is to run?

"Let's fit your makeup mirror and toiletries in this bag, shall we?" She points to the empty bag next to me on the floor.

"Okay." I pass the bag to her and continue folding my clothes into piles just like she taught me to do. A staggering ache pierces my heart when I'm reminded that this could very well be the last big milestone that she'll be lucid enough to help me prepare for. What will I do without her when I'm planning a wedding? Or when I have my future babies?

The thought is too much. I may desperately want to flee, but how am I actually supposed to leave her? What college student leaves for school without knowing if their mom will be here when they get back?

Maybe I should stay.

I sniffle and blink rapidly to clear my tears enough to see clearly.

"Hey," Mom says gently, reaching down to place her hand on my forearm. "Let's take a break."

"Okay." I nod, not needing much convincing. Pushing off the ground, I slump onto the bed next to her. She runs a hand over my hair while I puff my cheeks out with my exhale.

"I have something for you," she says with a small smile, reaching behind her back.

"You do?" I ask, running my fingers under my eyes, even though I know it's futile. More tears will surely come.

"It's a little going-away-to-college gift." She hands me a small black box with a teal ribbon tied across the top.

I swallow, nervously pulling it open, not sure how much more my emotions can handle today.

Inside the box is a silver chain with a snowflake pendant at the base. The light catches it just so as I hold it up, making the tips of it sparkle as it spins slowly in the air.

"It's so pretty," I breathe, tears welling yet again. I look over to find Mom watching me, her own eyes red at the rims—eyes that are the same shade as mine.

"Thank you," I whisper, my voice coming out wobbly.

"Here, let me," she says softly, clasping the necklace around my neck.

It's too much. All of this...it's too much.

She tips my quivering chin up with her knuckle until I'm looking into her eyes.

"I know this has been hard for you," she whispers, her own voice cracking.

I simply nod, pushing my lips together, not able to say the words out loud.

"It's been hard for me too. I need to say a few things to you while things are...clear at the moment. Would that be alright with you?" she asks quietly.

All I can do is nod slowly, bracing myself for what she's about to say.

"I want you to know...it's okay to give yourself permission to leave for college," she says quietly but intently. Her words validate my inner struggle, which she's always been so good at seeing. They both heal and break my heart all at the same time.

"But how can I leave you?" I croak out, my lips quivering with ferocity now.

"Oh, sweetheart." She offers a sad smile, gently tucking a strand of hair behind my ear. "It's okay, I promise. There's nothing I want more for you than for you to be happy and to live a full life. I wouldn't want you to miss out on college."

I hiccup on a sob while she continues through her own emotions.

"I want you to live a big, beautiful, fulfilling life without holding back or worrying about me, okay? I'll be alright. I want you to experience life. To find what you're passionate about and chase your dreams. To get your heart broken—maybe a few times. And then find a true love, letting that love put the pieces of your heart back together. I want you to have babies and bring them here to show them this piece of yourself and our history. You can't do all that if you stay here and watch me slowly fade. I know you. You are meant for more than this small town. Experience it all for me, please?"

I choke on another sob as my tears fall freely.

"And I hope like hell I get to be here for all of it. Truly, I do. But if I'm not...I want you to do it anyway. Can you promise me that?"

"Okay," I choke out, nodding, even though it breaks my heart to say it.

She shifts in place, wiping at a tear. "No matter where I am—physically or cognitively—I'll always be right here."

She taps a finger against my heart, right next to where the snowflake hangs.

"I promise you that. I will never ever leave you." There's a firmness in her voice now, along with a desperate plea to know that I hear her.

"I know." I nod my head, letting her words truly sink in. Her promise feels like a balm that warms the sharp cracks of my broken heart.

I also see them for exactly what they are. A promise to be a part of me forever, even when she's not physically here. And a promise I'm making in return to live a full life in spite of all that.

She pulls me in for a hug, and I latch onto her with all my might. As I cling to her, we both let the tears fall unabashedly and the grief be felt in its full magnitude. The depth of the pain feels like it's ripping apart the innermost part of me as I allow myself to feel it all.

We sit like that for a long time, neither one of us wanting to let go first. As I hang onto her, I'm fully aware that I should appreciate this rare moment of lucid realness with her. Appreciate the opportunity to have this conversation at all.

At the same time, I hate how absolutely unfair all of it is that we have to be going through this in the first place.

TWENTY-THREE
Sydney
Now

"Last chance," Graham says, keeping one hand on the dock post, looking at me expectantly.

All I can do is stand rooted in place. My body feels like a cement brick, pressing my feet to the dock. A part of me actually does want to go see Mom today—the biggest urge I've ever had, actually—but it still doesn't even come close to overpowering the reluctance I feel to do so.

"I...can't," I murmur, feeling every second of his and Blair's stares, as if it physically causes shame to wash over me.

"Alright," Graham says with his typical soothing voice, and Blair gives me a reassuring smile. "We'll tell her you say hi."

As they push the boat off the dock and motor out of the bay, I thumb the snowflake necklace that hangs near my heart.

She's in here.

Not there.

Mom's words ease my heavy heart, and I close my eyes, letting the wind blow through my hair.

My eyes are still closed, lost in the mental chaos of contradicting urges that pull at me, when I hear the crunch of leaves behind me.

"Can I show you something?" There's no greeting that comes with it. No small talk or flippancy. It's a straightforward question from someone whose voice is ingrained into my memory.

I turn around, finding Cole standing on the grass beyond the beach, looking serious as always, slightly hesitant as he shoves his hands in his pockets.

The sight of him brings a sense of relief in a way I can't quite explain. I shove down thoughts of my mom, burying them, and make my way off the dock toward him.

"You want to show me something? Like an object?" I ask, wondering what he could possibly want to show me.

He huffs, a twist to his mouth.

"No. A place." His brows rise as he says it, a question on his face.

"Okay."

"Yeah?"

"Sure. As long as you bring me back in an hour. I have a conference call this afternoon."

"Deal. Hop on." He gestures to his ATV that's parked next to the lodge.

As I walk, I pull my hair back into a ponytail to keep it out of my face on the ride. I climb on the back, and when I glance up, I find him watching me intently while he waits for me to get situated—studying me. My heart pounds in my chest as I find it's getting harder and harder to break from his gaze the last few days, especially when he stares at me like that.

The depth behind his stare was one of the things that drew me to him the most back then...and I'm starting to see that the same magnetic energy we had might still be there. A hint of a flame that I'm becoming more aware of now that our walls have come down enough to see it.

Call it the effects of forced proximity, or maybe it's the awareness of our shared past that's resurfaced. Whatever it is, it's getting harder to ignore, and I'm not sure how to feel about it. I spent the last eight years despising this man—to say my feelings are complex would be an understatement.

He blinks, snapping out of wherever he just was in his head, and climbs in front of me. As I've been doing every time he gives me a ride lately, I take advantage of the comfort his closeness gives me and scoot up just a smidge until my body is flush with his.

He doesn't seem to mind or flinch in the slightest, so I stay there. He simply starts it up and takes us along the trail. We travel the well-worn path all the way up to his cabin, where he parks along the tree line.

"Is this one of those times when you show me something inside your cabin to rub it in my face that I can't demolish it?" I snide as I hop off.

"No." He chuckles, passing me, gesturing for me to follow. "Besides, Shirley is in there. Come on, let's go this way."

With no clue as to where we're heading, I follow as he leads me all the way down the back side of his property. When we reach the beach, he hooks a left toward the tree line. As I look closer, I can see the tiniest of trails in an opening in the woods.

"Hiking wasn't exactly on my bingo card today," I mumble, but it doesn't stop me from wanting to follow him—not even in the slightest.

He holds a branch back as an invitation. "It's not far, I promise."

With an amused shrug, I follow behind him, ducking under the branch. Leaves scatter the ground, and random rocks push out from the dirt, making it hard to see where to take my next step.

"You clearly haven't maintained this trail, huh?" I tease.

"It's like this on purpose." He looks back to flash a smile. "I don't want anyone finding it."

The fact that it's a secret location adds a sense of intrigue, fueling me to trudge along behind him as we climb up an incline. Eventually, he comes to a stop at a small clearing.

A large boulder is nestled in the ground not far from where the edge drops off. Cole lowers to sit on it, leaving just enough room left for me. Before I join him there, I can't help but inch toward the ledge to see the full aerial view from all the way up here.

"Don't get too close," he warns.

"This is incredible," I breathe, my mouth parting in awe. I thought I knew every square inch of this island, but I can confidently say I've never been in this exact spot before. The beauty of the cliff rivals any other lookout I've come across, and it makes me feel full of energy as I take it all in.

"Cole." I can't help but laugh, stretching my arms out and tipping my head back, relishing the feel of the wind against my skin. "It's beautiful up here."

I twist over my shoulder to find him sitting stoically, studying me again. He doesn't have a trace of the same enthusiasm I do, but he does have a look of amusement—directed solely at me.

He nods, pursing his lips together as I join him on the rock.

"Look," Cole says, pointing a finger to the left. "See over there? Where the outline of the island curves to the right?"

"All I see are trees. Am I looking for anything in particular?" I whisper, all of a sudden feeling as if I don't want to disturb nature, as if this serene place deserves the respect of a quiet voice.

"See the tree that sticks out a little bit above the rest? That hangs over the edge? There's an eagle's nest in there."

I squint my eyes, and sure enough, there are two eagles sitting on top of the tree. The awe-inspiring beauty of it brings another smile to my face.

"I used to come up here when I needed to think. Or to find a quiet reprieve," he says, a hint of sadness to his tone that has a sobering effect on my carefree joy.

"To escape your dad?" I ask hesitantly, treading lightly. He may have opened up once, but that doesn't mean he'd want to do it again.

"Yeah." He runs his hand along his jaw. "Whenever my uncle was here, anyway. There were other spots I escaped to in town if he wasn't."

I nod. I'm fairly certain he doesn't want pity, but I'm not quite sure what else to say that doesn't have some sort of sympathy in it.

"I needed places to go after my mom left," he explains. "I didn't want to be in the house by myself once my dad stormed off. I couldn't stand being there alone."

My stomach drops in a heavy way as I think of everything he went through. "I'm sorry."

He falls quiet, picking up a stick to pick at while we watch another eagle fly into the nest. The mention of his mom brings the thought of my own to the surface, along with the lingering guilt for not going with Graham. There's still a strong urge to push it all down, but up here in the middle of nowhere, with him at my side, I feel an even stronger one to let the words out.

"I couldn't do it, Cole," I whisper, sharing my own vulnerability.

"Couldn't do what?" He turns to me.

"Go see my mom. That's where Graham and Blair were going. I just..." I let out a sigh. "I don't know why it's so hard to do. Every time I think I'm ready, I can't. It's like something holds me back."

I clamp my mouth shut, feeling the slightest relief at speaking my thoughts aloud but not certain I want to ramble further. Who knows what might come out of my mouth if I give myself permission to open all the way up.

He offers me the same supportive silence I gave him moments ago until he throws the stick into the trees.

"For the record..." He connects his gaze to mine, the sincerity behind his eyes sucking me in. "I think you're strong enough to do it. To go see her. Even if you don't think you are."

His words wash over me, bringing a wave of unsteady emotion along with it.

"How could you possibly know that?" I murmur, willing tears to be kept at bay.

He gives a close-mouthed smile. "It's not hard to see. You're a force, Sydney Peterson."

His words flood me with a warmth that seems to reach every corner of my body. As we keep our eyes locked on each other, second by second, anticipation builds. My heart rate picks up, and my breath hitches when he dips his gaze to my mouth.

Is he going to kiss me?

"Sydney?" he whispers.

The way he says my name sends a shiver straight down my spine—the same exact way my body reacted to him saying my name all those years ago.

I think I loathe and love it at the same time.

"Yeah?" I manage to squeak out.

"There's something else I've been meaning to apologize for. About back then."

I brace myself and clear my throat. "Okay."

"That night at the bonfire..." He looks down. "I shouldn't have kissed you."

My heart feels heavy as my stomach drops. He regrets it? I don't know why that thought hurts so much.

He looks back at me. "You were drunk."

I shake my head slightly in protest, my thoughts swimming.

"No, it was wrong," he insists. "I felt like I took advantage of you, and...I need you to know that I'm sorry."

"It's okay. I wanted it," I breathe out in a whisper. Something flashes behind his eyes, and my racing heart fills me with both hesitation and anticipation.

Do I really want to go back down this road with him? Is he safe? I think he is, but I'm not entirely sure.

As I sink deeper into his stare, I realize I already know the answer to that.

"Maybe I want it now too," I murmur, then bite my lip as I watch the way my words—and their implication—settle inside him.

My heart pounds wildly in my chest as he slowly leans forward, gently pressing his lips to mine. I lean in, resting my hand lightly on his chest as he slides a warm hand up my arm.

My chest blooms with each passing second that he moves his mouth gently against mine. My heart feels both wildly alive and oddly settled at the same time. All at once, I know this kiss is more than just a simple kiss between two people. I know, in my heart, it feels like a connecting of two lost souls. A coming-home kind of kiss with someone who sees me on a level that no one else ever has.

He squeezes my arm firmly, and when he reluctantly pulls away, he keeps his face close. As soon as I open my eyes, it's obvious in his heated stare that he felt the exact same thing I just did.

He moves his hand up to gently cup my chin, caressing my cheek with his thumb. I swallow, refusing to acknowledge the logical part of my brain that's demanding to know what this means. I just want to bask in this feeling as long as I can for now.

"Sit with me a while?" he asks, lifting his arm as an invitation.

All I can do is smile and slide under his arm, sinking into his side and the comfort of him as we watch the eagles fly in the sky.

TWENTY-FOUR
Cole
Now

Week Eight of Renovation

"Just a little to the left!" Blair shouts from behind us. Graham and I both hoist our side of the bear statue to swivel it a few inches over.

"Is that good?" Graham calls over his shoulder.

"A little to the right!" Sydney yells this time. With a sigh, I grunt, and we maneuver it back.

"Do you think they're just messing with us?" I ask Graham.

"That's very likely," he groans, standing up straight.

"Maybe—" Blair starts but doesn't get to finish.

"It's fine," Graham cuts her off curtly—yet respectfully, of course—brushing his hands together. I take a few steps to the side to study the placement of the statue. Graham wanted it right off the porch steps so guests will pass it when they walk in the lodge.

"Isn't it amazing?" Sydney gushes to Blair and Graham, the same sense of awe to her tone as when she first saw it.

I roll my lips to hide a smile, appreciating her attempt to brag, regardless of how unfamiliar it feels to me.

"It really is," Blair agrees. "Nice job, Cole."

"Thank you." I take a few steps to stand on the other side of Sydney, a force drawing me to her that hasn't relented since our kiss yesterday.

That kiss was as powerful and soul moving as the first time was all those years ago. Except, this time it felt even more like a choice. With all our cards having been laid out on the table—the good, the bad, the ugly—it felt like we were acknowledging our scars and baring our battle wounds for the other to see...and choosing each other anyway.

I don't know what this means for us moving forward, but that's okay. It doesn't need to be all figured out right now and wrapped up in a neat bow. When has it ever been with us? I'm content being along for the ride at this point to see how it will all play out.

From behind us comes the slow roar of a boat motor out on the lake that increases as it comes into the bay.

"Must be dinner time." Graham flashes a smile before he heads for the docks. Blair trails behind him, leaving Sydney and me alone for the first time all day.

"Neal and his team are over at the recreation site today, but he told me they got the floors installed in the main part of the lodge." Sydney smiles, a nervous excitement apparent in the way she bites her lip. "Do you want to come see it with me?"

"Sure."

"Okay, good." She leads the way to the steps. "I'm really nervous to see it."

"How could you be nervous? We spent two hours in the hardware store making sure it was the right color."

"You never know for sure until you see it in the space, Cole." She holds the door open behind her as I follow her inside.

"That's true, I guess," I chuckle.

The subtle fumes of a construction site hit me as soon as I walk in—dust, sealing compounds, and wood shavings fill the air.

"Whoa," I murmur, taking in the changes that have been made. The spot where the front desk used to be is no longer there, and the walls that separated the entry to the dining room are no longer, making it one big space that's pushed back farther than it used to be. The walls are white, still needing to be painted, but the stunning blonde, white oak flooring we picked out covers every inch of the floor.

I glance at Sydney, expecting her to be admiring it the same way I am. However, her face is stern as her gaze flitters back and forth. From the back of the room to the front, from the walls down the span of the floor, she's seemingly scrutinizing every little detail.

"What do you think?" I ask.

After a few sighs, she gives a hint of a shrug, nodding slightly.

"I think it'll work," she says, though not at all convincingly. I can see the way her brain is overthinking.

"Can I ask you a question?" I ask as I study her.

"Sure." She looks over her shoulder at me then walks around the perimeter of the room, eyes roaming over every surface.

"What happens if it doesn't end up perfect?" I ask the question as gently as I can. "This whole renovation...what if it's not flawless at the end?"

She huffs, a sad smile crossing her face while she ponders my question. Then she pushes her lips together before shrugging. "I guess I just feel like restoring this place is my way of honoring my family, honoring my past."

I nod in silence, giving her admission the quiet space it deserves before asking, "And you think you're not going to honor them if the wrong picture hangs on the wall or the paint color ends up being a tad too dark? Do you think anyone would care?"

She flicks her gaze to me, and as she holds my stare, her tension relaxes.

"No," she admits with a hint of a smile. "I know they wouldn't."

"That's what I was thinking too," I say quietly.

"I guess there's just a lot of things I feel guilty for," she admits before shaking her head. "I don't know. It doesn't make any sense."

I cross the room and slide my hand down her arm, squeezing at her wrist. "I get it."

She offers me a small smile before wandering to the far side of the room. I follow behind as we pass by the door to the kitchen, all the way to another doorway.

"This is Graham and Blair's apartment," she explains, pointing to the set of unfinished stairs that lead up to a living space without a door yet. "They're still working on electrical and plumbing in the addition portion of the lodge."

"That'll be nice for Blair and Graham when it's all done."

"Yeah. They deserve it," she says softly as we wander on. I stay as close to her as I can without crowding her. I'm finding more and more that I just want to be near her. Close enough to feel a hint of a spark that rushes over me when she's just within reach.

"Do you think you could ever live out here full-time?"

"Yup," I reply instantly, not needing to think about it long.

"Really?" She giggles. "I don't know if I could. I think I'd miss the city too much."

"The city is overrated," I mumble as we pass what looks to be the laundry room.

"Tell me about your place in Longville. What does it look like?"

"There's not much to it," I admit. "It's a rambler walkout with a kitchen and two bedrooms. Cheap, thrifted furniture and not a thing on the walls."

"Sounds perfect." She smiles. "Do you have land, or is it in a neighborhood?"

"I'm close to my neighbors, but I don't mind it. I'm not there often enough to need the solitude. I find that enough when I do my wandering."

I lift my gaze to hers to find that she's been staring at me with interest, as if she's enthralled by these small glimpses of my life that I show her.

"Can I take you on a date?" I blurt out suddenly. I might be moving too fast—I'm fully aware of that. But it feels as right as anything has ever felt before. *She* feels right.

She laughs, throwing her head back. "Where exactly are we going to go on a date around here, Cole? We're in the middle of a lake."

I hadn't gotten that far yet, so I lift a shoulder. "I'll think of something."

She stares at me, seemingly considering my offer.

"Okay...but can I make a request?" she asks.

"Of course."

"Could we not go into Baudette? Would that be okay?" She asks the question hesitantly, as if it would be a huge inconvenience on my end to not go into town.

"That's the last place I want to be too," I tell her. "I promise we won't go near the city."

The corner of her mouth tips up, a hint of excitement behind her eyes.

"Great. I'm looking forward to it," she says.

TWENTY-FIVE
Sydney
Now

"Did you get Graham's permission to take one of his boats, or are we stealing? I'm honestly fine with either," I quip as Cole unties the rope from the dock post.

"I got permission." He looks over to wink at me. "I didn't tell him what I was using it for, though."

I snort. "You mean you didn't tell him you were taking his little sister out on a date?"

"I did not. We aren't exactly close enough for me to know how he would take it. And to be honest, I don't really want to ruffle any feathers with him."

"It's probably good that you didn't tell him," I say honestly. While I know Graham truly only wants what's best for me, he is most definitely an overprotective older brother—to a fault at times.

With the help of Cole's hand, I climb into the boat and slide into the swivel chair next to the captain's seat. Then I peer around for any clues as to where he could be taking me. The only thing that looks out of place is a large blanket that seems to be draped over something in the back of the boat.

Interesting.

I sink against the back of my chair as he pushes the throttle into gear. I'm genuinely curious where he could be taking me that doesn't involve going into town. Maybe a different neighboring city?

The weight of the full day I've had presses on my shoulders. I roll them to loosen the tension as the sound of the lake water rolling against the boat seems to calm me. Simply being in Cole's presence seems to do that too.

This morning was spent glued to my laptop, connecting puzzle pieces in between virtual meetings, and poring over budget spreadsheets for the renovation. The afternoon was mostly taken up with overseeing the delivery of kitchen appliances that finally arrived via the barge—only a few days off schedule.

All of it is necessary work, of course, and I'm happy to be the one spearheading it, but that doesn't mean I don't feel exhausted by the end of the day.

Once we're out of the bay, instead of going left, which would take us in the direction of Baudette and Oak Island, he veers the boat to the right, heading north.

"Where are we going?" A burst of energy has me feeling like a little girl on Christmas morning, eager to uncover the magic

I know it will hold. I also know enough about the geography of this lake to know that any cities or operating islands in this direction are more than an hour boat ride away, and we're already running out of daylight.

"To Canada." He smiles, pushing down on the throttle.

I watch him with a lazy smile as the wind rushes through my hair, making me feel alive and exhilarated all at once. This kind of adventure is something I've admittedly been missing down in Minneapolis.

We pass several scattered islands, each one a different shape, all with wild brush and a varying number of trees sprouting from the bases. Some are small enough to be missed completely if you aren't paying attention, while some stand tall and majestic—a mini mountain of sorts in the middle of the water.

Eventually, he slows to a stop in the middle of the open water, not a single thing within sight other than an island a few miles ahead in the distance.

After he drops the anchor, I watch curiously as he slips the blanket off the pile, revealing a picnic basket, another blanket, and a small cooler.

"Aw, Cole," I say his name like it's the cutest thing I've ever seen. And it just might be. It really didn't matter what we were doing tonight. I just wanted to spend time with him. But the fact that he put thought into planning anything at all is what makes my heart flutter.

"There aren't a lot of places on Takini where we can be alone," he says, flashing me a subtle, perhaps a little timid, smirk. "I, uh...thought this would be nice."

"It is," I say emphatically, watching as he pulls a bottle of wine out of the cooler and pours some into two Solo cups. I take a moment to take stock of my emotions, concluding that I'm not feeling too out of sorts at the moment—honestly, probably a byproduct of being near him—so I accept the wine with a smile.

"We're going to sit here..." he announces, reaching for the blue-and-green plaid wool blanket, "drink some wine, and watch the sunset."

"Sounds perfect," I murmur, helping him lay the blanket on the bench that runs along the back of the boat. Then I have a seat on one side of the bench and bend to help unpack the basket.

"Did Shirley help you with this?" I pull out a perfectly curated charcuterie board, setting it on top of the blanket between us.

"Why? Do I seem incapable of putting this together myself?" He chuckles, a self-deprecating gleam to his smile.

"No," I retort with a giggle. "She's just known for packing a mean picnic basket."

He pulls out a container of fruit and a box of crackers then shifts so he's facing me. I bite at a slice of cheese as he takes a sip of his wine.

"So..." I start. I plan on taking full advantage of this uninterrupted time together. "I knew a little about Cole from high school. Tell me about Cole now."

"What do you mean?" He creases his brows.

"Like what's your favorite food? I want to know what you do for fun. What makes you tick? I'll even settle for knowing your favorite color. You know—the basics."

He swallows a bite of a cracker, brushing his fingers against his jeans as if he doesn't quite know how to broach the subject.

"I promise none of that is fascinating." He says it in a way that makes me wonder how many people have ever asked him about himself—if any at all. The thought tugs on my heart in an aching sort of way.

"Try me," I urge.

"Alright, let's see." He sighs. "My favorite color is brown."

"Shocker," I chide, pointing to his brown flannel button-up and caramel-colored vest. He ignores my comment and continues on without batting an eye.

"My favorite food is barbecued ribs, and what makes me tick..." He looks off into the distance, thinking.

"Besides me." I flash a snarky grin.

"Besides you," he mutters through a smirk. "Airports."

"Airports?" I laugh.

"Yup. Can't stand them—too many people."

"That's valid," I reply. "You forgot what you do for fun."

He shrugs. "Carving things."

"That's your job, technically," I point out. "But I'll accept it."

"Your turn." He tugs on a slice of salami that's been perfectly coiled into a bundle in the shape of a rose.

"Hmm. Okay, are we talking the same questions, or am I allowed to go rogue?"

"Whatever you want." He studies me in amusement.

"Okay." I sit up to prepare myself for the importance of this moment. "I love tacos in any form. I love to be organized, but I have a love-hate relationship with the planner that's hanging on my wall. Sometimes I'd like to just erase it all and disappear for a while instead. And my favorite thing to do with any free time is bike on the path in front of my apartment that runs along the Mississippi. That or do goat yoga—have you ever done it? It's where you do a yoga class, and goats roam around and jump on your back."

Clearly, he's never heard of that particular kind of yoga, judging by his face and emotionless shake of his head, but before he can comment, I blurt out one more thing that came to mind.

"Oh, and I have a bucket-list dream of going to France someday to admire the architecture there."

He nods, taking me in with a calmness that feels almost like an anchor of sorts. There's a calm look to his face like there's no place he'd rather be. He's simply content to be in the moment and present with me—even if all we're doing is talking.

The sun starts to set, the sky starting to ever so slightly get dimmer. I follow Cole's lead by placing the food back into the basket. Then he leans back against the side edge of the boat while bringing one bent knee up along the bench. It leaves plenty of room for me to slide in front of him if I were to choose to.

"Am I supposed to squeeze in there to snuggle and watch the sunset with your arms around me? Like in those romance movies?" I comment, feeling a rush of adrenaline at the mere thought of it.

He pins me with an amused, almost daring gaze that sends a prickling spark running across my skin.

"Only if you want to," he says so softly the words get carried away almost instantly in the wind. If he didn't gently tap the blanket in front of him, I would second-guess whether he said it at all.

A surge of exhilaration pushes me over to where he sits, lowering until my back is flush with his torso, my feet stretched out straight in front of me. His arms come around me like a cage, his right elbow propped on top of his bent knee.

Immediately, I feel safe and protected with his arms around me, in a unique way that I never have before. The beat of his heart thumps against my back, and his chest rises and falls with his breath. I'm comforted somehow, although I'm not sure from what.

"I made you something," he murmurs against my ear.

"You did?"

"Yup." He shifts, moving my body along with his as he digs in his pocket. He settles back, bringing a small object in front of me.

I take it, biting my lip when I realize what it is; a small eagle made out of wood perched on a branch with its wings spread wide.

"You carved this?" I breathe in wonder.

"I did," he says gently.

"Thank you, Cole," I whisper. The thoughtfulness behind his gift makes my chest swell with emotion.

"You're welcome," he says close to my ear.

"Did you have this in your vest pocket the whole time?" I tease, which earns me a chuckle.

"It was getting a little uncomfortable," he admits.

I run my fingers across the eagle, admiring the details of its beak all the way down to its claws, remembering the moment we shared while watching the eagle's nest on his property. Emotion continues to tug on my heart at his gesture, and the intensity of it sparks a subtle wave of anxiety with the next breath—an urge to put a name to whatever this is.

As I reach my hand up to hook it over the spot on his arm closest to me, my head laying against his chest, I whisper, "What are we doing, Cole?"

"Watching the sunset like they do in those romance movies," he states quietly.

"I mean with us?" I dare to ask, not sure I'm ready to hear an answer that might end us before we've even begun but needing to address it all the same. "I'm only here for the duration of the renovation, and we both live in different cities."

His heaving sigh has me lifting slightly along with his chest. "Honestly, I'm not really worried about that, Sydney."

"Oh, yeah? Care to clue me in as to why not?" I ask in amusement.

"Roaming is a part of who I am. It's in my blood," he explains softly. "I stay wherever I feel like for as long as I feel like. Whatever feels best in the moment. And right now...I think I'd like to be here. With you. If you don't mind. I don't have plans to go back to Longville anytime soon."

His words give me a rush of relief that further proves how much weight I was putting in his answer. This might not answer the question about the future, but at least we're on the same page for now.

"I think I'd like that," I murmur, turning my head to look up at him as best I can. His gaze immediately connects with mine, and he runs a thumb along my cheek. My skin burns under his touch. Anticipation has the air getting stuck in my throat as he peruses me with an intensity I can't seem to get enough of.

"You can't tell me you don't feel this," he murmurs.

As much as I might second-guess the reality and logistics of what we're starting, he's right. There's no denying what's between us. What has seemingly always been there.

"I do." The words come out a mere breath before he presses his mouth to mine—gently, of course—as he cradles the back of my head that's twisting to meet him. He slides his lips against mine as I open my mouth, deepening the kiss that's as intoxicating as it is soothing.

I get lost in the moment with him, relishing the high his kiss gives me. When he brings his arm across my chest to lightly run his fingers along my collarbone, I tighten my grip on his forearm in response and let myself sink even more into the rush of whatever this is.

It isn't until he pulls back and I slowly open my eyes that I realize the sun is almost completely down. I settle against him, our rapid breaths syncing together, slowing to a normal pace as our chests rise and fall in unison. We're a tangle of limbs, curled together as we watch the last sliver of the sun dip underneath the horizon.

TWENTY-SIX
Cole
Now

"Now that's what I call a swing set," I mutter as we step onto the sandy base of the recreation area that's connected to the Takini Island community land.

"Right?" Sydney looks around, her eyes scrunching slightly as she takes it all in. The structure has a winding tunnel slide, a large playhouse, three additional slides, and even a rock-climbing wall on one side. A makeshift boat, complete with a steering wheel and faux fishing rods attached, is built into the back side of it. Admittedly, it's one of the most creative ones I've ever seen. Not that I've seen many in my day, but still.

"I think kids will have fun playing on it, right? It was the biggest one I could find in our budget." She places her hands on her hips and tilts her head for one last scrutinizing perusal.

"I would say so," I agree, running my hand along the wooden base of the playhouse, admiring the finish.

"Is the craftsmanship up to your standards?" she asks, a hint of teasing in her tone.

A smile curves my mouth upward. "It looks good. Nice choice."

I turn to her. "Want to show me the rest?"

"Sure." She leads me across the sand, past a row of brand-new picnic tables with attached umbrellas that replaced the worn tables that were here before. I remember coming here once or twice with my uncle, but there wasn't a whole lot to play on then.

"We've got a tennis court over here and a small waterproof shed to store the balls and rackets." She points to the large slab of asphalt on the outer edge of the property. "The court still needs to be painted, but that should get done this week, I think."

She goes quiet as her gaze turns to the court with a hint of admiration. The fondness in her gaze has me wondering if it means something more to her.

"Did you used to play tennis?" I inquire.

My question brings a smile to her face for a brief moment before a faint twist of pain follows directly behind it.

"Not really. It was my mom's favorite sport," she says quietly. "I used to tag along when she would go to the gym every week to play. I'd watch her for hours on end."

I nod silently, not wanting to make her pain any worse by asking another question. I don't want to accidentally hit another nerve.

She seems to get lost in reminiscing for a few moments while I wait patiently for her to work through whatever she's reminiscing over. Eventually, she sighs, clears her throat, and turns to head toward the lake.

"We'll be setting up a volleyball net down here on the beach," she explains, the affliction now gone from her tone. I don't like that she's used to shifting out of pain like that so easily. "And we put in a new dock system to accommodate more boats."

I keep my gaze trained on her, on the lookout for any further shift in emotion, while she pans hers across the whole recreation area. Her hands come to her hips again as she sighs.

"I don't know. My plan was to make this a special place for families. Whether they walk over from the lodge or if they stop by boat. I'd like it to be a peaceful place for both kids and adults to play. Relax and alleviate the stress of life, you know? That's what I hoped for, anyway." She shrugs, and I can see the doubt behind her eyes.

"It's perfect," I tell her, using the words I know will mean the most to her.

She huffs a small smile, bashfully turning toward me. The roughness in her features softens as she zeros in on me. Then she lifts her brows as if an idea suddenly popped into her head.

"Hey, I'll race you down the slides," she challenges with a playful mischief.

"What?" I chuckle at the absurdity. "Sydney, I'll break it. I'm pretty sure I'm way beyond the weight limit for that thing."

That only seems to further her excitement, despite my rationale.

"Come on!" she yells, jogging for the playset. A sudden urge hits me to give in to her lighthearted challenge, and I make a split-second decision to do it. What do I have to lose? I break into a jog, her squeal fading into the wind as I pass by her.

I pause when I near the playground to wait for her, but she rushes past me to the vertical steps on the side. Following behind her, a youthful surge of energy runs through me. One that's carefree and light. One I don't remember ever feeling until this moment.

"Are you ready?" she asks, looking back at me from where she sits at the top of one of the wavy slides. I settle onto the one next to her as best I can, barely able to squeeze my legs in between the ridges.

"This isn't going to go well," I mutter, but I nod to her anyway. "I'm ready."

"Go!" she says, flinging herself down the slide. I push off with my hands, but my legs screech against the plastic of the slide, and I resort to using my feet to scooch my way down. When I finally make it to the very bottom, my foot hits the sand at an awkward angle when I try to straighten my leg, and I end up tripping over myself. My knees fall into the sand, and I catch myself with my wrist to avoid falling face first into it.

A hearty laugh escapes me as I attempt to regain my balance. It's an involuntary reaction that comes straight from my gut, fueled by this carefree, ridiculous moment. When I glance over at Sydney, I expect to find her doing the same, laughing at my expense.

Instead, she's staring at me, her expression void of any humor. In fact, she's frozen in place, pinning me with a look that I can't quite place.

"What?" I ask, slightly out of breath from my efforts.

She swallows, a subdued smile finally forming as she seems to come back into focus.

"Back then...I used to love when you smiled," she says quietly, stepping closer to me. "I didn't know what was going on in your life at the time, of course, but I assumed your smiles were hard-earned."

The breath gets caught in my throat as I roll my lips, feeling uncomfortable at her observation. Yet, a part of me desperately wants her to continue to find out what she has to say.

"I liked that I could bring out that side of you. It was comforting, in a way, to know that I could." Her mouth twitches with a smile. "I think the same is true when you laugh."

A warmth grips my chest, not making it any easier to breathe. As I process her words, the way they make me feel—this rush of emotion—has me leaning down to press a kiss to her mouth. It seems to be as involuntary and necessary as the laugh was.

When I pull back, she hovers close to my mouth instead of backing away.

"I like it, is all," she whispers, a small grin forming. Then she takes a step backward before racing back to the swing set for a second race.

I follow after her, deciding that I do too.

TWENTY-SEVEN
Sydney
Now

Week Ten of Renovation

"What do you think?" Neal asks the group, sliding a hand across the new bar top in the nearly finished dining room. I stand off to the side and study every facial expression that my dad and Shirley make, hardly able to contain my excitement.

This right here.

This is why I'm doing this.

Not only to honor my family's legacy but also for this moment. To see firsthand how it will bless the members of my family that are still here.

"This is incredible, Neal," Blair gushes, even though she and Graham already got the tour of this part of the lodge yesterday. Graham walks behind the bar to get a closer look at the new amenities back there, including a wine fridge, top-of-the-line ice maker, and two working dishwashers.

"Wow," my dad breathes, looking around in awe.

Emotion swells in my throat as I watch his eyes gloss over when he spots the same piece of art that was hanging above the original bar. The one of a cowboy on a horse that my grandpa bought at an auction many years ago and was always a staple conversation piece in the lodge.

My own eyes well up as he spins a slow circle, taking in every last little bit of the renovation. I watch as he takes note of the spacious open floor plan, the scattering of modern tables and chairs with leather seats in the same color that the old chairs were, the expanded bar top with trim made out of the original piece. It's a more modern space with touches that honor the past and true heart of Ruby Lodge.

That's been my goal all along. Nerves bubble in my stomach as I hope I executed it sufficiently. Judging by their faces, I think I may have.

"I was worried it would look too different," Dad admits quietly, glancing at me. "But it's not. It still has the same heart. It's pretty amazing, Sydney."

"Thanks, Dad." I grin as I slide my arm around his shoulders. He pats my forearm, and we rest our heads together to take a moment.

"Electronic pull-tabs?" Graham asks, picking up a tablet from the charging station behind the bar. "I didn't see these yesterday—and I don't remember seeing those on the master list."

"Those were a last-minute splurge." Neal winks at me and I smile.

"Want to see the kitchen?" he asks.

"Yes!" Shirley exclaims, clapping her hands together.

I trail behind them with a subtle smile still playing on my lips. I knew it would feel good to see their reactions, but I didn't think it would feel this good. It's a kind of satisfaction that runs incredibly deep, one that appeases some deep-rooted self-doubt I felt about completing this the right way. The perfect way.

Dad lingers back with me as the others head into the kitchen.

"You know, Graham and Blair are coming out to see your mother tomorrow. Maybe you could come? We could tell her about this," he suggests softly with a hopeful gleam in his eye.

My smile slowly fades as an ache forms in my chest. A foreign, primal urge that comes from the very bottom of my heart pushes me to say yes, but again...something heavy holds me back.

"Maybe," I tell him, although I know I likely won't. As the words come out of my mouth, another subtle urge hits. One that feels an awful lot like bravery. A strength that has me questioning if maybe I actually could do this. Maybe I should just try.

I haven't been able to write in the journal Blair gave me—as much as I've tried to. Yet I feel some sort of connection to it that has me carrying it around everywhere I go. I've been patiently waiting for the urge to write something to strike. It hasn't yet, to my frustration.

He nods sympathetically, accepting my words. Then he pats my back before turning to follow the others. A low whistle escapes him as we walk into the upgraded kitchen that's now double the size of what it used to be.

"Oh my," Shirley drawls, admiring the section of brand-new stainless-steel appliances. There's also ample counter space and floor-to-ceiling cabinets along the back wall for the pantry. It's nothing fancy, the kitchen, but it does give Shirley anything she could ever want back here.

"Is it functional? Ready to run?" she asks, the eagerness clear in her voice.

"It is," Neal boasts. "The whole front of the lodge is operational. There's still a bit of work left to do on the apartment and the rest of the addition—the library and exercise rooms—but it's minor work, and we can easily work around you while you're here."

"Really?" Shirley exclaims while Graham nods enthusiastically, seemingly ready to get back to work in here.

"Yup," I answer her. "I have some interior work to do on the library, laundry, and exercise room this week, but the kitchen and the dining room are fully functional and ready to be used."

"So I can move back down here?" she asks, looking positively thrilled.

"Yup," Graham cuts in. "Neal gave us the green light to move most of our stuff out of your cabin and into the apartment upstairs yesterday. I'd say you can make the switch whenever you're ready."

"I'll do it right now," she says, eliciting a laugh from us all. "Besides, I'm sure Cole is itching to have his cabin back."

The mention of his name makes my mouth go dry, and heat flushes the skin of my cheek when I notice Graham flick his gaze to me. I can't tell if he's gauging my reaction or not, but I avoid eye contact all the same.

The truth is, I'll be sad to see Cole go. I know he's not going far—as he said he wants to stay on the island for a while—but still. I'm getting used to having him around cabin twelve with me. It's been really nice.

"I'll let him know," I say, avoiding Graham's stare.

"Where do we go from here, Neal?" Blair asks. "What's next?"

"Well, I've got a crew finishing up the recreation area," he starts.

I make a mental note to swing by that area again tomorrow to sign off on the completion.

"And I've got a crew working on your apartment and one that'll start on the individual cabins tomorrow."

"Perfect. We're starting east and working our way west, right?" Graham asks. "I've got my bookings staggered so we can still rent the ones not being worked on."

"You got it," Neal confirms. A pang hits my chest as I realize that time is running out on my time here. Granted, we still have the individual cabins to finish, the glamping area, and landscaping, which will take a while, but I have a feeling it will fly by. I don't like that thought. I'm not quite ready for it to be over.

"Awesome," Graham says before turning to Dad. "You've got to see the exercise room."

"Show me," Dad says eagerly.

I bite my lip as I jog to stay close by. I want to be able to see my dad's reaction when he sees the rest of the lodge.

My feet ache with each step I take along the dirt path, tired from standing most of the day. By the time I reach cabin twelve, my eyelids feel just as heavy. A hungry grumble comes loudly from my stomach just as I push open the door.

"Hey," Cole says from the kitchen where he's standing over a sizzling pan.

"Hi. Wow, it smells amazing in here."

He throws a subtle smile over his shoulder. "Grilled cheese—it's about as gourmet as I can get in this small kitchen."

"I'm so hungry I would eat your sock right now. But your grilled cheese sounds much better. Thank you," I say while slumping down into a chair to untie my boots.

"Busy day?" he asks.

"Yes. We showed my dad and Shirley the lodge, and then I spent the entire rest of the day working on the interior. I stocked fresh supplies in the laundry room, moved some furniture around in the entryway, and helped Shirley get settled into the new kitchen. Oh...she's officially out of your cabin, by the way, so you're free to move back in." I hold my breath, waiting to see his reaction, hoping he doesn't seem overly excited about it. I'm expecting him to move out, but that doesn't mean it wouldn't hurt to see him eager to.

He pauses ever so briefly but doesn't say a word. Then he resumes flipping the sandwiches as if I hadn't said anything at all. If it weren't for a slight dip of his head, I would wonder if he even heard me at all.

"How was your day?" I ask him after a few quiet seconds.

"Pretty good. I went into town to drop a few client invoices in the mail, and"—he points his spatula at the pan—"picked up a few groceries."

I stretch my neck from side to side and roll my shoulders to ease the tension when he slides a plate in front of me, next to the puzzle.

"Here you go."

"Thank you." I smile gratefully as he sets his own plate in the spot across from me. As we eat in silence, I think back on the events of the day and to seeing my dad. Once again, the mixed feelings that were brought up about seeing my mom arise, and I glance up at Cole.

"I, um...I think I'm getting closer to wanting to see my mom," I admit quietly. He pauses, looking up, then sets his grilled cheese down altogether.

"Seriously?" he asks, staring intently at me.

"Yeah. I'm scared, though," I admit, trying my best to push down the emotion that threatens to surface.

He leans against the back of his chair while uneasiness swirls in my stomach. I don't know what else to say or, more accurately, how to put my feelings accurately into words, so I let the seconds stretch between us.

"I'm starting to feel anxious about leaving here at the end of the renovation without ever having gone to see her," I finally admit the root of it.

"What happens if you never do?" he asks softly.

"Never go see her?" I clarify, my brows furrowing.

"Yeah. I'm just playing devil's advocate here. Could you live the rest of your life not ever seeing her in person again?"

The thought makes the pang in my chest twist painfully sharp.

No.

The answer is a resounding no. I don't know how to get myself to go there, but for the first time in years, the thought that gives me the most pain is the one where I never see her.

I push my lips together and shake my head. He lets me sit with my words as I blink back a wave of tears.

"All I'm saying is, as someone who doesn't have much family left...I don't want you to have any regrets about not seeing a family member, especially one who's right in front of you."

"Yeah," I agree quietly, acknowledging the point he's making.

"But nobody would blame you if you can't. You need to do what's best for you. Whatever feels right."

"I guess I need to think about it some more."

He squeezes my arm as he stands, bending over to plant a kiss at my hairline. I stand too, ready to help clean up dinner, and offer to help with packing his things so he can head back to his cabin.

Except, after the dishes are all put away, he doesn't move to pack his bag. Instead, he pulls his sweatshirt off, slips off his socks, and lowers onto the cot—all without saying a word more than goodnight.

I bite the corner of my lip to stifle a smile, feeling a warmth course through me that he would choose to stay even when another option would be far more comfortable for him. Holding onto that warmth, I dim the lights and quietly head for the ladder.

TWENTY-EIGHT

Cole

Now

"Thanks for helping me carry this thing in," Graham says as I adjust my grip on the large reading chair. "I'm glad I ran into you in the dining room."

"No problem. You would have broken your back trying to get this in yourself."

He grunts. "Yeah, well, Sydney and I were supposed to bring it in, but I convinced her to go back to her cabin for the night. She needs a break. She's been working too hard."

I agree but refrain from saying it out loud. I'm pretty sure he would be able to see right through my tone or any sort of reaction I might unknowingly have. I'd rather not risk him potentially pummeling me on the spot for having feelings for his sister.

I haven't known Graham to be a particularly violent person in the time I've known him, but you never know where someone's limit might be...and I sure as heck don't want to test that right now.

"I think this goes back in this corner, but Syd will tell me I'm wrong tomorrow, I'm sure," he says, leading us to the open spot in the corner of the library next to the empty floor-to-ceiling bookshelf.

"I guess it's some viral reading chair?" He scratches his head as we step back to admire the oversized corduroy chaise lounge. "It's supposed to be all the rage on social media."

"It looks like a decent chair to me." I nod, not exactly sure what the fuss is about but keeping that to myself. It definitely adds to the cozy feel of the room, anyway.

"Well, thanks, man." Graham clasps a hand on my back as we maneuver around several boxes labeled 'books' and make our way out of the library.

"Anytime." I feel a sudden burst of courage and consider broaching the Sydney subject—I even open my mouth to do so—but as we approach the dining room, we both notice a long line of guests at the bar.

"Oh, shoot. Catch ya later." He rushes off, and I shove my hands in my pockets, letting the urge dissipate.

There's always tomorrow.

Outside the lodge, the night sky is dark as I trudge down the porch steps. Instead of tracking down my ATV to head up to my own cabin, as I briefly considered doing earlier, I follow the stronger pull I feel toward cabin twelve. I'm in no hurry to pack up and move back into my cabin—I'm perfectly content to spend any time I can with Sydney while she's here.

Twinkling lights hang between the trees, lighting the path in front of the cabins, and I admire the rustic beauty of the night, finding peace in it as I walk.

When I get closer, I spot Sydney sitting on the porch swing. In the dim light, I can barely make her out, but I can tell she's curled up under a blanket with a book of some sort in her lap.

"Hey." She smiles wide when I walk up the steps. She immediately lifts the blanket so I can slide in next to her. Crickets are chirping from somewhere in the dark, and the light from the cabin illuminates through the window behind us—just enough to see each other and not much else.

"How was your day?" I ask, sliding an arm around her, enjoying how she settles close into my side, as if it's the most natural thing in the world.

"It was good," she replies. "Blair helped me haul a ton of furniture into the lodge before Graham kicked us out."

She smiles, but it's not hard to see the exhaustion written all over her face. I'm glad he sent her back here.

"Graham thinks you're working too hard," I tell her gently.

She sighs, giving me a slight eye roll. "Yeah, well, I get my work ethic from him, so he can pipe down."

I chuckle at her snarkiness, wondering what it's like to have a sibling who cares for you like they do.

"How was your day?" she asks, peering up at me.

"It wasn't bad. I started making a new coffee table for the cabin. The old one needs to go."

"Oh, that'll look nice." She tilts her head up to look at me, and when her eyes meet mine, I hold them there, feeling the subtle buzz of chemistry that zaps down my spine when I do.

She lays her head on my shoulder, and I lean down to press a kiss into her hair, running my fingertips across the top of her arm. I could sit like this for a long time, I realize, and not get sick of it.

"What's that?" I ask, pointing to the book on her lap.

She runs a hand over the cover with gentle care. "It's a journal. Blair gave it to me a few weeks ago."

"That was nice of her."

She nods against my shoulder and sighs at the same time. "Yeah. I've been trying to use it to write down my feelings about my mom, hoping maybe that might help, but...I haven't had much luck. Every time I sit down to write, I can't seem to actually put anything onto the paper."

I squeeze her shoulder then slide it down the length of her arm. I'm at a loss for knowing how else to comfort her in moments like these. I feel majorly underqualified to know the best thing to do.

"But...I was thinking about our conversation last night." She tilts her head to look up at me again.

"Yeah?"

"I want to go see my mom." She says it cautiously, as if she's testing the words as she says them out loud.

"Really?" Pride blooms in my chest as the softest of smiles grows on her face. There's a confidence behind it that wasn't there before.

"Yeah." She nods and then dips her head down briefly. "Do you think you could come with me? I feel like I could do it if you're there."

My chest warms as her eyes go glossy. I squeeze her arm again when she lays her head on my chest. The fact that she trusts me enough to be there for her in a moment like that means more to me than I could possibly express. I'm more than willing to be there for her in any way she might need, and if simply going with her is all she needs, then I can absolutely do that for her.

"You calm me for some reason," she whispers, making the warmth in my chest even more prominent. "You keep me steady."

"I would be honored to, Sydney," I whisper back, brushing the hair away from her face. The faintest of smiles tilts her mouth, and I keep my gaze on it, absorbing it.

As I sit here with her under my arm, I realize that nothing has ever felt more true.

TWENTY-NINE
Sydney
Now

Week Eleven of Renovation

"It's going to be a great day," I sing to myself as I bound down the loft stairs, ready and eager to get to work. I mentally run through my checklist as I head to start my morning coffee. A barge is scheduled to drop off the flooring I picked out for the individual cabins later this morning, and I need to keep making headway on the interior of the lodge.

Cole must have left early this morning. I didn't even hear him get up, but his blanket is folded neatly over the cot that's pushed against the wall, and the pillow he's been using is laid on top of a nearby stool.

I push start on the Keurig and lean my hip against the counter while the coffee drizzles into the mug behind me. My eyes roam nonchalantly over the cabin, and when I glance over at the puzzle that's almost completed, I notice a slip of paper that's been tucked underneath it.

"What could that be?" I ask out loud, crossing the room to pick it up.

Something came up. I'm not sure when, but I'll be back soon.
~C

My good mood immediately deflates. He's not here? Where could he have possibly gone? Into town? Did he go back to Longville without telling me? I don't think he would, given our history, but if that's the case, there's no way he'll be back by tomorrow morning when I'm planning to go see my mom. The thought sends a sharp pang to my stomach.

"Okay, calm down," I tell myself. No need to overreact.

I pride myself on being a fairly reasonable person, and I don't want to get upset about something without knowing the facts. The last time that happened, I ended up inadvertently starting a childish rumor about someone who was actually hurting.

So I decide to give him the benefit of the doubt. He could even still be on the island—his message was vague enough. Worst case, he'll probably be back sometime tonight anyway, so there's no point in letting it ruin my day.

Brushing it off as best I can, I pour my coffee into a to-go cup, leave his note on the counter, and head out to start my day.

The first stop is always checking in with Neal, so I head toward cabin one. My muscles tense when I find him with his arms crossed, talking to one of his crew members outside the cabin. His face is gloomy, which brings a twinge of panic to my stomach.

"How's it going, Neal?" I ask with a smile, hoping I'm reading the situation wrong.

"Good morning, Sydney," he says, although his voice is a little clipped.

"What's going on?"

"It's not major." He puts his palms up in an attempt to reassure me right off the bat—not a great way to start a conversation. "But we have a problem with the electrical wiring in these cabins."

"Okay. Tell me about it," I say as we step out of the way for two of his men that are hauling the old flooring out of the cabin.

"Well, I'm assuming the wiring in here is original to when the cabin was built. Graham didn't seem to know if they had ever been updated, but I'm guessing not, because we are definitely not up to code." He cringes.

"Which we didn't plan for," I add with a sigh.

"Nope. Not only is it expensive, given how many cabins we have to do, but it'll set us back another couple weeks on our timeline."

"Alright." I lift my shoulders. "Well, do what you need to do. It needs to be up to code. There's no way around that. So we'll have to take the hit—both financially and timewise."

"Sorry, Sydney. I wish I had a better update for you this morning."

"It's not your fault," I tell him. "These things happen, right?"

"Unfortunately, they do. I'll keep you posted with what the cost is looking like."

"Great. Any other issues?"

"Not today." He smiles warmly.

"Sounds good. I'll check in later this afternoon," I say. With a wave, I head back to the main lodge.

"Perfect," I grumble to myself as I walk. We're at the very edge of maxing out our budget, so I'm hoping this will be the last roadblock we run into. We can't afford much more at this point.

Inside the lodge, I head straight for Graham at the bar.

"I'll take whatever comfort food Shirley is whipping up this morning," I tell him, struggling to keep my mood upbeat.

"Uh-oh. Is it something with the wiring in the cabins?" he asks, concern creasing his forehead. "Neal was asking me about that this morning."

I fill him in on the electrical setback with the cabins and the delay it will cause.

"That sounds like an expensive fix." He cringes.

"I'm sure it will be," I huff in agreement. "Hence why I need the comfort of Shirley's food."

"You got it." He smirks, wandering back into the kitchen to find Shirley. When he comes back, he leans over the counter onto his forearms.

"What's Cole up to today? He said he was going to find me this morning to help me move another piece of furniture in."

My stomach sours even further. The current Cole I've come to know is a man of his word, so for him to bail on Graham too makes me nervous. Where could he possibly be?

"I'm not sure. Haven't seen him yet today." I try to keep my tone as light and unbothered as I can. "I'll let him know to come find you if I see him, though."

"Sounds good." He pats the counter before grabbing a glass to fill with ice.

"How's the new bar working out?" I ask, shoving the uneasiness down.

"Great." He lights up. "It's a dream, Syd. I know there have been plenty of guests who've seen it already, but I can't wait for the grand opening—for everyone to see all the hard work you've put into this. It's truly incredible."

His words make me blush, and I wave him off with a subtle smile.

"For real. Have I said thank you lately?" he asks warmly.

I shake my head slowly while he grins at me.

"Well, thank you. Truly." He emphasizes the last word, really driving it home. His show of appreciation warms my heart, and the faintest of emotion prickles my eyes.

Before I can spiral into an emotional freefall, Shirley emerges from the kitchen with a plate.

"One ham-and-chive scramble for one special girl," she says, placing it in front of me.

"Thank you, Shirley. This is just what I need." I pick up a fork and dig right in.

"Where's Cole today?" she asks, looking around. Has it been that noticeable that we've been spending a lot of time together lately? Enough so that everyone assumes I'll know where he is?

"I'm not sure," I say through a bite.

"Alright, just wondering." She shrugs with a smile. "Enjoy, sweetie."

Shirley disappears back into the kitchen while Graham heads to the other side of the bar to help a guest.

While I eat, I feel increasingly unsettled and a bit agitated. Partially from the renovation hiccup, but if I'm honest, it's mostly due to Cole disappearing. It feels wrong that the one person who's been helping to soothe me when I feel this uneasy is actually the reason for it this time.

I finish my breakfast while going over the rest of my to-do list for the day, but I'm never quite able to bury the tension in my stomach. When I spot the barge coming into the bay, I push thoughts of Cole to the side and slide off the stool to forge ahead with what needs to get done.

The sound of the engine humming is the only noise filling the air as I stare out the window of Graham's pickup truck. What started as a moment to collect myself and work up the nerve to head inside has now turned into a half hour of me trying not to talk myself out of it.

I've made it all the way to the nursing home parking lot by myself, but I'm not convinced I can take another step on my own.

There's been no word from Cole since he left yesterday morning—which also doesn't help my general mood. Graham offered to accompany me, but I turned him down, assuming it might be easier to come by myself.

I'm starting to regret that decision with each passing second as the inevitable heartache that I know will come from this visit looms like a dark cloud. With a heaving breath, I pull out my phone and scroll through the contacts.

Sydney: Hey.

Laura: What's wrong?

I smile, appreciating the fact that I have a friend who can tell my mood just by a simple word.

Sydney: I'm going to see my mom. I'm currently sitting in the parking lot, working up the courage to go in…

Laura: You're the strongest person I know, Syd. You've got this.

Sydney: You think so?

Laura: I know so.

It's short and sweet, but it's enough of a pep talk to force me out of the truck. If it doesn't happen now, it never will. I can do this.

"I can do this on my own," I murmur to myself.

Just as I shut the door, a car I don't recognize comes peeling into the parking lot, screeching to a stop in the row next to mine. Annoyed, but unbothered, I keep my eyes on the nursing home and round the truck.

"Syd!"

I come to a halt, spinning around at Cole's voice. My mouth drops open as he comes jogging toward me. Is he serious? Shock morphs immediately into anger with each step he takes.

"So nice of you to show up," I spit, spinning on my heels to turn away from him.

"Syd, just listen—"

"No. Go away." I brush him off with a wave of my hand and pick up my pace. He continues following me, and I spin around in a spurt of anger.

"How could you do that, Cole? You said you'd be there with me every step of the way, and you weren't."

"Syd—" he says as his face falls.

"Don't worry about it," I say, spinning on my heels toward the door. I don't want to deal with him right now. "I can do this on my own."

"My uncle is back," he cuts in.

That stops me in my tracks, and I'm momentarily frozen in place before slowly spinning around. My anger swirls with something softer as I search his eyes.

"What?"

"He's back," he says, still breathless.

I skate my gaze over him for a moment, and when I see the glimmer of hope on his face, even more of my anger dissolves.

"Okay. Explain," I say, crossing my arms.

His shoulders slump with relief, and he runs a hand through his hair to compose himself.

"So I woke up to a text message yesterday morning asking me to meet him in Baudette the next time I rolled through. It's the first time I've heard from him in years, Syd."

My heart softens at the tone of his voice, and it's hard to not feel glad for him.

"I'll tell you all about it later, but I guess I, uh...lost track of time. I ran out to Takini this afternoon, but by the time I got there, Graham said you'd left already. I boated in as fast as I could, I swear."

He inches closer hesitantly, guilt creasing his features. "I'm sorry, Syd. I meant to be there with you before you left."

I roll my lips, absorbing his explanation. As hurt as I am, at the end of the day, I'm glad that his uncle is back. Can I really fault him for getting caught up in something as big as that?

"Come on," I say, hooking my head toward the nursing home. Another wave of relief crosses his face as he falls into step beside me.

"You really need to work on your communication skills," I mutter under my breath.

"I know," he sighs. "I'm...I'm not used to other people depending on me."

I know he doesn't say it for sympathy, but I feel it just the same. I reach between us and thread my fingers through his, needing to feel him, as he pulls the door open for us.

The reality of this moment hits me, and I tighten my grip on his hand. As much as I was prepared to do this myself—and I'm proud of myself for making it as far as I did—I'm grateful that he's here now. I draw strength from his presence as we make our way up to Mom's floor. My chest feels heavier with each step I take, and years' worth of avoidance tries to convince me to turn around and run. But I stand firm, determined to at least try today.

It's the least I can do.

The elevator dings once we reach her floor, and I spot my dad as soon as the door opens. He's leaning over the counter of the nurse's station, chatting amicably, and straightens as soon as he sees us.

"Hey, Dad." I wrap him in a one-armed hug, keeping a tight grip on Cole's hand. I'm not ready to let go yet.

When he pulls back, Dad's eyes are red around the rims. "Thanks for coming, honey."

I nod, unable to force actual words out of my tight throat at the moment. Dad nods in greeting to Cole and then points to the room I once visited frequently—one I haven't seen in years. A wave of guilt presses on me along with a fresh bubbling of nerves.

"Do you want me to come in with you, or do you want some time alone?" Cole whispers in my ear.

"Alone," I reply, looking up at him. "Thank you, but...I need to do this part alone."

He squeezes my hand, holding my gaze intently, letting me be the first to let go. With a deep inhale, I inch slowly toward the door.

Pushing it open softly, I squeeze my eyes shut, bracing myself for what state she might be in. The door creaks as I let it shut behind me. Slowly, I peel one eye open at a time, holding my breath as I immediately zero in on Mom, who's lying in the hospital bed.

Tears prick at my eyes, and my chest feels impossibly tight as I force myself forward. Mom looks almost the same as the last time I saw her. Her hair is a bit longer, and her skin is a few shades paler, but not much else has changed. I can't decide if that's comforting or not.

As I walk, Mom's eyes track me slightly, but there's no sign of recognition on her face. Her expression is stoic and empty, which sends a sharp pang of grief to my heart.

Finding my legs are much too wobbly to stand, I slide slowly into the chair that's set up next to her bedside. After a few quiet moments, I open my mouth to say something, but again, I can't force anything to come out. I clamp my mouth shut and sit there in silence, feeling like the oxygen is rapidly depleting from the room.

All these years of avoiding this moment, and it's finally here...and I have no idea what I'm supposed to do.

I study her hairline, the way her hair curls at her shoulders, rising and falling with her breath. She stares straight ahead, and I wonder if she even notices that someone is still in the room.

After several minutes of staring—her at the wall, and me at her—I lean against the back of the chair and rub my snowflake necklace between my fingers.

I'm not sure what prompts me to pull the journal from Blair out of my purse, but I act on the random impulse and open it.

I've hovered a pen over the second blank page many times over the last few weeks, but something has blocked me from writing every single time. This time, though, I'm surprised when the words actually come easily.

Hi, Mom.

An invisible weight lifts ever so slightly, even though it hurts to do so. I immediately put the pen back to the paper, not bothering to wipe away the tears that have started streaming down my face.

I'm sorry it's taken me so long to come. I haven't found the strength to until now.

It feels good to purge the words onto the page. It's an emotional release, and I push on, writing as fast as I can.

I hope it's okay that I write to you like this. It's the easiest way for me, I think.

So...I guess I should catch you up on my life and what I've been up to since I was here last. I finished my architecture degree and have been working at a firm downtown. I wish I could show you some of my latest designs. I think you'd really like some of them.

I'm sure Dad and Graham have told you already, but we're renovating Ruby Lodge. It's going to be incredible when it's all finished, Mom. I wish you could see it.

I'm sort of seeing someone—at least I think I am. It's complicated.

I glance up at Mom, who's moving her head side to side nonchalantly, scanning the room.

I love you.

I shut the journal and sit with her in the quiet for a few moments, feeling emotionally exhausted from the purge. Eventually, I slip the journal back into my purse and walk slowly across the room, feeling ready yet also reluctant to leave.

My legs feel heavy as a part of me wants to stay here in this room with her forever. It has taken me this long to get here...now I'm not sure how I'm supposed to leave.

I force myself to put one foot in front of the other, and with one last glance back at Mom, I head back out into the hallway.

Cole meets me immediately, lightly gripping my elbow.

"Are you okay?" he whispers. His presence feels like a steady wall, and I gravitate toward his comfort as he pulls me into a hug.

"Yeah," I croak out against his chest. I squeeze my eyes tight, emotion rising uncontrollably in my chest.

"Did it go okay?" Dad asks. When I pull away from Cole, I see the worry etched on his forehead.

"About as good as it could go," I reply shakily. All of a sudden, my flight response kicks in, and I desperately need to get out of this building. "I need to go. I'll talk to you later, Dad. Love you."

"Love you, honey," he calls as Cole and I turn toward the elevator.

Cole presses the button, and we ride down in silence while I process everything that just happened. What it felt like to be in the same room as her. A lone tear runs down my face, and I push my eyes closed, experiencing a new wave of grief that I've been trying to suppress for years now.

When we reach the lobby, I numbly follow half a step behind Cole. The outline of the furniture in the lobby looks blurred at the edges as I struggle to focus.

"Hey." Cole turns to me as we step outside. I look up, meeting his gaze, locking in on it.

"I have another place I'd like to show you."

THIRTY-ONE
Cole

Now

"This way." I clutch Sydney's hand, ducking under a tree as I lead her on the path in the woods I haven't walked since high school.

Sharp memories of when I was beaten down—quite literally bruised and battered—and came here seeking refuge flash through my mind with each step I take. I came here once to twist my own shoulder back into place after my dad dislocated it so I could yell out in pain without anyone hearing me. My stomach sours as I recall several other similar incidents.

The trees in the woods are overgrown, and the barely there path is unrecognizable, but I forge along purely on instinct.

Sydney is quiet behind me, which further fuels me along. The urge I had to comfort her when she came out of her mom's room was nothing short of overwhelming, and it hasn't dissipated one bit. Making sure she's okay is a need that presses heavily on my chest.

"Here," I announce when we reach the clearing. She comes to a stop by my side as we peer out at a large pond in the middle of the woods. It hasn't changed much except for an overgrowth of weeds along the edges, and I'm glad to find it still offers the same picturesque beauty I remember.

"This is so pretty," she whispers, the pain still evident in her strained voice.

I point to a hill along the shore of the pond and have a seat next to her, bending at the knees.

"This was another spot I used to escape to," I say quietly. "I thought you might need a quiet moment before heading back to the island."

I glance over and watch as she bites her lip, fighting back tears.

"Thank you," she says, her voice cracking. Seeing her like this hurts me in a way I wasn't prepared for, and I struggle to find the right words to say. Again, who am I to pretend to know the answers? How am I supposed to know which ones will take some of her pain away?

I settle for the only thing I know how to do.

To just be here—to be present.

We watch as two birds swoop around each other, dancing in the air above the pond, and I desperately hope that the scenery will provide the same solace for her that it once did for me.

"Are you okay?" I ask after a little while.

"Yeah." She sniffles before sighing deeply. "It was hard, Cole."

"I know." It doesn't seem like enough, but it's all I can think of to say.

"In a way, it feels like a weight has been lifted, but now...it's almost as if a new wound has formed in its place," she admits. "The image of my mother's blank stare used to be something that wasn't fresh in my mind. It was easier to push it aside when it was just a memory. Now it's fresh. And jarring. I don't know...does that make any sense?"

"It does."

"I don't regret it, though," she says softly, picking at a piece of grass by her foot. "I'm proud of myself for taking this step. It'll just take time, I think."

"You should be proud of yourself," I say quietly.

"Tell me about your uncle." She smiles softly, perking up slightly at the change of topic.

I've pushed the thought of him out of my mind to focus on being here for Sydney, so the reminder that he's back sends a rush of something light through my chest. I still can't believe he's here. I dip my head and dare to smile about it.

"Well, after I got his message, I left the island immediately," I explain, still feeling guilty about not being clearer with her yesterday morning. "He's staying at the motel up the street. I think he was surprised to see me so soon—he had no idea I was on the island. Anyway, he apologized profusely for dropping the ball on staying in touch. Apparently, he got caught up in a small-town romance in southern Texas that eventually went haywire."

"That's great, Cole—not the failed love interest, but that he's back. I bet it was nice to see him," she says sincerely with tired eyes.

"It was." I ensure eye contact before continuing. "I truly am sorry for not telling you where I was. We got caught up reminiscing and ended up talking all the way through the night. It's been kind of a whirlwind, to be honest."

She smiles. "It's okay. How long is he staying for?"

"I have no idea," I admit. "I didn't have a chance to ask before I realized I was late and booked it out of there."

"It's okay," she says with a subdued shrug. "What was your time like with him back then when you left Baudette? Did it take long to find him?"

"Not really. I knew he was in Albuquerque as of the last letter he sent, so I went there first. Luckily, he was still in town. All I had to do was ask around at a few of the local dives to be pointed in the right direction." I run a hand down my jaw as I recall the memories.

"He had been making ends meet by doing random painting jobs, so we ended up working together. I'd build something, and he'd paint it. Worked out for a while—a couple years, even—but then he got a hankering to head to Texas. I knew I didn't want to go there, and obviously, I didn't want to be back in Baudette, but I missed Minnesota. The seasons. The fishing and hunting—I do love it here. So I found myself a home in Longville."

I look over to find her watching me intently, as if she was hanging on my every word. She's resting her head against the arm that's folded around her legs, as if she's too tired to hold her head up.

"I'm glad you were able to find him," she says quietly.

"I am too." I twist my mouth into a smile before we fall into a comfortable quiet while watching the pond.

"Thanks for meeting me," she whispers eventually. "It really did help knowing you were right outside the door."

I roll my lips and slide my arm around her shoulder, not wanting but needing to feel closer to her. She scoots even closer to me and lays her head on my shoulder in place of her arm. We sit like that for a while, watching geese as they fly in to land on the water.

As we do, I ponder how, a few short weeks ago, Sydney was nothing but a thorn in the side of my painful past, and now...now she's quickly become a very significant part of my present.

I may not know how to put a name to this growing connection between us, or where it's heading from here, but I know without a shadow of a doubt that I'm willing to do anything to find out.

I pull her closer to my side, and as another goose flies in, I realize that right here, right now, with her pressed to my side, is the safest I've ever felt in this city.

THIRTY-TWO
Sydney
Now

Week Twelve of Renovation

"How did it go?" Graham asks quietly as he slides a book into place on the shelf. We've been in the library for twenty minutes now, and I can tell he's been champing at the bit this whole time to ask me that question.

I swallow hard from where I'm crouched in the corner on the other side of the room. It's only been a day since seeing Mom, and I'm definitely still processing the heavy emotions that came with it, trying to make sense of a new normal where seeing her like that is something that happens on a regular basis. Because I know without a doubt that, while it was hard, and there's been a raw, grief-filled cloud following me around ever since, it fueled a newfound resolve to see her again. An urgency, as if I need to make up for lost time.

Cole is in town, helping his uncle get settled into a short-term rental house, and Blair is helping Shirley feed the large group of fishermen who stopped by boat for lunch, so it's just Graham and me in here, getting the library put together.

"It went okay," I say softly, knowing that, out of anyone, he would understand the complex emotions that come with this situation.

"I know it's hard, but it does get easier," he says sympathetically. "As impossible as it sounds, you get used to it in a way. To seeing her like that."

"I don't know how you do it as often as you do," I admit.

"Maybe we could go together next time," he offers.

"I'd like that, Graham." I give him a genuine smile, taking a deep breath. I lift a stack of historical romances out of one of the boxes of donated books. With the lodge library nearly doubling in size with the renovation, more books was a necessity. However, I didn't want to cut into our budget to use a chunk of it on books, so Graham set up donation boxes in three neighboring cities, and I've been pleasantly surprised by the haul he brought in.

"We sure have a large selection of thrillers that were donated." I note five full boxes labeled with that genre.

"That would be the result of my fiancée," he chuckles. "Blair donated most of those. For some reason, she thinks those kinds of books add to the whole remote-island experience."

"She's probably not wrong." I smile, noting some of them look brand new. She probably purchased some at full price to add to the donations.

"So, are you going to fill me in on what's going on with Cole?" he asks after a few seconds of silence.

My hand stops midair as I freeze.

"What do you mean?" I feign innocence.

"You and Cole," he says firmly. "What's happening there?"

I blink at him over my shoulder, trying to gauge how much he knows.

"Come on, Syd. It's obvious to anyone with a set of eyes." He shakes his head, laughing as if he finds the whole thing amusing.

"Really?" I cringe.

"Yes. It wasn't hard to pick up on it once your little 'feud' pittered out." He climbs down the rolling ladder to grab another stack of books.

I wait for him to push for more info, but he stays silent, waiting patiently for me to respond.

"We're, uh...figuring it out, I guess. There's something there, obviously," I admit.

He nods, a slight smile on his face, but still, he says nothing.

"That's it? No big-brother speech? No threats of having a serious talk with him about his intentions like you do with every other person I date?"

"Nope. Not with him." He shrugs.

I probably shouldn't push, but curiosity gets the best of me. "Why not? Because you know him? I thought you weren't that close?"

"Because I know enough about him to know everything I need to," he says simply.

Graham has always been observant, so it's no surprise he would pick up on a person's character so easily. But I wonder how much of the truth of Cole's past he knows about.

"What do you know?" I ask as casually as I can.

He grunts as he climbs a few steps to hoist a stack of books onto the top shelf.

"Just that he was going through a lot back in high school. He kept to himself most of the time, but his face said enough. Clearly there was something going on internally, but he never missed a practice and always stayed after to help clean up gear. I saw him stay behind and clean up the locker room many times too, even though that was the last thing any of us wanted to do. Plus, he's always helped me check on properties on the island whenever he's here. He's got a good heart. That's not hard to see."

I smile to myself, silently agreeing with him. Cole does have a good heart, and for some reason, it feels not only good but necessary to have Graham's approval. It feels like a green light I didn't know a part of me was waiting for.

"I really like him, Graham," I say quietly, sliding the last book into place on the shelf.

"I can tell."

"I just don't know what will happen long term for us. We live in two different places," I say, voicing my concerns.

"You'll figure it out—if you both want to badly enough."

With a sigh, I stand back to admire the completed bookshelf on my side of the room. Rows and rows of books for guests to enjoy while they're here. I think it just might be one of my favorite rooms.

I stack the empty boxes by the door and move to the corner nook where I designed a beverage station, complete with a coffee bar and a mini fridge for cold drinks. Ripping the box of K-cups open, I get started filling the wire basket labeled *Coffee*.

"We should start talking about the grand opening," I suggest. "It's slated for six weeks from now. That'll be here before we know it."

"Do you think they'll finish the reno in time?" He huffs.

"I hope so. It'll be tight now that the electrical issue with the cabins are pushing us back, but I think we can still make it. Neal said they're almost finished with cabin one, so they must have been able to get a lot of the other work done while it was being fixed. Once all the cabins are done, we just need to do the glamping area, which shouldn't take too terribly long."

"Good, because word's been spreading through town already about the grand opening. I've been getting some calls about reserving cabins for that weekend already."

"That's not surprising." I chuckle.

"Well, you mention it to one grocery store clerk, and the whole town is pretty much in the know. Plus, anyone who's been out here has been raving about what's been done already."

"Yeah? Go ahead and book them, then."

"Yeah?" he asks excitedly.

"Sure. Let's fill the cabins up. It'll be our motivation for this last push."

"Alright. You don't have to tell me twice."

I finish organizing while my smile lingers. Once the beverage corner is completed, I place my hands on my hips, admiring the library as a whole.

"It looks great, Graham."

"It really does," he agrees. "I only have this box left, so you can go ahead and call it a night. I think it's getting late."

I check my watch and agree, a wave of exhaustion hitting me. "Alright, I'll see you in the morning. I plan to finish the workout room tomorrow if you need to find me."

"Sounds good. I'll come help you when I have a few spare minutes. Night, Syd."

"Goodnight." With another smile, I head out of the mostly quiet lodge and head into the darkness toward cabin twelve.

The walk is quiet and peaceful, with only the sounds of nature filling the air and the lake water rolling from somewhere in the dark on my left. Cabin twelve comes into sight, and an anticipation sparks inside me at the thought of seeing Cole. It's only been a few hours since I've seen him, but I miss him. There's an ache in my chest that doesn't involve pain or grief.

It's an anticipation that I know will be satisfied the moment I lay eyes on him.

I push the door open slowly, and a punch of disappointment hits me when I find him already fast asleep on the cot. It dissipates quickly, along with the ache now that I'm near him, followed by a heartwarming of sorts. He must have had a long day too.

I slip my shoes off as quietly as I can and creep inside. As I pass the table, I softly run my fingers along the puzzle we completed last night. The significance of working on it together over the course of many days, little by little, gives me a sense of pride I didn't know I could feel from just completing a puzzle.

On impulse, I slide my thumb over the wooden eagle Cole carved that I placed above the puzzle, and head quietly up to bed.

THIRTY-THREE
Cole
Now

"Wow, it looks great in here." I admire the interior of cabin one as I close the door behind me. Sydney's head pops up over the loft railing above me, and she beams.

"I think so too," she says, looking around, and I pick up on a slight difference in her expression from the other times I've watched her assessing the renovation. A softness that tells me perhaps she's starting to believe it.

"I'm almost done," she says, going back to putting sheets on what looks to be a brand-new king-size bed.

I slip off my boots and roam around, taking in all the changes. I know the cabins were nearly identical, so I assume the 'before' looks pretty close to the one Sydney and I have been staying in.

She already mentioned the electrical, HVAC, and plumbing upgrades, but it looks like the interior has had a nice facelift as well.

Black wrought-iron railings replace the chipped wooden ones in the loft and on the staircase, which, along with the new wood flooring, adds a more modern touch. The kitchen cabinets are freshly painted a slate-gray color, and the stainless-steel stove probably works a whole lot better than the one it replaced.

I head up the loft stairs. "Need some help?"

"Sure. Thanks." She tosses me a corner of the cream-colored comforter to spread across the bed.

"I'm assuming they're done with this cabin, then?" I ask. "If you're doing the interior?"

"Yup. They're on to cabins two and three now. This one'll be ready for guests as soon as I'm finished, which I'm just about done with—then we can go, I promise."

She grabs the quilted blanket I remember seeing from the original cabins and folds it neatly across the foot of the bed. I place the pillows at the top while she smooths the comforter with her hand. Then she steps back to admire her work, a hand on her hip.

"It'll do," she says, though not fully convincingly.

"It's perfect," I correct.

She smiles up at me, nodding her head.

"Just a couple more things to do." She cringes as an apology, walking briskly to the stairs.

"I'm not in a hurry. Take your time." I follow her down the stairs, where she quickly puts an extra set of bed sheets in the linen closet. I lean a hip against the kitchen counter, content to watch her as she places homemade soap and lotion from town by the sink. A rush of pride hits me out of nowhere—one that's intense and all-consuming.

It's not hard to find reasons to be proud of her. I am for many different reasons. For being courageous enough to go see her mom. For pouring herself into this renovation as much as she has. For simply being the kind of person she is.

My gaze snags on a picture that hangs above the new kitchen table. It's a modern white frame that holds a black-and-white image of a couple with a *For Sale* sign staked in the ground.

"Each cabin will have a different picture of my grandparents," Sydney says softly, the smile evident in her voice as she comes next to me.

"That's a nice touch." I can't help but slide my arm around her, pulling her in close. The little wheeze she makes when I do sends a spark to my chest. I like it so much that I squeeze again, enjoying the sound and the feel of her pushed against me.

"Okay, let's go," she giggles, pushing a hand against my chest to move away.

"After you." I reluctantly let her go and follow her outside the cabin, shutting the lights off before we leave.

"So, where are we off to this time?" she asks as our shoes crunch on the dusty path.

"We're going on an adventure." It's all I give her, and a rush of anticipation surges through me as we walk past a few guests who are headed into the main lodge. Having spent so much extra time with my uncle recently, I'm craving some alone time with her.

Just like the beginning of our last date, I lead her onto the dock.

"Are we doing another sunset cruise?" she asks, her voice perking up as if she would be just as excited as the first time. I know she would be too. I don't feel pressure to perform or to come up with an elaborate date plan to impress her. It's not like that with us—we just want to be together.

"Nope," I say, guiding her into the boat.

"A fishing competition? Whoever catches the biggest fish wins a carved wooden fish?"

"Nope," I say again with a smirk.

"An overnight camping trip?" She might be spit-balling ideas, but that one intrigues me enough to mentally log it for the future.

"Just sit down and get comfortable," I tell her, untying us from the dock posts.

We boat south of the island, the opposite direction as last time, while she keeps throwing out guesses for where we're going, none of them coming close to hitting the mark.

Eventually, I slow to a stop as we approach an island about half the size of Takini. There are no cabins or structures visible to the eye on this one, only thick brush and trees that cover nearly every inch of it.

The boat slides to a stop on the only small stretch of sandy beach I can find.

"Be careful." I grab her hand and lead her up and over the bow of the boat.

"Wait there." I hop off and square myself in front of the boat, one foot on the sand, one foot half in the water.

"Jump." I hold out my arms. She doesn't hesitate as she places her hands on my shoulders. I place mine on her hips and keep her steady as I guide her down until her feet are firmly planted on the sand in front of me.

She moves to pull away, but I have a knee-jerk reaction to grip her tighter, pulling her to me. I assess her reaction, watching as an intensity flashes behind her eyes, mirroring what's happening throughout my entire body. I bend to press my mouth to hers, keeping my eyes locked on hers until the very last second.

It's a sweet and innocent kiss. Quick and fleeting. But it's also intense enough to give me a rush that has me realizing I'm living for these stolen moments with her. With a squeeze of her hip, I pull back, tracking how slowly it takes her to open her eyes.

"Is this what you brought me out here to do?" she asks coyly. "Lure me away from civilization to have your way with me?"

"Don't tempt me." I smirk, my voice coming out low and gravelly.

She flashes a playful smile as we turn toward the trees.

"So what's the plan?" she asks excitedly.

"No plan," I admit. "We're just here to explore the island."

"Alright, let's do it."

She falls behind me as I use my arm to cut through the brush and clear somewhat of a path for us.

"Is this another one of your safe places?" she asks as we walk.

"Nope. Never been here before." I look back to offer a wink. "This one's just for us."

I step over a large tree stump, pointing it out behind me so she steps over it. There's something special about exploring a new place you've never been before with someone you care about. It feels intimate somehow. Exciting.

"So, how's your uncle doing?" she asks, slightly out of breath as we continue pushing through the thick woods. "I'm assuming he's still here, right?"

"He's still here," I confirm. He hasn't mentioned when he's leaving yet, but I know it's only a matter of time."

"Do you think he'll be better about keeping in touch this time?"

"I hope so. It seems like he really regrets losing touch. Hey, I've been meaning to ask you something." Nerves grip my stomach for some reason, although she's never given me a reason to be wary of asking her something like this. "Will you come meet him? Before he leaves?"

She's quiet for a moment behind me before saying a small, "You want me to?"

I stop in the middle of the woods and turn to look her in the eye. There are certain moments in life that require eye contact, and this is absolutely one of them.

"I want to let you into any part of my life that you're interested in being a part of," I tell her sincerely, the words coming from the deepest, most raw, part of me.

She bites her lip as she rakes her gaze over my face. I can't do a single thing other than stand there and wait for her to break the silence.

"I'd be honored to," she finally says, reaching out to squeeze my hand. "If he's important to you, I'd like to meet him."

I grip back, getting sucked into the way she's looking at me, like her agreeing to meet my uncle is a way of seeing a vulnerable part of me and my past—and accepting it.

"Come on, let's keep moving." I tip my head once the chirp of a bird brings me back to reality.

We trudge forward, crossing a small creek and narrowly avoiding a muddy patch. The land slopes higher and grows narrow as we climb. When we finally reach the very top of the island, there's enough room for only about a foot on either side of us.

"Whoa," she breathes, echoing my thoughts. From up here, we have a three-hundred-sixty-degree view of the entire island. The lake water spans for miles and miles on end, and another island, even smaller than this one, is only a stone's throw away.

We seem to gravitate even closer together naturally, and I pull her in front of me to wrap my arms around her collarbone.

She leans her head back against my chest and uses her hand to lightly grip my forearm. I rest my chin on her head and take it all in—both this aching feeling in my chest and the stunning view.

"This is nice," I whisper against her hair. She doesn't say anything. She simply nods, squeezing my arm. I don't pretend to be a man who knows a whole lot in this world...but I do know with every fiber of my being that there's no place I'd rather be in this moment than right here with my arms wrapped around her. That both scares and thrills me all at the same time.

THIRTY-FOUR
Sydney
Now

"Is this his Airbnb?" I ask the obvious question as Cole and I step up to the front door of an old rundown rambler along the river.

"Yup. It's, uh...it's nothing fancy." He looks nervous almost, embarrassed for some reason.

"It's fine, Cole." I place one hand on his arm and use the other to knock on the door. He runs his hand through his hair and looks unsettled, clearly not convinced despite my appeasing. I don't know why he's so nervous, but he should know by now that he has no reason to be.

The door creaks open, and a gentleman about my dad's age appears. He's got the same depth to his stare that Cole has, and aside from the beginning signs of wrinkles and the salt and pepper sprinkled along his hairline, he's nearly the spitting image of him too.

"Well, what do we have here?" he croons, studying me in admiration. Not in a creepy way, more of an 'I'm honored to meet you' kind of a way that feels warm. Soothing.

"Paul, this is Sydney," Cole says, wrapping an arm around my shoulder in a protective way that I secretly love.

"Well, I assumed so, with you showing up with her and all." He ushers us inside while throwing me a wink. "Didn't expect her to be so pretty, though."

I immediately feel at ease and wonder what it is about Fredrickson men that makes them ooze with this kind of re-latable tenderness.

Then I remember that these two might be the exception—it's most definitely not all of them that have this trait.

"Come in, come in. There's a couch right over here in the living room. Why don't you two have a seat?" His Minnesotan accent is so thick it makes me bite back a smile thinking of how many times he must have stuck out like a sore thumb down in Texas.

"It's a pleasure to meet you, sir," I say cheerfully.

"Oh, please. No formalities needed here." He brushes me off with a wave as I sit beside Cole on the couch.

"You're Peterson's little girl, right?" Paul settles into the La-Z-Boy across from us. "You've got your dad's cheekbones."

"Do I?" A hint of pride surges through me at the mention of my dad.

"Mm-hmm. Cole tells me you're renovating the lodge out there."

"We are! Have you ever stayed there?"

"Oh yeah. Many times. In fact, I remember you and your brother running around like you owned the place when you were kids."

I laugh. "Sounds about right."

"Is Shirley still out there?" Something shifts in his expression when he mentions her name—a softening of sorts.

"She is. She mentioned you two were friends."

A small huff comes out as nostalgia gleams in his eyes. "We were."

"So how long are you planning on staying, Paul?" Cole asks after a brief lull. Paul leans forward in his seat.

"That's what I want to talk to you about, actually." He rubs his hands together then scrapes one against his jaw.

"I'm planning on staying," he announces.

"Yeah, but for how long?" Cole asks.

"For good," he replies. My eyes dart to Cole, who's staring blankly at Paul, emotionless and struggling to comprehend, while I try to hide my gaping mouth behind my hand.

"I've been all across this country, and I'm officially sick of it. It took me this long to realize there's no place I'd rather be than here," he says. "Besides, I miss you, Cole. I can swing down to Longville from here a heck of a lot easier than I can from out of state."

"Are you serious?" Cole asks, his brows etched together.

"Yes. I've been feeling guilty about not being there for you as much as I should have been. I'd like to make up for that now."

The disbelieving look on Cole's face makes my heart crack in two as I realize how few people in his life have actually chosen him. How few have ever put him first.

"I'm here to stay," Paul insists, bringing a leg up to fold across his knee. "I'm getting too old to travel like I used to anyway."

"Wow." Cole breathes before clearing his throat. "I mean, that's great, Paul. I'm thrilled."

Paul beams at him from across the room, and from the way Cole grins back at him, it doesn't take much to see that these two have a special connection.

"Do you want your cabin back? It's yours if you do," Cole offers. "It's always been yours anyway."

As much as I had once desperately hoped to attain that land, I'm glad Cole never sold it to me. It belongs to them.

"Nope." Paul shakes his head vehemently. "Do whatever you want with that place. I'll find a new house. I feel like I need a fresh start up here."

"Are you sure?" Cole asks.

"Yup. I won't say no to you helping me find a house, though. I think I like being on the river like this."

"Anything you need. I don't have plans to head back to Longville for a while yet, so I'm here for whatever you need."

Cole's reminder that there's an impending end to our stay on Takini Island sends a twinge of panic to my core. I'm not nearly ready enough to say goodbye to him. That, and also the idea that we could go our separate ways without cementing whatever this connection between us is—to name it and validate it—makes me nauseated.

"Do you two want to stay for dinner?" Paul asks. "I don't have much for food, but we could order pizza?"

"I think we'll have to take a rain check," Cole says, rising to stand. "We should get going. I don't want to boat back in the dark."

"Another time," I promise as we walk toward the door.

"Sydney, it was a pleasure meeting you," Paul says, pulling me in for a hug.

"Likewise." I smile at him then step out of the way while he and Cole shake hands.

"I'll see you tomorrow," Cole says. Then he takes my hand to lead me back to the car.

"This is so exciting," I say once we head out of the driveway. "Your uncle is staying, Cole. This is big!"

"Yeah," he says flatly, scraping his hand down the side of his face.

"You don't seem as happy as I thought you'd be," I comment gently.

"It's just...kind of hard to believe he would settle down here. That he would come back to be closer to me." He says it so nonchalantly that it twists at my heart.

"Of course he would, Cole," I say as emphatically as I can. "You're important to him."

"Logically, I know that." He smiles over at me. "It just takes my heart a bit to catch up sometimes."

I run my hand along his forearm as we drive through town. My mind drifts to my mom, and I feel her proximity in a physical way, like a weight pressing on me.

"Hey, before we go to the marina, do you think we could stop by the nursing home really quick?" I ask. Now that I know what it's like to see her, it feels wrong to be in Baudette without stopping there.

"Sure," he replies right away. He doesn't hesitate or tell me that it'll be dark soon. He just does what he's always done—and what I hope I do for him. He blindly supports me.

"I'll make it quick, I promise." I shoot my dad a text to let him know we're coming, and before I know it, we've pulled into the nursing home parking lot.

Without me having to ask, he climbs right out of the car and walks next to me, offering his hand for support.

"Hey, Dad." I give my dad a hug when we make it up to Mom's floor.

"What a nice surprise," he says, a wide grin on his face.

"I just...wanted to say hi, I guess," I say, an unsettling energy creeping in at the thought of seeing her again.

"Anytime, Syd." He says it with a gleam in his eye, like maybe this is all he has wanted all along. "You don't need a reason to come."

I squeeze Cole's arm, leaving him with my dad while I head inside her room. Seeing Mom takes my breath away, and I'm not sure I'll ever get used to seeing her lifeless and without the things that make her...her.

I slide into the chair and open my mouth to say something, but just like the last time, the words get stuck. Remembering the journal, I pull it out and hover the pen over the paper to see if anything will come.

Hi, Mom.

I smile to myself, realizing how much easier it is to write my words down onto paper instead of speaking them out loud. Maybe this is how I do it—how I move forward. I highly doubt there's a right or wrong way to navigate this situation.

I met Paul Fredrickson, Cole's uncle, today. Did you know him? You probably did. He seems sweet.

The words aren't anything more than an update on my day. A rambling of sorts, giving her small details of my life that she would have loved to be included in once upon a time. My eyes catch on a tray of food by Mom's bed.

How's the food here? I hope it's not bad. Maybe I'll make you some cookies and bring them soon. Those chocolate pecan ones you like.

I glance at the clock on the wall, knowing we need to get back to the boat before dark.

Anyway, we're about to head back to the island. I'll give Graham a hug for you. I think we're all coming back tomorrow to visit. See you then.

Love you.

I look up, watching her for a few moments, soaking up the way being this close to her makes me feel. Then I shut the journal and head back out to Cole.

"I have a request," Cole announces as we step off the dock.

"Anything," I say in a sing-song kind of way.

"Do you think we could possibly spend the night at my cabin tonight?" He cringes as if it might be a huge imposition. "I just commissioned a wooden shed for a client yesterday and need to work on drawing up some plans. I figure there's some more space to lay them out up there."

"Oh, sure." The fact that he assumes we're a package deal as far as where we sleep has me feeling practically giddy. Sleeping under the same roof has become a given for us. A quiet agreement we can both count on at the end of the day, and I didn't realize how much I've been leaning on that predictable part of my day.

"I'll make us dinner and, uh…I'll bring the cot," he offers. His shy tone makes me bite my lip while a blush creeps across my cheek.

"Sounds perfect," I agree.

In my cabin, I pack a quick overnight bag while Cole grabs some food out of the pantry to take up with us. He's just about to reach for the folded cot when I act on a sudden urge to be bold and assertive.

"There's no need to take that." My voice comes out stronger than I feel on the inside. A rush of adrenaline at the prospect of sleeping in the same bed with him makes me feel anxious—and also exuberantly alive.

His gaze flicks to mine, and I watch with bated breath as he swallows thickly, the implication of what I said sinking in.

"Okay. Shall we?" he asks, offering a hand. I slip my bag on my shoulder and slide my hand in his.

We get to his cabin and hop off the ATV, both of us ducking our heads as the wind seems to have picked up the farther north we got. My hair whips across my face in a flurry, and I bury my head in his back while he leads the way to the cabin.

Inside, Cole shuts the door behind us with force. I set my bag down in the corner while he immediately gets a fire going in the wood-burning fireplace. The fire instantly warms my chill from the cold wind, and I relax while he starts some soft music on the record player that looks about as old as this cabin.

"How about sun-dried tomato pasta for dinner?" he asks, squeezing my elbow as he passes by to the kitchen.

"Deal, but I get to help cook."

"Fine by me. Do you want noodle or sauce duty?" he asks.

"Noodles, of course. I'm no Shirley. I don't think you want me putting the sauce together," I laugh as we get started in the kitchen.

"I knew a girl in college who hated pasta," I muse while we cook. "Can you believe that? Our friendship didn't last very long. Looking back on it, that's alright with me—I don't think I can trust someone who doesn't like pasta."

He chuckles at my random comment. "How dare she have food preferences."

"I know, right?" I smile, getting distracted from waiting for my water to boil by the way he moves with ease around this kitchen, easily throwing things in the pan to create a deli-cious-smelling sauce.

When I toss the pasta and the sauce together to finish it off, he dips a fork into it, collecting a bite.

"Careful, it's hot." He holds the fork out for me to taste. The pasta is flavorful and warm with the perfect amount of heat, and a hum escapes my throat.

"Yum. Here, you need to try this." I do the same for him, offering him a bite.

The flavor is so intoxicating that we end up eating it right over the stove, never making it over to the table.

Once we've finished eating, I help wash and dry the dishes then wander around while Cole rolls out a set of plans onto the table. The wind howls outside as I run my fingertips along the back of the couch, leisurely perusing the cabin while the fire crackles.

I roam through the living room, picking up small trinkets on the fireplace mantel to admire. A small wooden fishing boat sits on the very edge of it.

"Did you make this?" I ask, picking it up. Cole looks up from where he's hovered over the table and smiles when he spots the boat in my hand.

"I did." He slides his hands in his pockets and crosses the room slowly with a nostalgic calm to his face. "I think I was fifteen or sixteen when I made that."

He takes it out of my hand and rotates it around, studying it. "It's a replica of the boat Uncle Paul used to keep out here."

I watch him admire it and can't help but think back to the childhood he had, to all of the turmoil he went through. My stomach clenches as a thought dawns on me.

"Can I ask you a question?" I murmur, unsure if I want to know the answer...but needing to know all the same.

"Of course." He sets the boat on the mantel and turns to give me all of his attention. His brows crease when he sees the way I'm struggling to force the words out.

I swallow, my heart pounding in my chest. "Do you think this thing between us... Could we just be trauma bonded?"

His face softens as he steps closer, slowly shaking his head with resolution. He doesn't need to think about it long before saying a firm, "No."

I heave a shaky inhale, relief flooding me that he doesn't think so. Then he tucks a strand of hair behind my ear so gently that I barely feel it.

"This is the realest thing I've ever felt," he admits, speaking aloud the same thing I'm feeling. "I felt it back then, before I knew a single thing about you."

He moves even closer, bringing both hands to cradle my face. "And I sure as hell feel it now."

I nod, bringing a hand to rest on top of his, feeling emotion well in my eyes. "Our trauma just...complicated things for a bit, yeah?"

He smirks, nodding in agreement as he slowly lowers his head. I lift up to close the last bit of space between us and press my mouth to his, desperate to feel closer to him after acknowledging our feelings. His fingers slide even farther into my hair at the same time he deepens the kiss, a sense of urgency seemingly taking over as if he has something he needs to prove.

I run my hands down the sides of his torso, the wool fabric of his shirt feeling soft against my fingertips. Being close to him in this way feels right in every sense of the word. It feels eerily close to a sharp pang of homesickness, even though I'm right here with him.

He slips a hand on my waist, gripping hard to pull me flush with his body. It sends a warmth down my core and seems to awaken every cell in my body. I can't get enough of him and the way his touch makes it feel like a spark is being dragged across my skin.

He pushes me gently back a few steps until my legs bump up against the foot of his bed. He pulls back abruptly but hovers close with a hesitation in his eyes. There's a question behind the roll of his lips. Of course he would be gentlemanly enough to think that my staying here without the cot wouldn't guarantee anything more than sleeping.

What he doesn't know is that I want this as badly as he does. I need this moment with him like I need my next breath. It feels like a part of my soul has been waiting for this moment for years.

With a subtle nod of my head, he takes the permission and slowly lowers me onto my back while placing a warm kiss at the place just beneath my ear. He moves down the base of my neck, planting warm kisses at every stop while my nails run ever so softly down the span of his back.

He straightens, one knee pressing into the mattress between my legs, and he slips his shirt over his head. He flashes me a smile that looks both tender and devious at the same time, and I hook a finger in his belt loop and pull him down to me.

THIRTY-SIX
Cole

Now

I stir, rolling onto my side as the soft scrape of Sydney's hair on my cheek pulls me further out of sleep. With a contented sigh, I remember where I am and relish the way it feels to wake up next to her. To feel her skin under my fingertips. The warmth of her body tucked against mine.

Up until now, we've been taking our time, dancing around that line we crossed last night. We eased our way into this to be cautious and respectful of our feelings. But now that we've been together like this, the way my heart feels like it's about to explode has made one thing crystal clear to me.

I'm absolutely gone for this girl.

I'm in.

I'm all in.

I have been for a while, if I'm truly honest with myself, but it's never been more obvious to me than it is right in this very moment. Last night solidified something for me in a big way

Her breathing is calm and steady, the slow rise and fall of her chest telling me she's still fast asleep. So I climb out of bed slowly, not wanting to wake her.

Shuffling across the floor, I avoid the planks I know will creak under my weight and quietly get dressed for the day.

I slip my boots on, head outside, and click the door shut behind me as quietly as I can. As I walk to the shed, I pick up random branches that blew across the yard last night from the wind.

As I twist to toss them into the woods, I note that my back is pain free for the first time in a while. I'd happily sleep on any surface if it meant being near Sydney, but I can't say that I'm mad about sleeping on a bed with an actual mattress.

I pull the chainsaw and a few other tools out of the shed and gather a few planks of wood to set next to the tree stump I cut down yesterday. Then I get started crafting a small stool that I can set by the front door to use when taking my boots off at the end of the day.

Having a morning project to work on is my favorite way to start the day. It's the most peaceful time, and I often find myself zoning out, getting lost in my thoughts. Today is no different as the chainsaw blade has an almost hypnotizing effect, causing me to relive the entirety of my interactions with Sydney.

From the deep emotional connection in those first meetings in high school, to the way it crumbled in a split-second decision to leave town, all the way up to now. All of it further fuels the importance and weight of my feelings for her now.

Out of the corner of my eye, I catch movement on my porch. I stop the chainsaw and glance up to find Sydney wrapped in a wool blanket, her wavy hair a disheveled mess as it hangs past her shoulders. The sight of her loose and undone like that makes my chest ache.

Setting the chainsaw down, I slide my safety goggles off and head toward her.

"Sorry, did I wake you?" I ask with a cringe when I get closer to the porch.

"It's okay. I needed to get up anyway." She smiles in a content way—the look of someone who got a restful night's sleep. I also note that I can't find a trace of regret anywhere in her expression.

I rest my folded arms on top of the railing, craning my neck to look up at her. I resist the urge to reach out and pull on the blanket to bring her close enough to wrap my arms around her waist.

"How are you feeling?" Regardless of how comfortable she looks, I need to hear her say it out loud.

She locks me in with a tender gaze as she cups my cheek with her hand. As she slides her thumb across my skin, she smiles softly, leaving me weak at the knees.

"Great," she says quietly but firmly. "And you?"

"Never better," I mumble, slowly mirroring her smile.

"What's your plan for the day?" she asks, removing her hand to wrap the blanket tighter around herself.

"Paul sent me a message this morning. He's coming out to the lodge for breakfast and to visit the cabin. Then I told him I'd help him look for a house in Baudette."

"That sounds like fun."

"You?"

"I need to get down to meet Neal by the new glamping spot, but Graham, Blair, and I are heading into town as well after that to visit Mom."

I search her eyes for signs of anxiety about seeing her mom, and while the grief I find in them might always be there, it's not at the forefront as much as it was a few short weeks ago.

"Perfect. I can pick you up at the nursing home when I'm done with Paul?" I offer. "We can come back here together?"

"That sounds like a plan." She bends down, meeting me halfway to press her lips to mine. It sends a surge of electricity through my body—an awareness of what might happen if I follow her back inside and peel that blanket off of her ever so slowly.

"Same time, same place tonight?" I murmur against her lips, feeling them grow into a grin.

"Wouldn't miss it," she whispers.

I clear my throat, keeping my gaze locked on her as she backs away.

"Go ahead and get dressed while I clean up out here. Then I'll bring you down to the lodge," I offer.

"Okay." With one last smile, she disappears inside the cabin and I use every ounce of self-control I have to not follow behind her.

I wait patiently by the door of the lodge for Paul to finish up at the bar. I didn't realize he and Shirley were such good friends, but judging by the warm looks on both of their faces, I'd say they definitely have some sort of past—one that I'm obviously not privy to.

"Sorry," he says with a cringe when he finally joins me.

"No problem." I hold the door open for him, and he looks behind his shoulder one last time, his head swiveling as he takes in the updates within the lodge.

"This is looking amazing around here," he comments. "Your Sydney has done a phenomenal job."

My Sydney.

I like the way that sounds.

"She's worked really hard," I agree. His hand grazes the bear statue as we walk past, but for some reason I hold back on telling him I made it. I don't feel like I need the accolades from him. He's the only person from my past who told me he was proud of me often enough for me to actually believe it.

"Hop on." I point to the ATV. As I take him along the trail up to the cabin, a sense of normalcy comes over me. It's just him and me, roaming this island like we used to do so many times before.

When we arrive, he immediately takes off wandering toward the beach. I shove my hands in my pockets and follow along, content on letting him do whatever he needs to do while he's here. Roam around. Reminisce. Whatever he needs.

"Man, it's been too long," he breathes. As he looks around, taking heavy deep breaths, his soft nostalgic expression tells me that he holds all of the same memories I have in the same high regard.

"Did you miss it?" I ask, unsure of what his answer will be. It certainly didn't seem like he did, given he was gone for such a long time, but at the same time, I can't see how he couldn't.

"Of course." He nods with a grin.

"Are you sure you don't want the cabin back?" I ask cautiously.

He shakes his head vehemently.

"Nah. I'm not much for being attached to things. You saw the backpack of stuff I showed up with," he says with a chuckle.

I can't help but smile at that.

"The memories, though. That's what makes something special. And those have always lived here," he points to his head and then his heart, "and here."

An understanding washes over me, and I start to see what he does when he looks around. It's not the cabin itself that's special. It's what we shared here. The countless nights by the campfire. The canoe rides around the island. The way he would read *The Catcher in the Rye* aloud from the couch while I stoked the logs in the fireplace.

Whether he did them on purpose or not, those little things helped distract me from my reality enough to keep me hanging on. He saved my life in many ways.

"I'm proud of you, son." He says the same words he used to say, with emotion gripping his voice this time.

"For what?" I ask, my chest warming with my own emotion.

"For coming so far from where you were. For getting through what you did. And coming out the other side."

All I can do is nod and roll my lips, his words settling deep inside me as we watch the waves crash onto shore.

Eventually, he clears his throat, turning toward the cabin. "Come on. Show me what you've done with the inside."

THIRTY-SEVEN
Sydney
Now

Week Fourteen of Renovation

"We've got the ground fully graded, ready to begin constructing the glamping tents," Neal says as he shows me around the area behind the lodge that we've mapped out for the tents. "I just need the green light from you."

"Perfect. And you have space to fit five fully functioning, electricity-equipped tents in this space?" I ask, feeling skeptical as I note how tight everything is going to be here. We've downsized my original plan and removed several features in order to make it fit, but I'm still not convinced we'll be able to squeeze it all in this relatively small space.

"Yup." He nods, looking far more confident than I feel. "The crew should be finished with the last cabin tomorrow, so we can start out here the day after that if you're ready?"

"Yes, let's plan for that." I try to look excited, but I can't help the sigh that inadvertently comes from me. It definitely won't be as stunning as I initially dreamed it would be out on Cole's property. There won't be as many tents as I wanted, not to mention the million-dollar view, space to put an outdoor kitchen, or even room to put individual fire pits in front of each tent...but we'll just have to make the best of it. It's all we can do.

It will be perfect.

Cole's voice plays in my head, reminding me that it doesn't need to be exceptional. Sometimes it's okay to settle for good enough.

Perhaps that's true for more than just this renovation. Maybe it really is okay that it took years to come back to see Mom after she was gone, despite the guilt I still feel about it. Maybe trying my best and doing it on my own time has always been enough.

"Perfect. Thanks, Neal," I tell him. "Let me know how I can help. I've got the furniture for the tents being delivered sometime in the next week or two, so hopefully the timing will work out well for that."

"We'll get them done as fast as we can," he says confidently. "We're in the home stretch now, aren't we?"

"That's right." A flutter of butterflies hits me as I remember just how close we are to the end.

"Just a few more weeks and you can get back to your life down in Minneapolis. I bet you're antsy to get home." He chuckles, completely oblivious to how much emotional weight the word home holds for me.

This island and Baudette will always partially be home to me, of course, and the people I have here. But my life down in Minneapolis seems like home to me too. Even so, as much as both of those places do, another place that felt as close to home as anything else was in Cole's arms last night.

That realization further complicates my plans for after this renovation is finished and leaves my future path in question. I tuck that thought away for another time and smile at Neal.

"It's not so bad here," I say simply with a wink. "Alright, as always, thanks for everything. I'll be back to check in later."

"You got it." He smiles and waves as he heads toward his crew while I turn the opposite direction and head toward the dock to meet Graham and Blair.

Hi, Mom.

Graham showed me a box with some old photos yesterday. I found one of the four of us at a Twins game. I must have been seven or eight. Graham was all pouty because we lost to the Chicago White Sox and there was a huge ketchup stain on my shirt. Despite the minor looks of irritation on our faces, we still looked ridiculously happy. Dad was grinning proudly and you were tucked happily under his arm.

It made me smile, is all. Just wanted to tell you.

Blair's yelp of a cheer brings my attention up from the journal. Graham, Dad, Mom, and Blair are all sitting at the table by the window playing cards.

"Here you go, Mom," Graham says as he deals the cards, placing some in front of her. She looks a little lost and unfocused from where she sits in the chair, and each time I lay eyes on her, it sends a sharp twist of something heavy to my chest. But the sight of them doing a normal activity like that together is soothing to see. It reminds me of old times when the four of us used to play cards out at the lodge while we waited for guests to arrive. Now with Blair added in, it's truly heartwarming to see so many of my favorite people in one place.

I glance up periodically, watching them as I write from the chair next to Mom's bed, quickly losing track of time.

When a text message notification comes through from inside my purse, I dig it out. A buzzing anticipation flushes across my skin simply at the sight of the name on my phone.

> **Cole:** I got finished with Paul early. We found a house for him. He's putting an offer in tomorrow morning. I just got to the nursing home, so I'll be by the nurse's station whenever you're ready to head back. Take your time.

I ruminate over his words, staring at them while a thought comes to mind. I inhale slowly, contemplating whether I'm ready for this step or not. With one more glance up at my family, I realize I already know the answer.

> **Sydney:** Actually…do you want to come in?

He replies almost instantly.

> **Cole:** Are you sure?

> **Sydney:** Yes. Only if you want to, though.

I wait for him to reply again, but instead, a knock comes at the door less than twenty seconds later. With a sideways glance at Graham, who has his eyes pinned on me, I meet Cole at the door.

"Hi," I say softly, opening the door wide for him to come through. He runs a hand down my back in greeting, and I lead him over to the table.

Everyone's eyes fall on me—except Mom's, of course—and I know judging by their faces that they're also taking in the seriousness of this moment. The fact that I'm introducing Cole to my mom is telling of how significant he's become to me.

I open my mouth then realize I'm not quite sure what to say. Do I introduce him to Mom? I haven't gotten used to talking directly to her yet, so I falter. Do I announce him to the group as a whole?

Thankfully, Graham hops out of his seat, pulling me out of the awkwardness I seem to be frozen in, and reaches for another chair.

"Cole, I hope you know how to play gin rummy," he says, sliding the chair up to the table.

"I do not," Cole laughs softly. "But I'm a quick learner."

My heart settles—even soars—as I scoot my own chair in between Cole and Graham. Two steady sources of strength for me, which I'm finding comforting in this moment. I keep my gaze on Cole out of the corner of my eye while my dad rambles off instructions for the game.

"Does that make sense?" Dad asks when he's done.

"A little," Cole says, and I bite back a smile when I can tell that he still has no clue how to play.

"You'll pick it up as we go," I tell him, laying my head on his shoulder.

From this angle, I have a direct shot at Blair across the table, who gives me a wink and a knowing smile. This time, I don't attempt to hide my smile as I wink back to her.

Dad deals the cards to each of us, and we start playing the game. Mom may not know everyone she's playing with, but she somehow remembers the game well enough to play, which I find oddly comforting.

As the next hour passes, I note the importance of every single person at this table and how this moment feels absolutely perfect to me.

It feels like family.

THIRTY-EIGHT
Sydney
Now

"It looks good to me," I give my approval to the crew inside cabin eleven. "Nice work, guys. You should be done with this one today, right?"

"That's the plan." One of the workers who passes me on his way inside the cabin nods at me.

"Awesome. I'll get out of your way." I skirt around them to head back toward the lodge.

As I walk the path, I blow out a steadying breath, feeling exhausted and positively exuberant at the same time. I spent the entire morning furnishing and stocking the rest of the finished cabins. All Neal's crew has left to do is cabin twelve, which I need to move the rest of my stuff out of. That shouldn't be too much of an inconvenience since I've basically moved most of my things into Cole's cabin anyway. Then they'll round out the renovation with completing the glamping tents just in time for the grand opening, if everything stays on track.

The finish line is rapidly approaching, and aside from the uncertainty of Cole's and my future—and knowing I'll need to leave Mom, which stings more after each time I see her—there's also been a sense of pride that's been brewing steadily in my chest. I've been making a point to give myself permission to feel good about what we've accomplished on this project. Not only the physical upgrades but the way we were able to honor the legacy of Ruby Lodge.

When I get closer to the lodge, I spot Blair sitting in an Adirondack chair on the beach.

"Hey, Blair," I say.

She looks over at me with a grin. "Hey, Syd."

"What are you up to?" I come to a stop on the sand next to her.

"Oh, I needed some peace and quiet to go over some things. I'm filling in the calendar for my youth mental health wellness camps. Did I tell you we're completely booked for the next two months straight?" She lights up in the very specific way she does when she's talking about the camp.

"No, you didn't. That's amazing, Blair." I can't help but grin back at her. "I'm really proud of you."

She pushes her lips together and lifts her brows, a heartwarming smile growing wide. "Right back at you."

"I'm heading inside. Are you coming?" I ask.

"I'll be there in a bit. Just need a few more minutes out here." She waves before turning back to her calendar.

I head up to the lodge, letting a peaceful happiness wash over me. A happiness that is the result of so many different factors. Through the windows, I peer into the bar and catch sight of one very big one.

Cole.

My stomach does a flip, and the skin on my cheeks heats at the mere sight of him. It's as if my body involuntarily reacts to the sheer memories of the past few days with him.

If I think about it, it's somewhat unsettling how quickly my feelings for him have progressed. The foundation for a meaningful connection with him has always been there—even despite my best efforts to refute it for a time. Once we saw the truth for what it was—and gave ourselves permission to actually feel it—there was nothing holding us back from falling fast and hard.

What we have together is intense. It's rooted in an emotional connection that unnerves me at times. It often catches me off guard and steals my breath, just as it did all those years ago. But it's also genuine, and it's compassionate, and it's soaked in a chemistry that's somehow both soothing and scorching at the same time. I don't know what our future holds, but I'm in a place right now where I'm more sure of this connection between us than anything else in my life.

Inside, I spot Graham and Cole chatting over paperwork at the bar. As I walk toward them, I catch sight of Paul on the other side of the bar and Shirley emerging from the kitchen to serve him some food.

It might just be the hopeless romantic in me, and perhaps it's just a glow she's sporting from cooking in the newly renovated kitchen, but it's not hard to see that Shirley lights up on the inside when she's around Paul.

With a subtle smirk, I avert my gaze and slide into the chair next to Cole.

"What's that?" I point to the paper he's signing.

Cole finishes his signature and turns slowly in his chair, pinning me with an intense look—one laced with a sly smirk. I brace myself to remain steady under his stare and raise my brows, curious as to what he's about to tell me.

Graham quietly moves down the bar to give us some privacy, and my curiosity is officially piqued—so are my nerves.

"It's, uh..." Cole clears his throat. "Official paperwork to sell my land and cabin."

"Wait, what?" I murmur, not quite understanding the words I'm hearing. "To whom?"

He huffs a small laugh. "To you."

"I...I don't understand." I shake my head, trying to extract his reasoning through my stare alone. "That's your land. You have so much history there with Paul. You have to keep it."

"I've come to realize that what I was most attached to were the memories I had there with my uncle. My only connection to any sort of family I had was through that cabin. It was my connection to him." He flicks his eyes over to Paul. "Well, he's here now. I don't need the cabin anymore just to remember our history."

"I still don't understand." The logical part of my brain is refusing to hear his reasoning.

He runs his hand down his jaw. "The memories are what matter, Sydney. I'll always have those. Paul is okay with it too. I asked him first. Besides, when I come to Baudette to visit him, I'll likely visit his new house anyway."

"But what if..." My voice trails off, not wanting to say what I'm thinking out loud.

"What if he leaves again?" he finishes for me, again looking over at Paul. He shrugs. "Then I'll miss him. Not the cabin."

I stare at him, my mind daring to whirl with the new possibilities this opens up.

"You're really sure?" I need to know that he's absolutely positive about this before I let myself get excited.

"One hundred percent," he confirms.

A twinge of excitement flares as I slowly allow myself to accept what's happening. I can't help the squeal that comes out of my mouth as I jump into his arms. After nearly falling off the stool, he steadies himself with a chuckle and hugs me back, squeezing tightly.

"Thank you," I whisper against his ear, then plant a firm kiss on his mouth. My arm slides down his shoulder, and I hold his stare, getting lost in appreciation for his selflessness yet again.

Then I pick up the paperwork to glance over it, my mind still reeling.

"Graham!" I say his name excitedly as I motion him over.

"Pretty awesome, huh?" Graham grins, throwing an appreciative look Cole's way. Then he grows serious. "I sure hope it's not too late to do your glamping plan out there."

"It's not," I answer immediately. A rush of adrenaline runs through me as I work through how things can pan out from here. "Some of Neal's crew is supposed to start on the glamping portion tomorrow while the rest works on the final cabin. They haven't even touched the glamping area yet, except to make the ground level, so this is impeccable timing."

"Well, that's convenient," he says.

"I mean, I'll have to come up with another use for the spot behind the lodge, of course," I ramble, mostly to myself. "Electricity is already run out there, so I'm sure I can come up with something cool."

"Perfect," Graham says. Cole slides a hand on top of my knee under the counter. He gives it a squeeze as a show of support, and I place my hand on top of it, gripping it excitedly, my way of conveying my gratitude yet again.

"Oh, by the way, Syd," Graham says. "Since they're doing your cabin next, I have cabin one available if you want to move in there?"

I glance over at Cole and smile. "Sure, but...we won't need it until tomorrow night."

I automatically group Cole in my 'we,' not bothering to seek his input. I already know he'll be on board.

"We need one more night at his cabin," I say.

Cole's face softens, and my stomach swoops under the weight of his stare.

"Alright." Graham shrugs, once again backing away to give us space.

Cole immediately leans in for a kiss, one that feels more like a mutual understanding or, even better, a promise. Then he rests his forehead against mine as I soak in everything that's happening.

"I should probably start packing up the cabin, huh?" Cole smirks.

"I'll come with you," I say. "Just give me a couple minutes."

"I'll meet you by the ATV," he says, planting a kiss on my temple before walking over to Paul.

Then I slide my phone out of my pocket to shoot Neal a message to tell him about our last-minute change of plans.

THIRTY-NINE
Cole

Now

"Thank you. I'll see you tomorrow," I say before hanging up my phone. I take a long sip of cider before crossing the cabin where I rejoin Sydney and Paul, both of whom are sitting on the rug in the middle of the living room, packing boxes.

"I secured a storage rental in town," I tell them, lowering to sit between them. "He said I can pick up the keys in the morning when we bring boxes over."

"And you're sure you want to keep all this stuff?" Paul asks. "Aside from the pieces you made, I say you should just chuck it all."

Sydney bites back a smile, and I chuckle at his flippancy. "I think I'm a little more sentimental than you are, Paul."

"Ah." He huffs, shrugging me off.

"You definitely need to keep the table and stool you made," Sydney says, pointing to the furniture. "Those can go in the keep pile."

"Sure," I say before an idea comes to me. "Actually, do you want either of them for your new house, Paul? I don't have much of a need for them."

His eyes perk up as he considers my offer. "Oh, that's actually a great idea. Yes, I'd happily take them. I don't have much furniture in the house yet."

"They're all yours. Let me know if there's anything else you see that you want."

"How about this lovely duck lamp?" Sydney stands to pick up the old lamp on top of the shelf. As she lifts it, the bottom part of the duck breaks right off, falling to the ground.

"Oh no," she mutters under her breath as she quickly tries to gather the pieces. Paul and I simply laugh.

"Believe it or not, that was here when I bought the place many moons ago," Paul says.

I help Sydney place all the broken pieces into our trash pile and then I grab the end table to move to the keep pile.

"Be careful with that furniture now. Don't want those to break," Paul says under his breath. Sydney blushes at his teasing while I smirk.

"Oh, now these are deemed valuable enough for you?" I tease back. "Now that they're yours?"

"That's right," he says with a wink. Then he stands, brushing his hands on his jeans. "Well, Shirley is on her way to pick me up, so I'll see you two tomorrow."

"Oh, um...okay," I say, surprised by his sudden exit. I didn't even hear his phone ring. "Thanks for your help packing today."

"You bet. I'll be back in the morning to help you haul boxes down. Bye, darlin'," he says to Sydney before walking right out the door, pulling it shut behind him.

"Alright, then. I guess he's done." I chuckle and turn to find Sydney grinning to herself.

"I think there's a love connection happening," she says with a smirk.

"You might be right," I agree. Outside the cabin, we can hear the sound of an ATV approaching and then, moments later, disappearing again.

"We got a lot done today in a short amount of time," Sydney comments, placing her hands on her hips, looking around the nearly bare cabin. We successfully cleaned out the kitchen cabinets and packed up anything in our keep pile—which, admittedly, is not much. There wasn't a whole lot here to begin with, so between the three of us, the task didn't take long at all.

"We did," I agree. "Thanks for helping."

She strolls toward me in the middle of the cabin, our eyes locked on each other, and a buzz zips down my spine with each passing second—a primal reaction to simply being near her.

"We can pack up the bed tomorrow morning," I suggest softly, reaching out to pull her the rest of the way toward me.

"Okay." Her smile is coy as she steps into my arms. I wrap my arms around her in a tight hug as she lays her head against my chest.

"I feel bad that you spent so much time fixing this place up all to have it be torn down in the end," she says quietly against my shirt.

"Don't feel bad." I run a hand down her back. I'll keep repeating the same thing over again as many times as she needs me to in order to prove to her that I'm okay with this. Because I am. "These are just things. The memories are what's important."

"Okay." She nods slowly, her head sliding against my shirt. I run my hands down her arms, pulling her back slightly so I can give in to this overwhelming urge to feel my mouth against hers.

She reaches up on her tiptoes to meet me halfway, pressing her lips to mine. An instant flooding of warmth overcomes my body the same way it does every single time I kiss her. It's a rush I can't seem to get enough of. The way my pulse quickens and my chest gets tight. The way it feels like a wave of tiny electrical pulses sparking across every inch of my skin.

She fists my shirt at my lower back, pushing herself even harder against me. I hyperfocus on the way she tightens her grip around me. I respond by clamping under her thighs to lift her up in a jolt. My hands slide under her legs as she wraps them around my waist with a squeal.

I take a few steps forward until I'm able to set her on top of the back of the couch, all the while keeping her pressed tightly against me. I smile at the hum she makes when I explore more of her with my mouth, down the base of her neck to just below her collarbone, spending more than a few seconds there.

She slides her fingers through my hair, eliciting a shiver that runs all the way down my spine. It's then that my last thread of control snaps, and I'm officially consumed by desire for her.

After dipping my mouth a few inches lower, using my teeth this time to scrape against her skin, I raise back up to claim her mouth. She squeezes her legs tighter around me as she slides her hands down my chest.

"How about we make one more memory to take with us?" I whisper against her lips. She hums again, and I can feel it vibrate against my mouth as she smiles through the kiss. I take that as a yes, lifting her to bring her slowly, yet urgently, over to the bed.

FORTY
Sydney
Now

Week Sixteen of Renovation

The Bobcat creates a loud bang as it crushes Cole's cabin—my cabin, I guess—with ease. The four walls collapse on top of each other as a cloud of dust puffs into the air.

As I stand next to Cole, it's not lost on me that on most of the demolition sites I've been a part of, there's generally a sense of excitement in the air, an anticipation and eagerness to construct something even better in place of whatever we're tearing down. Aside from creating something entirely from scratch, that's what I love about being an architect: taking something that either doesn't exist or maybe isn't functioning anymore and bringing something new to life in its place.

While I am excited for what we're going to create here, I realize that I feel nothing but reverence in this moment. A quiet admiration and respect for the solace this place has provided for someone I care about very much. For being a comfort to him when he needed it the most. I make a silent vow to make sure this land will provide that same kind of peace and serenity to others.

"Are you okay?" I slip my arm through Cole's, lightly gripping his forearm.

"Yup," he says with certainty. There's no sign of regret or grief in his expression. He's calm and steady, as always. I squeeze closer to his side, resting my head against his shoulder, acknowledging—and appreciating—what he's letting go of.

We watch as the cabin gets leveled to nothing more than a large pile of wood and debris, and Neal's crew starts clearing the rubble.

"Well, should we head back?" Cole asks, turning to face me.

"Sure." I rise on my tiptoes and plant a peck on his lips, squeezing his arm once more before letting go.

As I climb onto the ATV behind him and scoot forward, I wrap my arms around his middle and lay my head against his back. I can feel the soft thumping of his heart against my ear and I close my eyes, feeling overwhelmed with emotion just like every time I'm close to him lately. It's become a force that grips my heart so strongly it almost hurts. One that terrifies me and exhilarates me all at once.

I stay wrapped around him like that while he takes us down the path. We pass by the rows of cabins, past the lodge, and come to a stop next to cabin one. Our 'home sweet home' until after the grand opening.

"Will you sit with me?" he asks, sliding his fingers through mine as we climb the stairs. He settles onto the newly upgraded porch swing that I'm happy to report doesn't creak in the slightest.

"Of course," I murmur, choosing to slide sideways across his lap instead of taking the space next to him.

He wraps an arm around my back, gripping me at my hips, and his other hand comes to rest softly on my thigh.

"I hope you don't have any regrets," I say quietly while I run my thumb across his cheek. My stomach feels uneasy as I wait for him to answer, unable to bear the thought that he might. He stares at me intently, taking his time, as if he's considering more than just his cabin.

"Not one," he mutters firmly, holding my gaze. "You know, that cabin used to be the only place in the world that I felt whole."

My chest aches as he continues.

"It was the only place I felt worthy and important. That I felt safe." He shakes his head ever so slightly. "Well, that's not true anymore."

His eyes break from mine as he trails the way his finger tucks a strand of hair behind my ear.

"You make me feel all of those things," he whispers, bringing his gaze back up to mine. "And so much more."

I'm overcome with emotion as I touch his cheek. His words stir up a whirlwind of emotions in my chest, and all at once, I feel the urge to put a name to what I know in my soul this is.

"I love you, Cole Fredrickson," I whisper, just loudly enough for him, and him alone, to hear it. Not even the nearby birds or insects are privy to it.

His eyes flutter closed, and emotion pricks at my eyes as I watch him take it in. I know full well how little he's heard those words in his life, which makes this moment that much more monumental for both of us.

"I mean it." I use both hands to tip his face up to mine, staring into his now opened eyes. I need him to hear me—I'm desperate for it. For him to feel this same ache in my chest as I do. "Do you know what an honor it is to love you?"

He inhales a deep breath, locking us in an emotion-laden stare before the slightest of smiles appears.

"If you say so." He says the words quietly, but I can tell from the way he smiles that he believes the words I just declared. He not only hears it, but he accepts it.

The warmth of his hand leaves my leg as he uses his thumb and forefinger to graze my chin.

"I love you too," he says just as intently as I did. My heart aches again, but this time there's a flushing of warmth that comes along with it. Hearing him say those words—to me—does something to me I couldn't dare put into words.

I drop my head, feeling weak, as if I couldn't possibly hold any part of myself up any longer, and press my forehead to his chest. His hand slides through my hair, and I feel the faintest pressure of his kiss against the top of my head.

When I've regained some strength, I lift my head to find him smiling softly at me.

"What does this mean for us, Cole?" I whisper the question that's been hanging over both of our heads the past few weeks. After a quiet moment, he lifts his brows along with a shrug.

"I'm open," he says simply, as if he's not overly concerned about it.

"I need to go back to my apartment after the grand opening. I'm slated to start another project right away," I tell him. Although I'm anxious for his reply, I know that whatever happens, we'll figure it out together. What we have between us...it can't be broken easily, no matter what obstacles we face. That, I'm sure of.

"Then that's where I'm going too," he says confidently. I didn't think it would be possible, but my heart swells even more.

"Do you think my apartment will approve of your chainsaw noise?" I tease.

"We can drop my loud tools off in Longville on the way down," he says with a grin. "I'll just bring my small carving tools if you don't mind."

"Not at all."

I get lost in watching the way he looks at me, my mind going over what a future with him will look like, until my phone beeps in my pocket.

Shifting on his lap so I can pull it out, I read the message and huff a laugh.

"Graham wants to know if we are interested in playing a rematch of gin rummy against him and Blair. I guess the lodge is quiet at the moment, and he says he's in the mood to kick our butts."

"Let's do it," he says with a nod.

He pats my hip, helping me slide off his lap. I follow him off the steps and he bends slightly, pointing to his back.

"Want a ride?"

"Duh," I say excitedly, using the bench to climb onto his back. I wrap my arms around his neck as his arms grip under my legs, and I note—and adore—the carefree way he takes us to the lodge.

FORTY-ONE
Cole
Now

"Hi," Sydney says with an exhausted sigh as she comes inside cabin one.

"Hey." I meet her at the door for a kiss. "Rough day?"

"Not rough, just busy." She smiles, wrapping her arms around my waist. "I was up at the glamping site all day. Neal's crew is working hard. I can't wait to show it to you."

"I can't wait to see what all the fuss is about," I murmur, placing another kiss on her forehead. It's something I can't help, this automatic need to be touching her, to be holding her. But I pull away reluctantly so she can bend over to untie her boots.

"How was your day?" she asks, slipping them off.

"It was good. I spent most of the day over at Paul's house building some more furniture for him. It's a good thing we're storing all my tools over there. It's the perfect setup for me to work."

"Oh, I bet he appreciates that." She straightens, and it's then that she notices what I have set up on the table.

"Oh, what's this?" she asks with excitement, noticing the package of cupcakes next to the laptop.

"Have a seat," I tell her, sliding the chair back for her to sit. "This is yet another take on trying to be creative for a date night around here."

"Hey, if it involves cupcakes, I'm already sold." She smiles at me. "Did Shirley make these?"

"No, I picked them up in town before I came back to the island. I also dropped some off with your dad to give to your mom and the nurses too."

Her eyes soften and go misty at the edges, and I think I'll happily do anything I can for the rest of my life to get her to keep looking at me like that.

"Thank you," she whispers.

"You don't have to," I say quietly, yet again getting sucked in for another kiss. Then I wake the computer up and open the package of cupcakes while the screen loads.

When what I have planned pops up on the screen, she gasps, her eyes going wide.

"Is that what I think it is?" she breathes, her mouth dropping open.

"If what you're thinking is doing a virtual tour of the Palace of Versailles, then you would be correct," I say with a smirk.

A squeal escapes her this time, and she covers her mouth with her hand. "Really?"

I nod. "I know it's not the same as seeing it in person, but it's the best I can do for now. You said you wanted to admire some of the architecture in France, so I thought this would be nice."

"It's wonderful," she says, her voice cracking slightly.

"Have at it," I tell her, pointing to the start button. I watch her face light up as she uses the mouse pad to start the tour and immediately gets sucked into it.

I settle into the chair next to her, fully aware that I'm looking at her the same way she's looking at the screen. I get caught up in simply watching her as she takes a bite of the chocolate cupcake, completely enthralled with what she's seeing on the screen.

I get up to grab us some napkins, and when I come back, instead of sitting down in the chair next to her, I opt for coming behind her. I bend, curling my arms around the top of her chest, and rest my chin on top of her shoulder.

She sighs, leaning into me as I nuzzle into the crook of her neck.

"Look at those beams," she says in awe, running her finger across the screen to show me the interior structure of the palace.

I admire the design and craftsmanship of the sprawling palace right along with her, pointing out my favorite sections and listening to hers.

"Stunning, isn't it?" she breathes.

"It really is," I agree, keeping my arms folded tightly around her.

"Someday I'll take you there, babe." I whisper the promise into her ear, relishing the way goosebumps cascade across her skin in response.

"Okay," she whispers back, squeezing my forearm while she keeps her eyes glued to the screen.

We move on to the tours of the gardens and many statues on the estate, soaking the beauty in. When the tour comes to an end, my arms lift slightly with her chest as she inhales deeply. I place another kiss on her hairline and back away as she stands, turning to face me.

"That was lovely." She slowly wraps her arms around my shoulders, and I don't waste the moment to slide my own around her waist.

"I'm glad you enjoyed it." I use the back of my hand to brush her hair behind her shoulder and then run my hand down the length of her arm.

Her eyes lock with mine as her own hand runs up the base of my neck. It sends a shiver straight down my spine, slowly and deliciously, and I can't get enough of the way her affection makes me feel.

"I love you." I mutter the words that I know will be the most important ones I'll ever say in my life, no matter how many times I plan on saying them.

"I love you too," she replies with a soft smile, making my chest feel like it's about to explode.

I don't know if I'll ever get used to hearing her say 'I love you' to me. I hope I never do. I hope every single time feels just like this.

She leans up to connect her mouth to mine, and I tighten my grip, pulling her tight against me. A warmth flushes down my core as I deepen the kiss, running my hand up the length of her spine.

An urgency runs through me when she uses her fingernails to scrape through my hair. I instinctively move us until she's flat against the wall next to the loft stairs, and a tiny sound comes from the back of her throat when I push myself into her.

I pull away, breathing hard, and search her eyes for confirmation that she's on the same page as I am. I find not only that but an even deeper desire in her eyes that further fuels me.

"Take me up?" she asks with a sultry smirk, and I waste no time gripping her by the thighs, wrapping her legs around my waist.

"Hang on tight," I say. She wraps her arms around my neck, squeezing tight as I carry us up the stairs.

FORTY-TWO
Sydney
Now

"So this is a glamping tent," Cole murmurs under his breath.

"Yup." I wiggle my brows at him as he helps me reposition the small couch along the canvas wall of one of the tents.

"It's like a mini cabin," he points out skeptically, as if he's not understanding the appeal.

"Precisely." I move to where the rectangular table is set up and straighten each of the chairs to fit underneath.

I look around, my hands on my hips as I take in the completed interior. He's right. It is very much like a mini cabin—complete with a king-sized bed, rustic light fixtures, a bathroom tucked in the corner, and even a mini kitchen.

"I guess I still don't understand what all of this is for... Isn't the whole point of camping to be outside?" He scratches his head.

"Trust me, some people like to be in nature without actually being in nature, okay?"

"That makes no sense, but I trust you." He chuckles, shaking his head.

"The ones who need it will appreciate it." I pat his back as we step out onto the small deck portion of the tent and look around.

Now that we were able to build on Cole's property, we've been able to execute my initial plan for the glamping tent area. We constructed six fully functioning tents, each with a million-dollar view and a personal fire pit of their own.

"They got a lot done in such a short amount of time," Cole says, watching Neal's crew as they work on the last tent. Another group is working on the brick outdoor kitchen that has a grill and a flat top for the guests to use.

"Yeah, Neal actually recruited some help from another construction company so we could make the deadline on time," I tell him. "Since it was a last-minute change—and we added three more tents than we would have had in the space down by the lodge—I don't think we would have made it without the extra manpower. With the grand opening only a couple days away, we're just barely going to make it as it is."

"Wow."

"But yes, they did move fast. I think the most time-consuming part was running water, plumbing, and electricity to each one, but with that many workers, they were able to cruise on it."

"Do we need to do the interior for the rest of the tents?" he asks, seemingly along for the ride to do whatever needs to be done.

"Nope. The last three cabins won't have furniture for a little while since I had to order those last minute."

I can feel him studying me out of the corner of my eye.

"Those'll be empty for the opening," I admit. "It won't be perfect, but that's okay. I'm pretty proud of it as it is."

I breathe in, taking a full breath while a slow smile lingers on my face. The view alone from these tents is enough to lure flocks of people here from miles away. It's going to be great—I just know it.

"It's just like I envisioned," I say quietly, wrapping my arms around Cole's torso, taking comfort in being near him. He slides an arm around me, squeezing tightly.

"Have you come up with anything for the space behind the lodge yet?" he asks.

"I did." I grin up at him. "Do you want to hear about it?"

"Of course."

"That area will officially be The Ruby Lodge Event Pavilion. We'll have a gazebo and a large concrete slab where chairs can be set up, and we can host events—weddings, family reunions, you name it."

"I love that. It's perfect." He squeezes me once as a show of excitement.

"I think so too. It'll be completed after the grand opening, of course—another thing that won't be perfect on the day. But

I'm okay with that. They can do that without me. There's not much I need to oversee there."

"Well, it'll be fun to come back and see the progress the next time we're in town."

He says it as if we're a package deal, which I have to agree, we are. My heart warms at the way he says it, though—so matter of fact and nonchalantly, as if it's the most obvious thing in the world.

"Yes." I smile up at him. "What do you think? Should we head back down?"

"Sure," he says, offering a hand to help me step off the deck platform. "I have to do some work back at the cabin. I need to make arrangements for getting the shed I finished for my client delivered."

"That's at Paul's currently, right?"

"Yup. His garage has also become a second storage space for me," he chuckles.

"I'm sure he doesn't mind."

We hop on the ATV and head all the way back down to the lodge. Instead of passing by the lodge to get to cabin one, Cole brings us to a stop near the dock where we notice Paul and Shirley on the very end of it. Behind them, the ferry is just now coming into the bay.

"I'm going to go check in with Paul before he heads back to town, okay?" Cole asks me, squeezing my wrist briefly.

"Sure, go ahead."

I wander to the beach and smile as Shirley walks off the dock toward me.

"How are you doing, honey?" she asks, sliding an arm around my shoulders.

"I'm good," I tell her, and it strikes me how much I mean it. So often in the past when I've been here and people ask me that question, it hasn't been the full truth when I say I'm fine. But this time...I truly mean it with every fiber of my being.

I really am fine. More than fine. The renovation is nearly done. My soul is full from so much quality time with Graham, Blair, and my dad. My relationship with my mom is different than I'd hoped it would be, of course, but at least I'm at a place with my own grief where I can physically be in the same room as her, which is more than I could say as of a few months ago.

And then there's Cole. I flick my gaze out to where he's helping Paul climb in. What do I even say about the man who has given me so much? The man who strengthens me. Who supports me unconditionally. Who loves me with an intensity I've never known before.

Shirley elbows me in the side. "Easy, there. You might look too happy if you're not careful," she teases.

I huff. "Look who's talking. Are you going to fill me in on what's happening with you and Paul yet? Or are you going to keep us guessing?"

She pushes her lips together while lifting her shoulder in a shrug. "I'm not sure what it is yet. But I can tell you one thing about life, Sydney...sometimes your past has a way of coming back to surprise you."

I hum under my breath, watching the wistful way she looks out at Paul, and then my own gaze finds Cole again.

"Yeah. It sure does."

FORTY-THREE
Sydney
Now

Week Eighteen of Renovation

"Hey," Cole says, using a gentle hand to stop me from racing back out the cabin door. "Before we go out there, let's just breathe for a minute, okay?"

The features of his face come into focus as I zero in on him, calming me from the adrenaline that the grand opening has me running on.

"Just breathe," he reminds me. "You've been going nonstop all day. Don't forget to stop and take it all in, okay?"

I take a deep breath in, letting my heart rate slow down to an appropriate speed. "Okay. You're right."

For the first time all day, I take the time to appreciate this quiet moment. I'm suddenly glad that we needed to run back for the stack of flyers I forgot to grab earlier this morning.

"It's a big day, Sydney. You should be feeling proud of yourself, not stressed out."

He leans in to kiss me, and I latch onto him, holding him against me for longer than I'm sure he intended. I just need to feel connected to him for a moment before we go back outside. When he pulls away, my eyes flutter open slowly, feeling notably calmer.

"That's better," he says with a wink.

"Okay, I'm relaxed," I say, looping my arm through his. He leads me out of the cabin, and the live music by the lodge can be heard immediately as well as the general buzz that comes with a large crowd of people all talking at once. Streams of people pass us, going the opposite way to check out the new recreation area, and I smile as they walk past, wishing I could see the reactions of every single person here as they see each area for the first time. If only that were possible.

As we get closer to the lodge, hand in hand, I take Cole's advice and truly soak it in for the first time today.

All these people are here to enjoy and appreciate the updated Ruby Lodge—the project I poured so much of my blood, sweat, and tears into over these past few months. I can't count how many people from my past have congratulated me so far today, bringing up memories and stories from when my grandparents were alive and running the lodge. It feels like more than a celebration of a renovation here today. It feels like a celebration of a community in a way. One I'm proud and honored to be a part of.

Cutting through the crowd, we pass the long table where Shirley has her catering set up, and Paul and Blair are helping her serve the food. Blair winks at me as we pass by, and I wave to Laura and Jimmy, who are in the long line for food. I make a mental note to find them later, the next time I feel like I need a break.

On the far side of the property, Neal is running an ATV to shuttle people back and forth to check out the glamping area. I wave to him as Cole and I head up the lodge stairs, past the band, and in the door under the *Welcome to Ruby Lodge* banner we hung yesterday.

Inside, the dining room is filled to the brim with people. Every chair in the entire room is taken, and there's a long line at the bar. We reach the corner and wait patiently for Graham and my dad to get the line under control, chatting to ourselves quietly. When Graham comes to our side of the bar, I pass him the fliers.

"I put some at the front desk, but I figured it wouldn't hurt to have some back here too," I say with a smile. "Just in case anyone asks. It has all the information on the updates we made and the list of new amenities we have to offer guests."

"Awesome, thanks," Graham says, a little out of breath. There's a swirl of both excitement and exhaustion behind his eyes, but I know he loves every bit of today just as much as I do.

"Graham, I hate to do this to you, but I need to get back to your mother," Dad says, coming up behind him. "I've stayed as long as I can for the day."

"No problem, Dad." Graham nods. "I hired extra staff for today. They'll be here any minute now."

I meet Dad when he rounds the bar, intent on saying a quick goodbye so he can be on his way. Instead, he pulls me in for a long hug before I have a chance to even lift my arms.

"Tell Mom I'll see her soon, okay?" I whisper as he pulls back.

"You bet I will," he says, emotion brimming in his eyes. He pushes his lips together as if he doesn't know how else to articulate his feelings at the moment.

The feeling is mutual.

I pull him in for one last hug, although I plan to say goodbye to him and Mom tomorrow before Cole and I head back down to Minneapolis.

He throws one last wave to Graham, Cole, and me before disappearing into the crowd. Cole is at my side instantly, sending a comforting scrape of his fingers down my arm. Somehow, he always seems to know when I may need an extra dose of comfort.

"Come over here," he suggests quietly, leading me to the windows. From this corner window, we have a perfect view of the whole crowd outside. He comes behind me, wrapping his arms around my collarbone.

"You did this," he whispers in my ear, his chin on my shoulder. "I'm proud of you, Sydney Peterson. And I love you."

I squeeze his arm, feeling the weight of his words in the center of my chest.

"Thank you," I whisper back. "I'm proud of you too, Cole."

His arms squeeze me tighter in response, and I twist my neck to look up at him, wanting to look into his eyes. I haven't been able to get enough of the way he looks when I tell him this next part.

"And you already know I love you too."

His face softens the same way it always does, and he heaves a slow inhale. I like to believe that the words are healing a small piece of him every time I say it.

He presses another kiss to my lips, and then I straighten, resting the back of my head against his chest. I scan my gaze from side to side, watching the ferry full of people coming into the bay, the kids that are dancing in front of the band, and the people that are pointing out the new bear statue with excitement.

All of it warms my heart, and I find myself feeling exhilarated. For the many memories that will be made here for years to come. For the newfound love that I get to carry with me when I leave. And for once in my life, I'm already looking forward to when I get to come back home.

EPILOGUE
Sydney

Eighteen months later

"Here you go, babe." Cole hands me a glass of lemonade, then slides under the blanket I have draped across my lap.

"Thank you." I smile as he kisses the side of my head. He wraps an arm around my shoulders, pulling me into his side, where I nuzzle against him, warming from the inside out.

Three torches along the deck's edge blaze against the night sky, illuminating just enough light to see the outline of ourselves on the couch but keeping it dark enough to see the scattering of stars in the sky.

What we can't see behind the veil of the dark night sky is the stunning view we soak up every single time we come up here—the one that offers a bird's-eye view of the cliff drop off and an eagle's nest in the distance. The exact same one we bonded over not too long ago.

You see, after the grand opening, and after Cole came with me down to Minneapolis, I immediately added an additional design project to my docket.

Up here, on the far corner of Ruby Lodge's property—just past the glamping tents—is where we built a dwelling just for Cole and me. We now have a cabin of our own in the very same spot he once brought me eagle-watching.

One that we come to when we need a reprieve from the real world or from our travels. We split our time between the apartment in Minneapolis, bouncing around to other cities across Minnesota to deliver pieces for Cole's clients, and then we come up here when I get the urge to come visit Mom—or Dad, Shirley, or Paul. Or Graham and Blair, of course, who are fully enjoying the bliss of newlywed life. They were the very first couple to get married at the Ruby Lodge Event Pavilion six months ago and have been almost nauseatingly happy ever since.

So far, this has been the perfect scenario for us, especially since I'm no longer tied to my architecture job. I realized shortly after the Ruby Lodge renovation that my heart was really in doing mostly freelance design work that better suits Cole's and my nomadic lifestyle.

"What are you thinking about?" Cole asks, his whisper tickling my ear.

I rest my head on his shoulder and smile. "How much I love you and this life we have together. How proud I am of how far we've both come."

I shrug, feeling silly at the random admission. "I don't know. A lot of things, I guess."

He squeezes me tighter as I reminisce on the last year and a half together. I find it fitting that we sit in the dark as I reminisce on our relationship thus far. Because that's exactly where we found each other all those years ago in high school, amidst our own personal darkness, when we were just two lost kids looking for something real to grasp onto. And while it may have taken a few years—with both of us fleeing as fast as we could—we finally found that what we were looking for was right at home all along.

"I'm going to grab my journal. I'll be right back." I carefully slip out of the blanket and head inside the cabin, passing the plans that are laid out on the kitchen table. We're working on a plan for a home I'm designing, with Cole's help, for Paul and Shirley. It turns out that the home Paul bought along the river needed enough repairs that he decided to level the whole thing and start fresh—with Shirley by his side. I'm designing the home, and Cole will help build it as he's expanding his woodworking skills to include carpentry now.

I cross the cozy living room to the floor-to-ceiling bookshelf next to the fireplace. On the middle shelf—underneath the framed loon puzzle we built together and the eagle Cole carved me—is where I keep my row of journals. There are six of them in all. Completely filled to the brim with my conversations with Mom. I'm currently working through the seventh.

When I went back down to my apartment after the renovation, I found myself writing to her nonstop, spilling all of my day-to-day details, even though I wasn't physically with her anymore. I've continued that habit, writing in it every single night. It's been my way of keeping her close to me and a part of my life no matter where I am.

I'm eager to write to her tonight to tell her all about the canoe ride Cole and I took today to Oak Island for lunch, and how I have a sneaking feeling he's going to propose any day now. I know she would be ecstatic right along with me.

With a smile, my gaze flicks to Cole, and I head back outside to him, clutching the journal close to my chest.

ACKNOWLEDGMENTS

If You Say So proved to be the most difficult story to finish out of any others I've written so far. In full transparency, my dad was diagnosed with cancer when I was about halfway through writing this manuscript. Naturally, my mind was consumed with more important things than writing, and I seriously considered putting this book on hold indefinitely. Attempting to focus on a fictional story, especially one with a parental grief storyline, was often the very last thing I wanted to do. However, I gave myself patience and grace, leaned heavily on my trusted beta readers, and slowly pushed through to the finish line. Publishing this book brings feelings of pride and excitement, as every book release does. However, this one also comes with even more complex feelings of self-doubt, hoping I had the mental capacity to give this story the attention it deserves, and hoping it will resonate with readers the same way Say You Mean It has.

That said, I want to thank you, dear reader, for giving this story a chance. For holding space for Sydney and Cole's journey.

I also want to say thank you for your endless support of me and my stories! Whether you have been along on this author journey of mine from the very beginning or have just now found me, thank you for being here and giving my books a chance! You quite literally make my world go round—thank you endlessly for supporting my author dreams!

To Brooke, Lexie, Shelby, Hannah, Megan, Erin, Taylor, Court, and Darci for reading this story in its various stages! Without each and every one of you, I truly don't think I would have been able to get to 'the end.' Your support and encouragement got me through to the finish line and I do not take that lightly.

To my editor, Jenn, thank you so much for helping me polish this story into a clean manuscript! I'm grateful for you!

Thank you to Sarah for proofreading for me, and another HUGE thank you to Lorissa for creating another stunning cover that is better than anything I could have dreamed up myself! Your talent is astounding and I'm oh so grateful for you!

Last but certainly not least, a big thank you to Nick and my kids. None of my stories would ever get written if it weren't for all of you and your endless love and support. I love you to pieces!

ALSO BY MEGAN REINKING

The Ruby Lodge Series
Say You Mean It
The Hawaiian Getaway Series
The Ohana Cottage
The Summer Break
The Perfect Tide
The Holiday Prize

About the Author

Megan Reinking is a wife and mother who lives in Minnesota, where she spends her days reading, writing, and chauffeuring her three children around town. She enjoys writing heartfelt romance stories that her readers often tell her feel like a warm hug!

www.ingramcontent.com/pod-product-compliance
Lightning Source LLC
Chambersburg PA
CBHW032342310726

48973CB00007B/1811